Cash and the Sorority Girl

What Reviewers Say About Ashley Bartlett's Work

Cash Braddock

"There were moments I laughed out loud, pop culture references that I adored and parts I cringed because I'm a good girl and Cash is kind of bad. I relished the moments that Laurel and Cash spent alone. These two are really a good match and their chemistry just jumps off the page. Playful, serious and sarcastic all rolled into one harmonious pairing. The story is great, the characters are fantastic and the twist, well, I never saw it coming."—*The Romantic Reader Blog*

"This book was amazing; Bartlett has a knack for being able to create characters that just jump off the page and immerse themselves into your heart."—*Fantastic Book Reviews*

The Price of Cash

"The chemistry between Cash and Laurel is fantastic. This match has tension, heartache that pulls you deep into their dilemma. You want them to go for it and damn the consequences. It is so good! The whole book is fantastic, the love story, the crime, supporting cast, really top notch. Ashley Bartlett has written a fabulous follow-up. I cannot say enough good things about this one. I am absolutely hooked on this series!"—*The Romantic Reader Blog*

Dirty Sex

"A young, new author, Ashley Bartlett definitely should be on your radar. She's a really fresh, unique voice in a sea of good authors. …I found [*Dirty Sex*] to be flawless. The characters are deep and the action fast-paced. The romance feels real, not contrived. There are no fat, padded scenes, but no skimpy ones either. It's told in a strong first-person voice that speaks of the author's and her character's youth, but serves up surprisingly mature revelations."—*Out in Print*

Dirty Money

"Bartlett has exquisite taste when it comes to selecting the right detail. And no matter how much plot she has to get through, she never rushes the game. Her writing is so well-paced and so self-assured, she should be twice as old as she really is. That self-assuredness also mirrors through to her characters, who are fully realized and totally believable." —*Out in Print*

"Bartlett has succeeded in giving us a mad-cap story that will keep the reader turning page after page to see what happens next."—*Lambda Literary*

Dirty Power

"Bartlett's talents are many. She knows her way around an action scene, she writes *memorably* hot sex, her plots are seamless, and her characters are true and deep. And if that wasn't enough, Coop's voice is so genuine, so world-weary, jaded, and outrageously sarcastic that if Bartlett had none of the aforementioned attributes, the read would still be entertaining enough to stretch over three books."—*Out in Print*

"Here we have some rough and tumble action with some felons on the run! A big plus is the main characters were very engaging right from the start. …If you like your books super chocked full of all manner of things, this will be a winner. I definitely ended up enjoying this wild and woolly whoosh through the world of hardcore criminals and those who track them. Give it a try!"—*Rainbow Book Reviews*

By the Author

Sex & Skateboards

Dirty Trilogy

Dirty Sex

Dirty Money

Dirty Power

Cash Braddock Series

Cash Braddock

The Price of Cash

Cash and the Sorority Girl

Cash and the Sorority Girl

by

Ashley Bartlett

2019

CASH AND THE SORORITY GIRL

ISBN 13: 978-1-63555-310-9

This Trade Paperback Original Is Published By
Bold Strokes Books, Inc.
P.O. Box 249
Valley Falls, NY 12185

First Edition: May 2019

Credits
Editor: Cindy Cresap
Production Design: Susan Ramundo
Cover Design By Megan Tillman

Acknowledgments

The previous Cash novels debate morality and criminality and social constructs. This book is not concerned with existential wrestling. Rape is not debatable. At the same time, I am not offering grand solutions—or any solutions, really. I am condemning sexual assault and suggesting our emotional, physical, and social survival is contingent upon being respectful and kind. It's harder than we imagine.

The research for this novel gutted me. Mary Alice, I cannot fathom the courage it takes to be a sexual assault and domestic violence counselor. You are heroic.

Once again, Sydney, you lent my cops authenticity. I'm sorry the authority figures in your life probably think you do weird drugs now.

This book was most challenging, of course, when I had to dress a femme girl. Aurora, thanks for responding to my inarticulate questions with coherent answers and pictures. You're swell, doll.

My mental health was not great when I was writing this. Carsen, I don't know what to thank you for. Everything? You make me laugh and you build my confidence and you fight my battles—even when I'm fighting with myself. Ruth, my bro. I'm certain our text conversations would baffle any scholar. Thanks for getting how my brain works. I love you guys.

Cindy, I know you hate texting. And talking on the phone. Really, any communication before three a.m. But you do it anyway and I know that means you love me. Thanks for lecturing me and talking me off ledges.

Bold Strokes Books is the best home I could ask for. Radclyffe and Sandy, you have created something exquisite and I'm lucky to be part of it.

Finally, a massive thank you to my audience. You guys are pretty great. Thanks for sticking with me and Cash on this strange journey.

Dedication

For my wife.

Because you get me.

And because you don't suffer fools.

Chapter One

The phone ringing didn't wake me. Laurel had perfected the art of stealthily answering a barely audible phone in the middle of the night. There was probably some woman in the past for whom she had developed that skill. I'd never given it much thought. The women in the past, that is. The ninja phone answering I'd thought far too much about.

As she spoke, I pulled her closer, pressed my face to the warm cotton draped over her shoulders, and continued to doze. It was her lack of movement that made me wake up. The usual subtle catches and shifts of her breath when I splayed my hand against her stomach were strangely absent. Her breathing was deep and too even—like she was holding it at the top of each inhale. Her exhalations were measured, cultivated. That was what woke me.

I opened my eyes and rolled away. I couldn't see through the haze of sleep and I couldn't understand what Laurel was saying. Words were too hard to process. But the control, the curt urgency in her tone was chilling. She tapped the phone to hang it up. The pad of her finger against the glass echoed dully through the room. She sat up. I pushed myself up too.

"I need to go to Mercy."

"The hospital?" I asked.

Laurel nodded. "Lane is there."

"Your sister? Is she okay?"

Laurel started to shake her head, then shrugged instead. "I don't know."

I waited for her to expand. When she didn't, I knew she couldn't. "I'll drive you."

She nodded once. "Thanks."

We moved around each other, dressing, finding shoes, blinking away sleep. The efficiency of her movements was the product of a detective's hours. Mine weren't born of habit, but panic. I'd never seen Laurel quite this coiled, subdued.

We drove out of midtown into East Sac. The lights on the dash rolled to three a.m. Laurel kept both feet on the floor. Her hands were folded in her lap.

"Do you need to call anyone? Your parents?" I asked.

"No."

I pulled into the hospital lot and followed the signs to the emergency room. Laurel didn't say anything so I assumed that was the right place. I parked and Laurel walked to the brightly lit entrance. Her pace slowly accelerated so we were almost jogging by the time we got inside. She walked through the waiting room, turned down a hallway, and took a hard corner.

"Where are we going?" I asked, but she didn't answer.

We stopped outside a closed door. She knocked twice, then let herself in.

A woman sitting on a rolling stool just inside vaulted to her feet. "No, absolutely not, Detective." She blocked Laurel's forward movement. Lane was sitting on a hospital bed in the center of the room. She looked at us but said nothing as Laurel was forced back into the hallway. The woman closed the door and stood directly in front of it. "You cannot be in there. The waiting room is back around that corner." She pointed. Her hand, her voice was steady. "When she is ready, I'll bring her out to you."

"I'm sorry. You misunderstand. I'm her sister." Laurel tried to edge around the woman.

"I'm not misunderstanding anything. You absolutely cannot be in that room. If you try, I will have you removed." The woman crossed her arms. She was older, early sixties, maybe. She was a good six inches shorter than Laurel and probably weighed a hundred pounds. She looked South Asian, Indian maybe. Her dark hair was faintly graying, tucked into a loose bun. She was wearing shapeless jeans and a casual shirt. It looked like she had rolled out of bed and come directly to this room to yell at Laurel. There was something commanding in her presence.

"I'm not trying to break protocol here. I'm not just a family member. I'm also a detective with Sac PD. I just want to be present when she is interviewed."

"I know who you are. Lane has already been interviewed by the police."

"She wants me in there. She asked you to call me for a reason."

"I'm sorry. She doesn't want you in the room." The woman's unrelenting stare broke for a moment. Pity came through. "You know how this works, Detective. It's better if you're in the waiting room."

Laurel deflated. "Yeah, okay." They stared into each other's eyes for a long second. "Thank you," Laurel said before she broke and turned back to the waiting room.

I followed. I thought I understood what was happening, but speculation felt like a violation. So I sat in an institutional chair and held Laurel's hand. She brought our joined hands to her lap. With her free hand she traced the bumps and cracks in my knuckles. We sat there for a long time. Or maybe it was only five interminable minutes. The doors slid open, and a wall of sound came at us. Laurel jerked. Lance Kallen came through the door. It was his uniform making all that noise. The radio on his shoulder, the creak and groan of his equipment belt, the partner in uniform trailing behind him. Laurel extracted her hand from mine.

"You tell them to find that little bitch motherfucker. I want him. I'm taking him in. You let them know I'm the arresting fucking officer. I don't give a goddamn fuck what precinct he's in." Lance turned back to make sure his partner was receiving the message.

The partner held his hand over his radio but wasn't touching it. "Kallen, calm down. I get it, but we need to do this by the book."

Lance's hand shot out and grabbed his partner's shirt. The other guy rocked back, pissed, but he stopped himself from reacting. They stared hard at each other. Lance dropped his hand. They sighed and walked the rest of the way into the room.

"Lance." Laurel stood.

He crossed the room in two big steps and swept her into his arms. It took me a second to realize she was holding him. He hunched and buried his face in her neck. She cupped the back of his head. Their voices were indistinct murmurs.

Lance's partner hung back. We made awkward eye contact. The doors slid open again. Seth—Lance's childhood best friend—came in. It was less loud this time. His radio was already turned down. He stepped lightly, purposefully. There was only a faint creaking of leather. And he wasn't shouting. That helped. The door closed halfway, then changed course and slid back again. A fourth uniform followed Seth. She stepped to the side and stood at casual attention next to Lance's sweating partner.

Laurel and Lance broke apart. Seth stepped forward. He gripped Laurel's shoulder so tight his knuckles went white. Lance fell to Seth. Seth let go of Laurel and wrapped his arms around Lance. Their forearms bunched and bulged as they squeezed each other. Lance finally stepped back and straightened to his full height. Lance's partner stepped forward hesitantly. Lance rounded on him.

"Did you call it in? Did you tell them?" Lance asked.

"No. I—I don't know if that's the right call," the partner said.

Seth stepped between them. "Dispatch doesn't know she's a Kallen?"

"No." Lance shook his head once. "I want Sac State flooded with uniforms. The detectives who interviewed her have the description of the perp. Every available body needs to be on this."

"And tell them Lance and I want to take the guy in. Make sure they tell everyone," Laurel said.

Seth nodded and reached for his radio.

"Wait," I said.

All five cops turned and stared at me. Lance and Seth seemed a little surprised to see me there at all. Laurel seemed surprised that I was slowing down this tar and feather party.

"Why?" Laurel asked.

I stood and stepped close to Laurel. "You guys can't announce on the radio that Lane was raped." I whispered it, but Laurel and Lance drew back like I'd slapped them.

"That's not what we're going to say," Lance said.

"Not in that language, but whatever you do say is going to involve her, and you can't do that," I said.

"Why?"

"Because it will make her a perpetual victim."

"I don't know what the fuck that means. Call it in." Lance shifted his weight. He was ready to bolt or fight someone. Or both.

"Hold up." Laurel gestured at Seth and he nodded. "What do you mean a perpetual victim?"

"If you put out a call for help in finding the guy who raped the Kallens' youngest daughter, you're branding her for life. Every event she goes to, every fundraiser, every cop she runs into in a grocery store will suddenly know this intimate detail of her life."

"But it's not her fault," Seth said. "I know cops aren't known for their sensitivity, but no one is going to blame her."

"That's just untrue." It was a nice story, but all of them knew better than to believe it. "And even if your entire department suddenly pays attention to their cultural competency training, it's not our story to tell. It's hers. So radio in and say it's a family friend of an officer, tell them this young woman deserves nepotism, but do not label her further. She's already had her consent stripped away tonight. Don't compound the problem."

"That's bullshit," Lance said.

Seth shook his head. "It's not." He waved Lance's partner over. "Don't let him contact dispatch. I'll be right back." He bypassed the radio and pulled out a cell phone.

Lance flexed and spun in a tight circle. Laurel let him. After the third spin, she grabbed his arm and pulled him into a chair. His partner crossed his arms and stood over them. I think he was aiming for protectiveness, but it just read as threatening. Laurel shot him a look and pointed at the chair on Lance's other side. He rolled his eyes carefully and sat. Laurel turned her gaze to me and I quickly dropped into the chair next to her.

Seth's partner hovered behind him, just out of earshot. When he hung up the phone, she stepped forward and they had a whispered conversation. After a minute, they crossed the waiting room and sat facing us. Seth nodded at Laurel. She nodded back.

Everything felt very quiet. I waited for a follow-up. Something to make me feel better or worse. It felt common. As though I'd already heard the story, but I didn't know what happened. I only knew why. Lane was a girl. Girls were for raping.

Lance stood abruptly. "I need to help them look." His eyes were wide, the muscles in his jaw and neck were tight. He looked caught.

"Go ahead." Laurel said it softly.

They sized each other up. Lance seemed to realize at the same moment I did that Laurel desperately wanted to trade places with him. She lacked the capacity to wait for Lane and deal with the aftermath. But she knew Lance was even less equipped. So she had chosen to stay and let him charge off. At some point, each of them would realize he was getting a bum deal. If no one caught the perp that night, it would forever be Lance's fault.

"We'll help too." Seth stood.

Laurel nodded. The four uniforms awkwardly made their way back to the doors. The mass was quieter this time but pervasive. When the doors slid shut behind them, Laurel slumped slightly. There was nothing to say, so I said nothing.

Laurel didn't last long before she got up and started pacing. I wanted to go and wrap her in my arms. I wanted to take her back home and throw our phones out the window. I wanted to break Lane out of that sad, institutional room and undo the night. I wanted Lance to catch the perp in an epic, painful flying tackle and march him to the courthouse. But that wasn't how nights like this ended. All I could do was hug Laurel and try not to lie to her.

She slowed when I stepped into her path, then she altered her course to go around me.

"If you don't want me to touch you, tell me now," I said.

She stopped walking away and fell into me. Her arms went around my shoulders. She tucked her head low and pressed her forehead to my neck. I pulled her close. My arms felt too long for her narrow waist. Her body fit against mine. The warmth and comfort and impotent strength were perfect and familiar. She breathed deeply, which turned into a shuddering sob. Her breathing evened out. The muscles in her arms tightened. She mumbled something into my shoulder.

"I can't hear you," I said.

Laurel leaned back a little so my body wasn't muffling her. "I don't know what to say to her."

I shrugged. "Just be there. You don't have to say anything."

"What if I say the wrong thing?"

"Don't blame her. That's the only wrong thing."

"Are you sure?" She blinked at me. Her eyes were dry but rimmed in deep pink.

I thought back to the few times Shelby and I had talked about her assault. Like really talked about it. That was my only frame of reference. "Don't make it about you."

"What does that mean?" Laurel asked.

"You will be traumatized. Just knowing your sister was assaulted is traumatic, or it will be when you start to think about it."

She went through a full range of emotion in an instant. Confusion played across her face, then comprehension and fear. She looked at me, stricken. "Okay."

"And you're going to have questions about what happened and how she's doing and what to do. But don't put that burden on her."

"What does that mean?" She started to trace the seam of my sweatshirt. Her fingers dragged along the back of my neck.

"Just that you're not entitled to her experience," I said. She nodded but dropped her eyes to my chin. "If she wants to share, that's good. But she doesn't owe you anything."

"So basically, I shouldn't bombard her?" She made eye contact again and almost immediately dropped it.

I shrugged and attempted a smile. "Yeah. And if you need to yell or rail against someone, tell me."

"How will she know I care?"

I sighed. The simplicity of her question was heartbreaking. "Say it."

"Say what?"

"Say 'I love you and I'm here for you.'"

"Just like that?"

"I mean, you can write it in a card if you want, but that seems unnecessary." I succeeded at smiling finally.

Laurel smiled too. "Yeah, okay."

We sat back down to wait. I thought waiting was the worst, but then I remembered Lane was getting a rape kit.

The woman who had kicked Laurel out finally entered the waiting room. I waited a moment for Lane to follow, but she wasn't there.

"Detective Kallen, I'm sorry for the abrupt response earlier." She held out her hand. "My name is Neeru. I'm a counselor with WEAVE."

Laurel shook her hand. "Thank you for being here. This is Cash." Neeru smiled kindly at me. "I'm sorry I was rude earlier," Laurel said.

"Your reaction is understandable." Neeru gestured at the chairs. "Can we talk for a moment?"

Laurel nodded and sat. Neeru began to explain what Laurel could expect from Lane. She used very careful language. The cadence of her speech was soothing and practiced. That more than anything saddened me. This woman's job was literally to come sit with sexual assault victims and hold their hand. When she finished with that, she came out and patiently explained to their families how to not hurt them further. What conviction did that require?

Neeru slowly transitioned the conversation into an explanation of familial trauma. She handed Laurel pamphlets with highlighted phone numbers for the family members of survivors. Laurel stared fiercely at the thick paper as she agreed to bring her brothers, her parents to counseling.

The conversation circled back to Lane—as though they hadn't been speaking around her for the last fifteen minutes. As I watched, Laurel fractured. Each splintered piece seemed to only be held in place by the need to lie to Lane, the need to be whole enough to carry her home.

Eventually, Neeru went to retrieve Lane. They returned moments later. I finally realized that we weren't in the normal waiting room. This one was reserved for the family members of assault survivors. Laurel had known exactly where to go.

Lane stopped in the doorway and looked around. When she saw it was only the two of us, her shoulders relaxed. She stepped forward—the echo of her cheap flip-flops deafening in the empty room. She was wearing a set of shapeless gray sweats. I imagined her clothes and shoes were in evidence bags. Laurel hesitated until Lane moved to hug her, then pulled her in tight.

"Thanks for coming," Lane said.

"Yeah. Of course." Laurel released her.

Lane hesitated, then hugged me as well. I'd been expecting fragility, but I should have known better. We'd only met a handful of times, but Lane was not fragile.

"Do you want to go to your dorm or my place?" Laurel asked.

Lane slid her arm around Laurel's waist. "Your place."

"I'll get the car and meet you guys out front," I said.

Laurel thanked me with a glance. I nodded and rushed outside. When I pulled up at the doors, Laurel had her arm slung around Lane's shoulders. For sisters, they really looked nothing alike. Both were brunettes, but that was about all they had in common.

I got out and opened doors for them. It had less to do with chivalry and more a need to do something. Neeru waited until Lane was in the car, then stepped back.

"Are you parked close by?" I asked.

"Close enough, thank you." Neeru smiled. "I need to go back inside, but security will escort me to my car when it's time to leave."

"All right. Thank you." I tried to imbue as much appreciation as I could, but there was no way to thank her for such service.

She nodded again and went back inside. We were on our own.

Chapter Two

Laurel's couch was not comfortable. Or I was too old to sleep on couches. When I heard Laurel moving around in the kitchen, I figured that was enough of an excuse to get up.

"Please tell me you're making coffee," I said.

Laurel looked up from the coffee grounds she was pouring into the gold basket. "Nope. I'm actually doing my taxes."

I rolled my eyes. "She still asleep?"

"Yeah." Laurel nodded in the general direction of her bedroom. We hadn't discussed it the night before. It was just obvious that Lane needed to sleep next to Laurel.

"Did you guys sleep okay?"

Laurel shrugged, nodded. "She tossed and turned a bit, but then she was out." She smiled to herself. "She still sleeps diagonal with her arms splayed." She spread her arms to demonstrate.

I chuckled. "Sounds comfortable for you."

"Oh, yeah." Laurel started the coffee. She looked at me and sighed. I stepped into her space and hugged her. We breathed each other in. Her phone chimed and she sighed again. I let go so she could check it. "The guys want to come over."

"Which guys?"

"Lance, Seth, maybe their partners. They are all off shift."

"That sounds like a terrible idea," I said.

Laurel shook her head at her phone, which was an effective communication method. "I agree, but I think Lance is going to show up anyway."

"It's fine," Lane said from behind us.

"Hey, baby sis. You're up." Laurel tucked her phone away.

"I heard the coffee grinder."

"I can tell them you're not up for it," Laurel said.

"Let's just get it over with. He won't give up. If I do this now, I'll get two or three days of peace." Lane grimaced.

The irony of their brother's entitlement did not seem to be lost on them.

"Okay. After that, you want to swing by your dorm for some clothes?" Laurel asked.

Lane nodded. "Please. I need my meds too. You sure you're okay with me crashing?"

"Yeah. I'm glad you want to stay here."

They held eye contact until I was uncomfortable watching. But it seemed to comfort them.

"Do I have time for a shower before they show up?" Lane asked. She'd showered the night before, but as far as I was concerned she could have all the showers she wanted.

"Definitely. I'll grab some clothes for you," Laurel said.

Lane looked down at the boxers and baggy T-shirt she'd borrowed the night before. "You don't think this is a good look?"

"It's a super look. It's just, you know, fifty degrees out."

"That's bullshit. I blame the patriarchy," Lane said with conviction.

"I'll write the patriarchy a note on your behalf."

"Make it angry."

Laurel scoffed. "That's the only way to write a note to the patriarchy. Especially notes about the weather."

Lane turned to me. "My big sister is smart."

"It's one of her better qualities," I said. Lane and I nodded at each other.

Laurel shook her head as if she was irritated, but she wasn't. They left the kitchen together, Lane muttering something disparaging about Laurel's fashion choices. A few minutes later, the shower turned on. I poured a cup of coffee and folded the blankets I'd used. Laurel came back as I was tucking away the linens. She had changed into pale blue chinos and a vaguely nautical crewneck sweatshirt. She sat on the very edge of the couch, her fight-or-flight instincts still riding high, apparently. I brought her a fresh cup of coffee from the kitchen. She wrapped her hands around the mug and breathed in the warm steam. Her shoulders dropped a scant half inch.

"How long until they get here?" I asked.

Laurel shrugged. "Fifteen, twenty minutes."

"Are you sure that's a good idea?"

"It's a terrible idea." She shook her head. "But baby sis is right. If Lance sees her, he will leave her alone. If she avoids him, he will get real annoying, real quick."

"I want to say that's sweet, but it isn't."

"Nope. It's obnoxious. But that's Lance." She took a sip of her coffee and groaned. "It's only ten and I'm already done with today."

I leaned down to kiss her. "I know."

When I started to stand back up, Laurel cupped the back of my neck and pulled me in for another kiss. The press of her lips was hard. I kissed her back, conscious that her coffee mug was tilting precariously and her brother would arrive soon with a cadre of off-duty cops and her vulnerable sister was only a few walls away, but not caring because Laurel needed me. I'd never felt needed quite the way she made me feel in that moment.

She drew back slowly. "If you don't want to be wearing sweatpants when they get here, you might want to go change."

"Maybe I don't care." I did care.

"There are fewer than ten people in this world who have seen you in your pj's. Somehow I doubt you are interested in expanding that number."

"Your attention to detail is disgusting."

"I'm a cop."

"Don't remind me." I grinned.

Laurel pushed me away. Since she was sitting and I wasn't, her leverage was nonexistent. "Go." She was trying for stern, but I could hear the hint of mirth in her tone. It was enough.

In Laurel's bedroom, I rooted through my drawer until I had underwear, socks, a T-shirt. With the shift in weather, I was going to need to add some long sleeve shirts to my collection at her place. In the meantime, I snagged a flannel from her closet. It smelled faintly of cedar and salt when I pulled it on.

"You can borrow a flannel if you want," Laurel said.

I stuck my head out of her closet. "You're hilarious."

"I know. Toss me my Clarks."

I looked at the shoe rack along the wall. "You have three pairs of Clarks."

"I only have one pair that goes with what I'm wearing."

I grabbed the tan pair and hoped they were the right ones. Laurel was sitting on the edge of the bed pulling on her socks. I held up the shoes and she nodded.

The click of the bathroom door opening echoed down the hallway. Lane appeared in the doorway, towel-drying her hair. She was wearing a tank top with an open lightweight shirt over it. Her chinos were a little loose, but she'd cuffed them to mid-calf which made the cut look intentional.

The doorbell rang. Lane froze, then started breathing hard. Laurel immediately went to her. She took her hands and made her sit on the floor.

"Cash, get the door, will you?" Laurel asked without breaking eye contact with Lane.

"On it." I stepped past them.

Granted, I didn't have much experience in the whole sibling dynamics thing, but I truly couldn't understand why they were so resigned to Lance's invasion. He had a tendency to take over rooms, but he also appeared to respect his sisters.

I opened the door to a dude who was definitely not Lance. Same forgettable white boy face, but not Lance. He was built more proportionally, as if he worked out more than just his arms at the gym. He was wearing bland khakis with a bland cream colored cashmere sweater.

"Logan?" I asked.

"Yes. Who are you? Where is my sister?" He stepped inside without being asked. Laurel's front door opened into a smaller room that contained Laurel's office. An open double doorway led to the larger, central room of the apartment. Logan got as far as the living room before I managed to move or respond.

"I'm Cash."

"Cash?"

"Yes." I barely stopped myself from making it a question.

"Okay, Cash. Who are you?"

"I'm a friend of Laurel's."

"Fine. That's fine."

So glad I had his support in existing. He continued toward the back of the apartment. Short of physically stopping him, I didn't see a way to keep him from walking away. So I followed him down the hallway to Laurel's bedroom.

Laurel looked up when she heard him coming. "Fuck."

Lane looked over her shoulder. "You came."

"You asked me to." Logan stopped next to Lane and glared at Laurel until she moved. He sat where she had been.

Laurel stood and left the room in a huff. I followed her.

"What was that?" I asked.

"Fucking Logan."

"Yeah, I figured that part out."

"She told him," Laurel said.

"Why wouldn't she?"

The doorbell rang again. Laurel answered it. Lance, Seth, and Seth's partner from the night before filed in. They had changed out of their uniforms, but doing so didn't make them look any less like cops. They wore their jeans and field jackets like uniforms. Their boots were shined. Their hair was slicked. Even Seth's partner had her long hair pulled back in a wet ponytail. The only mild improvement from the night before was the lack of obvious weaponry on their hips.

Laurel hugged Lance and said, "She called him."

"Fuck."

Seth sighed. "She didn't."

"Of course she did. He's her big brother," Lance said in a tone that was decidedly acerbic.

"Who?" Seth's partner asked.

They all turned to her. "Logan."

She looked at me, but I didn't know what was going on so I shrugged. Logan and Lane chose that moment to enter the central living room. The room felt very full. The three older Kallens glared at each other.

"It was good of you all to come, but I think it's best for Lane and me to leave now," Logan said.

His proclamation was met with a lot of shouting from his siblings. Laurel's response consisted of a lot of big words designed to make Logan feel very small. Lance was focused pretty solidly on profanity.

Lane began to claim that she wasn't a kid anymore, which kind of made her sound like a kid.

Seth waited a minute, then joined the fun. After he had shouted "hey" about ten times, they all stopped and stared at him.

"I don't actually have anything to say. I just don't think yelling is helping anyone," Seth said.

Laurel closed her eyes and took a deep breath. Lane sat on the couch. Logan checked his watch. There was a beep and everyone checked their phone. It was Laurel's.

"You fucking asshole." She looked at Logan. I'd seen varying levels of anger and hatred from her, but this brand was new and scary. "You called them."

Logan clenched his jaw and looked away from her. He sat next to Lane. "Listen. I know you asked me not to, but they only want to help. You have to trust me."

Lane stared at him. She drew into herself. There was a long period where she breathed deeply and blinked back tears. "I didn't ask. I told you not to." She stood and stepped away from him. "This is why they think you're a dick." She wrapped her arms around herself.

Seth backed away from Lance's side. He leaned against the doorway opposite his partner. They had the right idea.

"Come on. That's not fair. You're not seeing the full picture here. We can never fully see the picture in the moment," Logan said

"Don't do that."

He stood and looked at Lane with misguided pity. "Do what?"

"Regurgitate that shit. I'm not twelve years old and having an anxiety attack in the grocery store. You don't get to big brother this situation."

"But I'll always be your big brother," Logan said. The sad part was how believable it sounded.

"I'd settle for someone who listens to me." Lane angled away from Logan, toward Laurel. "Are they coming here?"

Laurel grimaced. "Yeah. I can delay them, but that's probably it."

"What is wrong with all of you? Our parents are the best people to help Lane through this. They can get her help," Logan said.

Lance started muttering about what an idiot his brother was.

Lane looked pissed. "That's my call to make, not yours."

"It amazes me how stupid you are," Laurel said to Logan.

Logan crossed his arms. "Asking for help doesn't make me weak."

"I said stupid, not weak. You're arrogant too, for the record."

Logan faced Laurel for the first time. "Says the woman who is fucking her CI."

Well, that shut Laurel up. Not for long, though. She turned to Lance. "You told him?"

"No, he didn't tell me. I'm not that stupid." Logan huffed.

"Thanks for trusting me, dickwad." Lance crossed his arms and glared at Laurel.

I realized that I was getting a reenactment of fifteen years in the Kallen house. Somehow I doubted that anything aside from some intensive therapy would help them communicate better. Regardless, Lane was dealing with enough already. She didn't need to regulate her siblings' argument over who loved her more. And I didn't really appreciate my relationship—regardless of how inappropriate it was—being weaponized.

I touched Lane's shoulder. "You want some coffee?" I asked quietly.

Her mouth quirked in an unspoken question. "Sure."

"Come on." I nodded at the doorway to the kitchen. She followed me. Behind us, the voices swelled. Once we were in the relative safety of the kitchen, I waited a beat to make sure everyone was occupied. "Listen, I don't know how your family works. I'm sure it would be healthy or some shit for you to deal with them, but I also think the last twelve hours have been a lot for you. So maybe today is not the day for all of that." I gestured vaguely at the raised voices.

"Yeah." She nodded wryly. "I'm feeling all of that, but I don't know what to do about it. You want me to tell them all to leave me the fuck alone? Because I'm open to it at the moment even though I don't think it will work."

"Or we could just sneak out of here."

Lane's eyes went wide. A slow grin spread across her face. "Are you serious?"

I nodded. "We can go out the back door. When we're far enough away, I'll call Laurel. My apartment has coffee." I thought about the usual contents of my fridge. "And zero groceries, but I will totally buy you groceries."

"Sold." Lane looked down. She was barefoot. "I don't have shoes."

"What shoes were you wearing last night?"

She looked embarrassed. "The woman from WEAVE gave me flip-flops."

"Where are they?"

"Laurel's room?" She shrugged.

"Okay. You go down the back steps. I'll get the flip-flops and meet you out there in two minutes."

Lane took a deep breath and smiled. "See you in two minutes." She eased the back door open and stepped out on the porch.

I made sure the door was closed tight. It tended to blow open with the right gust of wind. You'd think a cop would be averse to a door that opened itself, but Laurel had never seemed concerned.

When I stepped back in the living room, they were all still bickering. Seth had joined in, which was a mistake. His partner was trying to calm him, which was a bigger mistake. Laurel made eye contact with me. I motioned with a wave of my hand that she should keep them going. I wasn't sure if she got the message, but then she started in on Logan's daddy issues so I was really hoping that was a ploy and not just conversation.

The flip-flops were on the floor in front of Laurel's dresser. I grabbed them and one of Laurel's leather jackets. Lane would probably swim in the jacket, but I didn't want her to get cold. I arranged the jacket over my arm so it would hide the shoes. The Kallen boys barely noticed when I came back in the room. I went straight to Laurel.

"I'm taking off," I said quietly.

She frowned. "Okay. Is Lane all right?"

"She just needs some time. Give her five, then check on her, okay?"

"Sure," Laurel said. She could clearly tell something was up, but didn't say anything.

"I'll call you." I didn't bother to say anything to anyone else, just skirted around them and left.

I hustled down the front stairs. There wasn't anyone noteworthy on the sidewalk. I'd never met Laurel's parents, but I'd seen photos. When I was pretty sure we were clear, I rounded the corner and opened the gate to the backyard. Lane was sitting on the lower deck, smirking at me.

"Come on." I tossed her the sandals.

She kicked into them. "Thanks."

"Here." I handed her the jacket as she fell into step beside me. "In case you're cold."

"I thought you were supposed to be a hardened criminal or something."

"Oh, I am." I smiled at her. "You can't tell anyone I'm secretly nice." We paused again at the sidewalk to look for anyone related to Lane.

"That will be difficult. I know lots of criminal types."

"I sensed that about you." I unlocked my car and held the door for Lane.

She climbed up. "The chivalry is really killing your rep."

Chapter Three

Hey. What's up? Did you forget something?" Was how Laurel answered the phone.

"No. Have you gone to check on Lane yet?" I asked.

"Not yet. Should I?"

My phone was plugged into the car stereo so Lane could hear our conversation. I glanced at her. She half smiled at Laurel's question.

"Well, she's kind of not there. I snuck her out the back," I said.

"What?" Laurel asked.

"Hey, big sis," Lane said.

"I don't understand."

"Don't be mad at her. It was my idea. I just thought she was already dealing with a lot and your family is also a lot and maybe she needed some time," I said.

Laurel started laughing, which she turned into a cough. "I agree."

"We're going to her dorm, then my place."

"Excellent. I'll call you later."

"Thanks for getting it," Lane said.

"Anytime."

I hung up. "That wasn't terrible."

"It was the opposite of terrible. Laurel is an excellent human."

"One of my favorites."

Lane pointed at a small street. "Turn there."

We were at the back end of Sacramento State's campus. She directed me through another couple of turns to a visitors' lot. I parked and cut the engine.

"You want me to wait here or come up with you?"

"What do you want?" she asked.

"Whatever makes you more comfortable. If you just want a buddy, I got your back. But if you don't want a drug dealer following you around campus, I'll hang here."

She seemed nervous. "Yeah, okay. You should come up with me."

"Done." I pulled out my keys and got out of the car.

We were quiet on the way to her dorm. After a couple of minutes, Lane stopped walking so stiffly. I wondered if I was making her nervous or if it was just being back on campus.

The dorms were relatively empty. I'd expected them to be busy at this time of morning.

"Where is everyone?" I asked.

"We're a month and a half into the new semester. The shine of dorms has worn off so a lot of people go home on weekends."

"I remember that feeling. But I was in queer housing so it was a different vibe."

Lane unlocked the door to her room. It was empty. Both beds were still made. Her roommate clearly had slept elsewhere as well. "Queer housing would be way cooler."

"It was. I'd never been around so many gay people, so many people who got me."

She pulled a duffel bag from under her bed and started stuffing clothes in it. "I was hoping to get a room in my sorority house this year, but it's by seniority."

"I didn't know you were in a sorority."

"Epsilon Epsilon Epsilon." She nodded at a large flag with three Es above her bed.

"Well, yeah, once you point that out it's pretty obvious."

Lane laughed. "I'm not surprised you didn't know. Laurel wouldn't have told you. She thinks it's dumb."

"Yeah, she's not the sorority type, I guess."

"She's not. But I like it." She grabbed a bag of toiletries. "My mom was Tri Ep too so I'm a legacy."

"That's got to have some perks, right?"

"Mostly it means the pre-law sisters all want to be friends with me. Judge Kallen has clout."

"So it's just helpful if you need a pre-law tutor?"

"I think my mother would die of happiness if I took a pre-law class." She opened a prescription bottle and tapped out a round, pale pill. Then she punched another pill out of a blister pack. The first pill was an anxiety med. The second I didn't recognize. Professionally, I was curious. Personally, I was indifferent. She dry swallowed them, which was just a little too badass for my taste. It takes a certain type of person to dry swallow pills. She shoved the bottle and blister pack into her bag and zipped it. "I think that's everything."

"Shoes?"

"Good call." She kicked off the flip-flops and stuck them in the trash can under the desk on her side of the room. She slid on a pair of ballet flats and stuffed a few more pairs of shoes into her duffel.

I slung her bag over my shoulder and followed her back into the hall. "Back to my place?"

"Yeah, as long as you weren't lying about having coffee."

"I don't lie. I mean, not when it matters." Lying to cops I wasn't sleeping with didn't count as lying. Ethics said so.

"Coffee matters?"

"Coffee is very serious."

"Then I'll be a happy camper," she said.

"One condition."

"Yeah? What's that?"

"If we are hiding out, you have to pick out something utterly mindless to watch."

Lane nodded. The whole way back to the car she really worked on her pensive face. After we climbed in, she turned to me. "When I had shitty days when I was little, Logan and I watched nature documentaries."

I nodded slowly. "Right. I don't think I have any nature documentaries. Netflix probably does. I will find you nature documentaries." I mentally scanned my movie collection and Netflix queue.

"You sound so certain. And shockingly uncertain. It's an interesting juxtaposition."

"I'm an enigma."

"We don't have to watch nature shows."

When she said nature shows, I knew exactly what to watch. Semantics were important. "Oh. I've got it."

"Got what?"

I pulled onto H Street. "How do you feel about Shark Week?"

"Everyone likes Shark Week."

"Yeah, but new Shark Week is all fast sharks and blood. It's not sciencey. They aren't documentaries."

"Okay?" Lane twisted in her seat so she could see me better.

"Old Shark Week is where it's at."

"Because they are sciencey?"

"Yep." I cut down to Folsom Boulevard. No need to drive by the hospital again if we could avoid it.

"Sold. Are they on Netflix?'

"No. They are impossible to find. Luckily for you, my uncle spent my first year in college transferring all my childhood recordings of Shark Week to DVD."

"That sounds pretty healthy."

I shrugged. "He had trouble coping with me leaving for college." We passed under the freeway and entered midtown. "You want to stop for groceries?"

"I'm good. I don't think I want to be around a ton of people."

"That's valid." I turned toward my house and away from the store.

"So why did your uncle have trouble with you going away to college?"

"Empty nest, I guess. He raised me. Shark Week was our thing when I was little, thus the painstaking recordings."

"That's slightly less weird. Still weird, but less so."

"It's totally weird. But it was kind of great every time I got a care package."

"My parents aren't the care package type. One day, they'll manage to package disappointment and dreams that will never be realized, but it hasn't happened yet," she said brightly.

"You're not interested in law school either?"

She laughed. "Absolutely not. I'd hate studying law so I'm not going to."

"That seems reasonable."

"Not to Janice and Randolf."

"So is Logan the favorite or something?" If they wanted their children to be lawyers, a twenty-five percent success rate was pretty pathetic.

"God, no."

"But he's the lawyer."

"Yeah, but he's also the crazy one."

"Huh?"

"They hospitalized him briefly at fifteen," she said. At my questioning look she expanded. "Institutionalized him. He was suicidal. I'm pretty sure he only went to law school to redeem himself for sullying their name."

"Wow. That's…" I didn't know what that was. These people sounded like shadowy monsters when their children described them. Horrible, but always in intangible ways. Yet, everyone else appeared to love them. What truths did the children see that no one else could?

"Yep."

We pulled into the driveway. Robin's car was gone. She'd mentioned switching shifts with someone. I'd have to check my texts to see when she was supposed to be off.

"They blamed him for being a suicidal teenager?" I asked.

"Never." She said it with conviction that veered a bit close to sarcasm. "They assumed he was fundamentally broken and could never function without them. After that, he got perfect grades, went to the perfect schools, read the perfect books."

"To prove he could."

"Exactly." Lane got out of the car.

I grabbed her duffel and led the way up the front steps. I held the door for her. "So what's the plan?"

Lane leaned against the back of the couch. "I'm going to change into my own clothes and you're going to make coffee and then we're going to watch Shark Week."

"Cool." I pointed at the open doorway. "You can change in the study. I'll make up the couch in there for you later. Make yourself at home."

"Thanks, Cash."

"Of course."

"No, really. Thank you." She threw me some of that meaningful eye contact.

I wanted to argue the sentiment, but that was probably a useless endeavor so I went to make coffee. I glanced at Nickels's food bowl, but either Robin or Andy had fed her that morning. My neighbors were the best.

A couple of minutes later, Lane came into the kitchen and sat at the table. She had changed into yoga pants and an off the shoulder sweatshirt. Her shoes had been replaced by fuzzy socks.

"I didn't actually get to drink any coffee this morning." She sighed meaningfully.

"It'll be ready soon."

"Okay." Another deep sigh. "Laurel text yet?"

I checked my phone. "Nope. But she knows we're just vegging all day."

"All day?"

"Yeah. You get all of the snacks. And all of the mindless television. And later we can drink all of the beer." I sat across from her at the table.

"This is an excellent plan."

A strange thought occurred to me. "Wait. You're not twenty-one."

Lane chuckled. "You're not going to let me drink beer now are you?"

"Your big sister is a detective and your big brother is a cop."

"So?"

"Your mother is a judge."

"Valid points, I guess," she said.

The coffee pot beeped. I got up and poured each of us a cup. "You should actually drink this one."

"I'm looking forward to it." Lane took one of the mugs from me on her way into the living room. "Bring on the sharks."

I followed her. "And the science."

"All of the science."

I dug out a stack of plain cases holding burned DVDs. Clive's blocky handwriting identified the title and year. We were deep into the late nineties when my phone started vibrating. I ignored the text messages, but then it started ringing. I looked at the screen. Andy.

"Sorry. I have to take this," I said.

"It's fine." Lane waved her hand.

I paused Shark Week and swiped to answer the call. "Hey, tiger. What's up?"

"Whatcha doing?" Andy drew it out.

"Watching Shark Week."

"Cool." She apparently wasn't going to volunteer the reason for her call.

"What are you doing?" I asked.

"Standing outside of school."

"It's a Saturday."

"Yeah, but Sloan and I had an SAT prep course."

"Do I know Sloan?" I was pretty sure I knew all of Andy's friends.

"Yeah, but you know them by a different name." Andy did not offer up the different name.

"Okay. Why are you calling?"

"Oh, well. See, I was responsible for writing down the time of the SAT course. And I texted the time to Sloan so their mom could pick us up. And apparently I wrote it down wrong because I thought we were going to be here for another hour and Sloan's mom is at an appointment and Mom is working until later this afternoon."

"So you and your friend are stranded at McClatchy?" I asked. Lane cocked her head at me.

"A little, yeah," Andy said.

"Just a sec." I covered the mouthpiece so I could talk to Lane. "I'm really sorry. I have to go pick up the neighbor kid."

Lane shook her head. "It's fine. Don't worry about it."

"Thanks." I uncovered my phone. "I'll be there in fifteen."

"Rad. Thanks, dude."

I ended the call. "You want to chill here or come with?"

"I'll come with you. If that's okay."

"Yeah, of course. But how strong is your stomach?"

She looked at me like I was crazy. "My stomach?"

"Andy has her permit. Her mom and I decided that anytime Andy is traveling in a motor vehicle until she gets her license, she will be operating that motor vehicle." I grinned.

Lane laughed. "You and her mom are brave people."

"Nope. Just stubborn."

"Sometimes, that's the same thing."

Chapter Four

We pulled into the circle in front of McClatchy High. Sophie—or maybe that was Sloan—and Andy were lounging on the steps in front of the school. It was cloudy and dreary, but their posture suggested full sun in the middle of July.

When Andy saw my car, she poked her friend and stood. I stopped the car and got out.

"Hey, Cash, thanks for coming," Andy said.

"Yeah, thanks." Sophie nodded.

"Anytime, kid," I said. Lane got out of the passenger side. "This is Lane, Laurel's sister."

"Hi." Andy formally extended her hand. "It's nice to meet you." When had she started growing up? When did she get so charismatic? "This is my friend Sloan." So this was Sloan.

Lane shook Andy's hand and grinned at me. The charm was working.

"Sloan now?" I asked. Sloan and Andy nodded. "Pronouns?"

Sloan smiled with a mix of relief and shyness. "They."

"Got it." I tossed my keys to Andy. "Let's get out of here."

The keys hit the ground next to Andy. She looked at me in horror. "I'm not driving. You know Freeport scares me."

I grimaced. "That sucks. It's a long walk home. Hop in, Sloan."

Andy knew I was bluffing, but that didn't stop her from panicking. Walking was much worse than driving. She picked up the keys. "Fine. But if we die in a fiery crash, it's your fault."

"What if it's not a fiery crash? What if a light rail crossing malfunctions and you stop on the tracks and we're crushed to death?" Sloan said.

"Sloan," Andy whined.

Sloan laughed. "Or the freeway collapses and your reflexes are too slow because you're too inexperienced and we are pulverized?"

Andy stomped around to the driver's side.

"Or what if you drive so cautiously you get pulled over for driving too slow?" I said.

"It happened one time," Andy shouted.

Lane and Sloan and I laughed at Andy's frustration. She pouted, but I was pretty sure she wasn't actually mad. I climbed in the passenger side and Lane and Sloan piled in back. Andy handed me her backpack, and I tucked it at my feet. She carefully adjusted her seat.

Lane leaned forward. "When I was learning to drive, my brother had just graduated from the police academy. His buddies pulled me over forty-seven times the first month I had my license."

Andy turned. "Forty-seven?"

"Forty-seven." Lane nodded. "They had some sort of bet going."

"What an asshole," Andy said.

"What did you do?" Sloan asked.

"You mean to get back at him?" Lane asked. Sloan and Andy nodded. "I stopped pulling over. They had to either chase me when they had no cause or turn off their lights and back off. After two days of looking incompetent, they left me alone."

"Did they get in trouble?" Andy asked.

"Of course not. But Lance had to buy a lot of guys a lot of beers. He said it turned out to be the most expensive prank he ever played on me."

"Lance doesn't really have much forethought, does he?" I said.

Lane shook her head and scooted back to buckle her seat belt. "He does not. But he's fun and handsome. So, you know?"

"Boys will be boys," Andy said.

We laughed. The patriarchy was funny.

"Are you planning on starting the car any time soon, tiger?" I asked.

Andy huffed and turned the key. She gave it just enough gas for us to creep to the exit of the circle. Cars flew by on Freeport. Andy took a couple of cleansing breaths. She nodded at herself, paced the oncoming traffic, then pulled smoothly across the lane and merged perfectly. Laurel was right. This was too easy. We should have started her on a stick.

"Well done," I said.

Andy gave a short nod but didn't take her eyes off the road. In her defense, the lanes on that stretch of Freeport were barely wide enough to accommodate an SUV. We were almost kissing the line on both sides.

Sloan and Lane kept a reverent silence as we drove north. When Freeport split and turned into 21st, the lanes widened. Andy relaxed a little.

"We're coming up on the turn for Sloan's," I said.

Andy nodded. "Yep. I see it."

She signaled sooner than necessary but turned without issue. In anticipation of the next turn on the grid, she changed lanes. She took the final turn real slow and coasted to a stop in front of Sloan's house. We sat for a moment. Andy mouthed her checklist as she shifted into park, set the brake, and removed the keys.

"Great job."

"Thanks." Andy spun in her seat to look at Sloan. "Text me about the history project?"

"Yeah, when I hear from Bella." Sloan grabbed their bag. "Way to not kill us."

"Hey, Sloan?" I said. They stopped scooting out. "Do your parents know about the name? I don't want to out you."

They dropped their eyes briefly. "Mom does. Dad doesn't yet."

"Noted."

"Thanks." They hurried to get out. Nerves made their movements jumpy.

"Am I still driving?" Andy asked. I just stared at her. "Right. Got it. Whatever." She put the key back in the ignition.

The drive home was uneventful. Which was good. I handed Andy her bag as we walked up to the porch. She slung it over her shoulder.

"What time does your mom get home?" I asked.

"Three?" Andy asked. I obviously didn't know so making it a question was not helpful. "What are you guys up to? Where's Laurel?"

I glanced at Lane. She shrugged. "We've been bingeing Shark Week," I said.

"Shark Week?" Andy stopped and glared. "You're watching Shark Week while I'm studying for SATs? That's some bullshit right there."

Lane laughed. "So join us."

"Can I?" Andy asked. "Wait, why are you watching Shark Week in the middle of the day?"

I glanced at Lane, but she didn't look too capable of answering. "We were at Laurel's last night, but this morning the whole Kallen clan descended and we decided to run away."

"Run away?"

"Like adults." I unlocked the door to my side of the duplex. If Andy wanted to go to her side of the house, she could use the back porch.

"Yeah. Running away seems pretty adult." Andy led the way inside.

Lane followed. She was taking deep, measured breaths, but didn't seem nearly as panicked as she had that morning.

"I'd offer food, but I don't have any. We were thinking about ordering pizza later," I said.

Andy looked back outside. "It's not pizza weather." Whatever remnants of sun had been there were gone. It looked dreary. And the temperature was dropping. She wasn't wrong. "It's soup weather." Her eyes went wide at her own suggestion. "Can we make soup? Lane, do you like soup?"

"Doesn't everyone like soup?" Lane asked.

"Some people don't like all kinds of soup." Andy smirked pointedly at me.

I stared right back. "Tomato soup is just warm ketchup."

Andy dropped her bag in the middle of the floor and flopped dramatically on the couch. "It is not."

Lane laughed. "It kind of is."

"Thank you," I said.

"Okay. No tomato." Andy sat back up. "But we could make soup. We could make two kinds. Or three. We could have a soup party."

"What is a soup party?" I asked. It was clearly a very silly question.

"A party. With soup." Andy rolled her eyes so hard she had to flop back again.

"I'm kind of not hating the soup party idea," Lane said.

"See." Andy gestured at Lane. "She understands me."

"Fine. Sure. Let's have a soup party."

"Yes." Andy threw her fist in the air. "I'm making chicken tortilla. Or minestrone. Oh, man. This is a conundrum."

"I like minestrone." Lane sat next to Andy.

"Deal. Minestrone it is. Cash will make that potato thing with the cheese."

Good to know I had an assignment. "Right, sure. Whatever you say."

"What kind of soup does Laurel like? Is she coming to the soup party?"

Lane shrugged and looked at me. "We should probably call her and see if she's escaped."

"Plus, you know, invite her to the soup party," I said.

"Are you mocking the soup party?" Andy asked.

"Never."

Laurel kicked the door instead of knocking or letting herself in. I got off the couch to answer it. When I opened the door, I realized why. Her hands were full of groceries. I took the bags from one of her hands.

"Thanks." She slid past me to drop her bags on the kitchen table.

Andy hopped up from the couch and bounded into the kitchen. "Are those soup ingredients?"

"You're a strange child," Laurel said.

"Wait until you taste my minestrone. Then we will see who is strange."

"You're kind of adding credence to my whole 'you're a strange child' theory."

Andy sighed and started unpacking groceries. She separated the ingredients into different piles for different soups. When she came across a leek, she held it up and examined it from different angles.

"It's a leek. For mine," I said.

Andy looked at me skeptically and put it next to the bag of potatoes. Next she found a bag of salt and vinegar chips. "Okay, these are definitely not for soup."

"In my defense, I didn't know there was a rule that all groceries had to be soup ingredients." Laurel took the bag from Andy. "Lane, I got snacks," she called.

Lane shuffled into the kitchen. She looked taken aback by the chaos of Andy's sorting system, but then she saw the chips Laurel was holding. "You're the best." She grabbed the bag, then started poking around in the still packed grocery bags.

"Here." Laurel dug into a specific bag and pulled out a huge bag of M&Ms. It was at least two pounds. "But, for the record, you're sick."

Lane took the candy. "Maybe my palate is more developed than yours."

"It's unlikely."

"You're not going to mix those are you?" Andy asked with barely disguised disgust.

"Don't take her side." Lane nodded at Laurel.

"It's not a side. One person does not constitute a side. You're the only person who thinks that's okay," Laurel said.

I could hear the echoes of childhood battle in the cadence of their speech. "Leave her alone. If she wants to pollute her taste buds, that's her business."

Lane made a face at Laurel. Laurel made it back.

"What's this?" Andy held up a pepper.

"Poblano. Mine." Laurel pointed at her pile.

Lane settled into a chair and opened the bag of chips. After a handful, she opened the M&Ms.

"Heathen. Barbarian," Laurel said.

"Bite me, La La."

Andy and I turned and stared at Lane.

"La La?" I asked.

Laurel's face slowly dropped in horror. "Dammit."

"What?" Lane started to smile. "They don't know?"

"Now they do," Laurel said.

"You call her La La?" I struggled to keep the glee from my tone.

"When I was a baby, I couldn't say Laurel very well. It became La La."

"This makes me unspeakably happy. I hope you realize this."

"Oh, I do." Lane poured a handful of candy into her mouth and smirked at Laurel.

Laurel just shook her head and continued unpacking groceries.

Andy wouldn't let anyone start cooking until she had unpacked all of the grocery bags and sorted them. The pile of not-soup ingredients on the counter grew until it was larger than the soup piles. I realized Laurel had just gone grocery shopping for me. It was almost as if she was judging my empty fridge.

Lane went back to Shark Week. Somehow, I got stuck cutting all the veggies for Andy's minestrone while Andy migrated to the couch with Lane.

"So how bad was it that we left?" I asked quietly.

"It was goddamn brilliant, honestly," Laurel said.

"Were they all angry though?"

Laurel started in on her own pile of produce. "Livid. If I hadn't been the one to catch their collective ire, I'd think it was hilarious."

I grimaced. "Sorry."

"Don't worry. I'll think it's funny in a couple of days. My brothers are shockingly unimaginative in their responses. Lance wants to fight someone. Logan wants to go see his therapist to process why Lane doesn't trust him. And then he wants us all to go to group therapy to process why Lane doesn't trust him."

"I don't know why you didn't introduce us sooner. That Logan is a hoot."

Laurel scraped the diced peppers off her cutting board into a bowl while holding scary eye contact with me. "You're so funny."

"What? I liked how he layered beige over beige. Bold move, but he really nailed it."

Laurel tried not to smile. "It's his signature color."

"To match his soul."

"Yep. He's just a dude who stands by and can't intervene because he sees the value in both sides. He is what's wrong with moderation." She started going a little harsh on her onion.

"What exactly did I miss?"

She sighed and set down the knife. After a minute, she pulled out a chair at the table and sank into it. "My mother's first question was about which frat Laney was at."

"Okay." I sat next to her.

"I didn't know because why the fuck would I know that? So I told her it wasn't really important who was hosting the party." Laurel looked at me for confirmation. I nodded emphatically. "She was going on about Sig Eps and the type of girls who go to their parties or some shit."

"The type of girls?" I hoped I was misunderstanding. "So Sig Eps are rapey and girls who go there deserve it?"

Laurel just nodded. "Logan thought I was being too harsh on Mom. She was just stating facts." She rolled her eyes hard on facts.

"That's really more of an interpretation of facts. Like the fact that they are rapey doesn't—" I stopped talking when I realized Laurel was glaring. "Yeah, okay. You already knew that."

"Anyway. I said it probably was the Sig Ep house and she was probably wearing a tight skirt and was probably drunk. And then I volunteered to be the one to tell her that she deserved it. So they all got even more mad at me. That's when I kicked them out of my apartment and I think I might have disowned them. It's all a blur. I'll be honest, it wasn't one of my better moments."

"It sounds like a damn good moment to me," Lane said.

Laurel jerked. I looked up. Lane was standing in the doorway.

"Shit. You weren't supposed to hear that. I'm sorry." Laurel stood and got halfway to Lane before she stopped.

Lane closed the distance and hugged Laurel. She said something, but it was muffled by Laurel so I couldn't hear.

I left them in the kitchen. Andy was still entranced by sharks. I leaned over the back of the couch and poked her.

"Did you know they can like train sharks to do tricks?" Andy asked without turning around.

"That's way cooler than dolphins."

"Dolphins are overrated," Andy said.

"Hey, I have to run back to the store. I need you to drive me."

"Cash." She drew it out. I sighed. She turned and caught sight of Laurel and Lane hugging in the kitchen. "Oh. Right. Okay, I'll drive you to the store."

"Thanks."

She turned off the TV and grabbed her shoes off the floor. "I need a sweatshirt."

"You want to run next door, then meet me out front?" I asked.

"Yeah. Two minutes." She went out the back door. After a second, the door on her side slammed.

I collected my wallet and keys. "Hey, guys?" I said quietly. Laurel and Lane separated enough to look at me. "Andy forgot to add some ingredients to the grocery list so we're going back for them."

Lane nodded. Laurel half-smiled at my weak attempt to give them space.

"See you in a bit," Laurel said.

Andy was leaning against the car when I got outside. "Everything okay?" she asked.

I shrugged. "It will be."

Andy took my answer at face value. I hoped she held on to that sweetness a little longer.

Chapter Five

"I really am sorry." Laurel barely glanced at me as she tied her oxfords.

"It's fine. Lane and I get along just fine. We will probably watch sharks and eat soup. It's basically a perfect day." I stretched and tried to grab Laurel, but she stood and shrugged into a blazer. Foiled by my lack of desire to get out of bed.

"I feel like I'm making you babysit." She grabbed her phone off the nightstand.

"You're not. I mean, I'm still hoping you'll tip me." I winked.

She hid a smile and slid the phone in her pocket. "You're kind of the worst."

"I am. But you like it."

She leaned over and kissed me. "I only kind of like it."

"You should come back to bed." I tugged at the edge of her jacket.

"I can't." She straightened. I pouted and refused to let go of the blazer. "Cash, let go."

"If I let go, you'll go do boring police things."

She stared at me pointedly. I let go. "Thank you."

I sighed. "I guess I should tell you that you put my phone in your pocket. Yours is still plugged in."

"Funny."

"I'm hilarious. But right now I'm not being funny," I said. Laurel pulled the phone back out of her pocket, realized it was mine, and rolled her eyes at me. "I know you think the dealer gig is much more glamorous, but you chose the cop route. Now you have to stick with it."

"That was very inspirational," she said.

I grinned. "You're welcome."

"Reyes said we wouldn't be long. It's just a consult."

The last time I'd seen Reyes, he was still in a hospital bed. "How's he been?"

"Obnoxious. He's only cleared for light duty and he's milking it for all he's worth."

"I thought cops were supposed to hate being assigned to a desk," I said.

"Oh, he does hate that part. But Duarte has been his lap dog for three days. He brings him coffee and files and won't let anyone near him without a written statement of intent, confirmation of health, and a signed declaration by either a holy person or a judge."

"That's not extreme." I accepted that Laurel wasn't getting back in bed so I got up and searched for pants.

"A couple of days ago, I had to stop him from setting up a temporary desk next to our desk."

"So Duarte has a desk next to you now?" I asked.

"He did. I convinced him he had a cold and was going to infect Reyes."

"How do you convince someone they have a cold?"

Laurel tossed me a pair of jeans. "You get fifteen random people to stop them throughout the day and ask if they are feeling all right because they don't look so good."

I laughed. "That kid is going to figure out how to fight back one day and make your life a living hell."

She waved a hand like the idea was inconceivable. "I'll be back in a couple of hours." She kissed me for not nearly long enough. "Don't forget to call Kyra about tonight."

"Yeah, yeah."

I heard Laurel say bye to Lane, then the front door closed. A minute later, Laurel's truck started up. I went to the kitchen to start coffee. When I passed the living room, I found Lane wrapped in a blanket watching another nature documentary.

"Morning," I said.

Lane turned and smiled faintly. "Morning. There's coffee." She lifted her own mug as evidence.

"Thanks." I poured a cup and sat opposite her on the couch. "What are we watching?"

"*Planet Earth*. Thanks for showing me how to launch Netflix last night. I never would have figured out your television."

"Yeah, Beverly is a complicated broad."

Lane turned in slow motion. "Your TV has a name?" she asked. I shrugged. "And her name is Beverly?"

"No, actually. I just made that up. But I think I like it. I hereby dub thee Beverly," I said to the TV.

She chuckled. "I can see why Laurel likes you."

"You mean La La?"

"God, she's going to kill me for that one."

"You're not wrong," I said.

"In my defense, it's my sacred duty as her younger sister to torment her."

I couldn't dispute that.

The episode ended and the next started. Some British dude started talking about trees.

"Hey, we're not in the ocean anymore," I said.

"You seriously have never seen this? It was like a staple of my childhood."

"I was in college during your childhood."

"Oh. Well, each episode is a different habitat. This one," she hit the information button, "is 'Seasonal Forests.'"

"How are you ten episodes in?"

"I, uh, couldn't sleep."

"Got it."

"But I talked to my therapist. We have an appointment Monday morning," she said.

"Cool."

"I probably don't need to sleep between now and then, right?"

"Sure. Humans function well on zero sleep. Especially when they are already in a vulnerable state and they remove something that is both a coping mechanism and necessary biologically."

"So you're saying I'm doing good?"

"The goodest."

We watched two episodes of *Planet Earth*, then transitioned back into Shark Week. We attempted to make a dent in the leftover soup supply and were wildly unsuccessful. We were halfway through another Shark Week when Laurel came home. I immediately remembered that I was supposed to call Kyra.

"I thought you were joking when you said you would spend the day watching sharks and eating soup," Laurel said.

I leaned toward Lane without looking away from the TV. "Is she judging us?" I asked. Out of the corner of my eye, Lane nodded. "What a jerk."

"Such a jerk. You were nothing but honest with her."

"You guys know I can hear you, right?" Laurel asked.

"And now she's interrupting a very important experiment," Lane said.

"I know. We're never going to know why the sharks' feeding patterns suddenly changed in this specific area, twenty years ago." I shook my head.

"Which is pretty pivotal in our day-to-day lives."

"So pivotal."

"Whatever." Laurel walked down the hallway.

I laughed. "Laurel, wait. Come back." I paused the show.

Laurel emerged from the hallway looking skeptical. "What?"

"Did you bring us Juanita's?" I looked around. There were no grocery bags, no chips.

"Seriously?"

Lane started giggling. She hid under a blanket, but the blanket shook with her laughter.

"Your sister has never had Juanita's. They are the greatest tortilla chips to ever exist. Are you trying to set her up for failure?" I asked with the utmost sincerity.

Laurel looked pissed. It was possible I'd gone too far. She went back down the hallway.

Lane pulled her head out of the blanket. "Uh-oh."

"Shit. I'll be right back."

"Good luck."

I found Laurel sitting on the floor in my room. Her oxfords were untied and loosened, but that was as far as she'd gotten.

"Hey, we were just fucking around."

Laurel looked up, seemingly surprised to see me. "Oh. I know. Sorry."

"You okay?"

She nodded deliberately. "Yeah, sure. Of course."

I sat next to her and started to pull off her shoes. "How did the consult go?"

"Not great, honestly."

"What happened?"

"We met with a couple of detectives assigned to Sexual Assault. They've had four reported rapes in the last two weeks on Sac State's campus. All at Greek parties. All the victims were young women."

"Shit." That seemed to cover it. I knew I should be upset at the high rate—and I was—but all I could think about was Laurel sitting in that meeting discussing her own sister.

"That's not including Lane."

I was confused. "But she was at a party on campus. And it was less than forty-eight hours ago."

She nodded. "Yeah. But these cases were all connected. They just found out. That was the consult. All of the victims were dosed with ketamine. They just got word from the Sexual Assault nurse at the hospital."

"Was Lane drugged too?"

She started to shrug, then changed it to a nod. "Yeah. Of course she was. The nurse didn't include her, but I'm sure when they get her blood panel back it will show ketamine."

"Okay. So what did they say when you mentioned your sister was likely part of their investigation?" I asked. Laurel jerked in response. I tried asking a different way. "Did Ionescu pull you?"

"No. Of course not."

"Of course not what?"

"I didn't tell them. It's not my case so it isn't relevant. There's nothing to pull me from."

"I'm pretty sure it's still relevant. If nothing else, your sister was just raped so you're not going to be able to stay neutral."

She looked up and held my gaze. "I'm perfectly capable of determining when my judgment is compromised."

Well, that tone was not good. "Okay."

"How could you even suggest that?"

"I'm not suggesting anything. I think the last couple of days have been rough. I imagine sitting in a meeting discussing sexual assault on the college campus where your sister was just sexually assaulted is difficult."

"Fuck." She hung her head. "Yes. I'm sorry. I didn't mean to jump on you."

"It's fine. Like I said, it's been a rough couple of days."

"Yeah." She reached blindly for my hand. I scooted closer and pulled her in. She braced her forehead against my shoulder and breathed me in. "Thank you."

"For what?"

"I don't know." She shrugged. "Letting me be a dick. Not condemning me for it."

"It's cool. Seriously. You're dealing with a lot." I ran my fingers through her hair and she sighed. "And you're not being a dick. You're just not filtering your usual dickishness very well."

She chuckled. "So I'm naturally a dick and usually I just hide it."

"Exactly."

She sat up and made eye contact with me again. Her eyes looked a little pink, but she was smiling. "That's good to know."

"Now, I'd like to confess that I didn't call Kyra. In my defense, I forgot."

"That's your defense?"

"Yep."

Laurel rolled her eyes. "All you need to do is add two names to a guest list."

"And I'm going to. Just as soon as I remember."

"The event is tonight."

"And your point?"

She realized I was messing with her. "You're obnoxious."

I grinned and pulled her in for a kiss. She held back to force me to move in closer. When I did, she rested a warm palm against my rib cage. The other hand, she placed on my chest, just above my heart. Her fingertips pressed into the dip above my collarbone. She exhaled, inhaled deeply as I moved closer. She smelled like freshly split wood, warm and crisp. Her lips slid against mine, smooth and familiar. Her grip on my ribs tightened and I drew back.

"Your sister is in the living room."

Laurel groaned. "Christ, that's inconvenient." She dropped her hands and scooted backward. We shakily got to our feet. Or maybe that was just me shaking. She looked at the floor instead of me. Her shoes seemed to fascinate her. She stared at them as if she didn't know how they had been removed. She shook her head a little. "Okay, you call Kyra. I'll go convince Lane to go out with us tonight."

I saluted exaggeratedly at her. "On it, Detective."

"And maybe consider showering."

I glared. "Now you've gone too far."

Laurel glared back. Her glare was better.

A few hours later, Robin, the Kallen sisters, and I were granted access to a private opening of the Scholten Gallery. Which surprised me not at all.

Kyra caught my eye from across the room and smiled briefly before continuing her conversation with a handful of old dudes. It looked super fun.

Robin looped her arm through mine. "I need wine. I need to meet Kyra's new boyfriend. And I need to look at art."

"Girl, I've got just the night planned for you," I said.

"I'll get wine. You see if Kyra needs rescuing."

"On it."

Laurel and Lane followed Robin as I ducked around people to get to Kyra. The gallery had cultivated an impressive showing. When I was about ten feet away, Kyra shot me a pleading look. It was brief but desperate. I sidled up to her just a little closer than was appropriate.

"Excuse me. I'm sorry to interrupt, but I need to borrow Ms. Daneshmandan."

The three men she was talking to exchanged looks. I couldn't tell if it was my queerness throwing them off or the fact that my queerness had made Kyra's queerness impossible to ignore. Or maybe they just didn't like the cut of my pants. It was hard to tell old men's expressions apart.

As soon as they were out of earshot, Kyra turned and hugged me. "Ugh. I hate art. What am I doing here?"

"You're the artist." I waved my hand at the fifteen-foot canvas behind Kyra.

"There's no need for you to point that out. I'm having a moment of weakness."

I chuckled. Kyra could lie to herself, but she couldn't lie to me. "Where's Van? Robin is dying to meet him."

"Oh no. I put names on the guest list in exchange for meeting Laurel's sister. I'm collecting Kallens like Pokémon cards."

I held back an eye roll. "Lane's with Laurel and Robin." I nodded at the trio weaving through the crowd toward us. "They are coming over here to meet Van. You going to deliver?"

"Yes. I'll introduce my dreamy boyfriend to you."

"You have a dreamy boyfriend? Damn. I was going to ask you out," a deep voice behind us said.

Kyra and I turned. She smiled and drew a guy with dark, curly hair and an unruly brow into our circle. "I'll lose the boyfriend immediately."

"My night is looking up." He smiled back at her.

"I'm really hoping you're Van. Otherwise this is going to be awkward," I said.

"I am." He held out his hand. "You must be Cash."

I nodded and shook his hand. I felt Laurel come up behind me before I heard her.

"Robin. Laurel." Kyra dropped her grip on Van's arm to hug the newcomers. "This is Van Bertram. Artist. Professor. Boyfriend."

"You forgot dreamy," Van said.

"I thought that part was obvious," Kyra said.

"It's good to meet you." Laurel shook Van's hand.

Robin opted for a hug. "It really is. I was starting to wonder if she had invented you."

"Same." Van grinned. "Kyra's far too antisocial to have actual friends."

Kyra looked at Laurel pointedly, then slid her gaze to Lane.

"Sorry. This is my baby sister, Lane." Laurel put her arm around Lane's waist.

Kyra rolled her eyes. "Finally. You're not a cop, right? I can flirt with you without hating myself?"

Lane didn't really know what to make of that. "I'm definitely not a cop. I actually have self-esteem."

Kyra started laughing, then saw Laurel's expression and laughed even harder. "Yep. She's my favorite." She pointed at Lane. "And you said there's one more?" she asked me.

"Yeah. Another brother," I said.

"He's a hoot." Laurel didn't even try to curb her sarcasm.

"Another cop?" Kyra asked.

"Is this like a whole cop family thing?" Van asked.

"No, only two of us. We're disgraces because we aren't lawyers," Laurel said.

Kyra gasped. "Same here. Of course, I went the complete opposite route." She waved at the canvas behind her.

"Oh, that's a good point. Next time my mother gets pissy about the detective thing, I'll remind her of the semester I changed my major to theater," Laurel said.

We all stared at Laurel.

"You did what?" I asked.

"Oh, yeah. I was a theater major."

"On purpose?" Robin asked.

"Yep."

"Have you met you?" I asked.

"Oh, whatever. I was good," Laurel said. We laughed. She didn't look like she appreciated the laughing.

"Hey, I feel you." Van spoke over us. "My first semester in college, I studied biology." He shuddered.

"Oh, my God," Lane said.

We all turned to her.

"You look familiar. Do I know you?" Van asked.

"Umm, yeah. I'm taking your seminar. I guess I didn't recognize you out of the classroom."

Van smiled, which frankly, made him look pretty dreamy. "No way. Are you enjoying it?"

"Say yes," I stage-whispered to Lane.

She laughed. "I am, yeah."

"You're taking an art seminar?" Laurel asked.

"Yeah. It's Queering American Art in the Twentieth Century," Lane said.

Kyra turned to Van. "That's what you called the seminar? You are such a douche." He smirked.

"Why did you choose that one?" Laurel asked.

"I don't know. I needed an art seminar. My sister's queer." Lane glanced at Van, then immediately looked away. "Plus, Professor Bertram is kind of a celebrity on campus. I mean, he's one of the few trans faculty members. He's an actual artist. And he's not ninety years old like half the professors."

Kyra groaned. "Why, Lane? He's going to be impossible now."

"What?" Lane asked.

"A celebrity? Professor Bertram? Ugh. You used to be my favorite Kallen."

"Oh. Sorry."

"It's fine. I'll forgive you. But you have to spend the next twenty minutes telling me how brilliant I am. Come on." Kyra looped her arm through Lane's and led her away.

"I'm so giving that kid an A," Van said as soon as they were out of earshot.

"It's good you have standards," I said.

"Absolutely. Accidental sucking up is the best kind."

"Well, now that I know you're a professor, I expect a fantastic discussion about art," Robin said.

Van grimaced. "That sounds like work. How about I escort you around and tell you all the dirty secrets about the art collectors."

"That sounds much more fun."

Van led Robin upstairs where they leaned against the railing and looked down. He pointed someone out and leaned close to tell Robin a story. She started laughing.

"Is she going to be okay?" Laurel asked.

"What? Yeah. Why wouldn't she be?" I looked away from Van and Robin and realized Laurel was watching Lane across the gallery. "Oh. Yeah. She's a strong kid. She can get through this."

Laurel slid her hand into mine. "Thank you."

Chapter Six

Nate looked like shit. He had a scruffy beard that didn't look cultivated. His hair was still wet from the shower, but it wasn't styled. But the ultimate sign of dissonance was his inside out varsity jacket.

"Hey, man." I pulled the coffee I'd gotten him out of the cup holder.

"Oh, God. I love you." He wrapped his hands around the paper cup.

"How's the dissertation going?"

He groaned. "Would you ask a pregnant woman at eight and a half months how the pregnancy was going? No. So don't ask me how the fucking dissertation is going."

"Right." I pulled out of his parking lot and turned back the way I'd come. I couldn't believe I'd driven to Davis just to pick him up. But then I saw how pathetic he looked and remembered how sad he had sounded on the phone. "When's the last time you went outside?"

"What's today?"

"Monday."

"Hmm. Is it still October?" he asked.

"Wow."

"I will accept pity or tough love from you, but judgment and scorn are not approved."

"Okay. Did you know your jacket is inside out?"

He screwed up his face and made a strange sound. "That explains a lot." He put the coffee back in the cup holder and shrugged out of his jacket. One of the big patches caught on his sleeve and it took him way too long to disentangle it. He wrestled it right side out and pulled it back on.

"I didn't know if you were going for a look or something," I said.

"If that's a look, I've been inside for way too long."

"If it is a look, I think you're too old to pull it off."

Nate flipped me off. "I don't suppose you know why we've been summoned?"

"Sac State has had a recent increase in sexual assaults. All the victims had ketamine in their systems. So I'm guessing they are looking for a ketamine connection."

"Huh. Ketamine is back in vogue?" he asked.

"Apparently."

"It's good we are up on trends."

"Between that and the jacket, I feel like you might be too advanced for this world." I wove through traffic to hit our exit. Nate did that grandma thing where he pressed his foot to an imaginary brake until I got off the freeway. "It's good they called us in to consult on a drug we don't sell that we didn't even know was being used," I said.

"Yeah, I mean, we probably are going to learn a lot. I love when they put on these private seminars for us," he said.

"I just wish they would take requests."

"Hey, you're sleeping with a detective. Shouldn't that garner you some influence? Can you tell Kallen I'd like one on trying to get out of the drug business while on the homestretch of finishing a PhD?" Nate's phone beeped and he wiggled it out of his pocket. "Also maybe stress management."

"Sure. No problem."

"Are you getting texts like these?" He held up the phone for me to read. I was driving so I didn't read it.

"You know I can't see that, right?"

"Oh. Got it." He pulled the phone away. "It's one of my Sac City kids. Haven't heard from him in months."

"I assume he's one of the customers Jerome poached? I'm getting texts too." I finally pulled into the parking lot of the Sacramento Police Department headquarters.

"Have you responded at all? What do you want to do?"

"I don't know. I've only had enough product to fill the few customers who didn't stray. I wanted to see if you had enough demand to justify a larger order."

"I do. I'm just not sure how long they will stick around," he said.

I parked. Nate took off his seat belt and grabbed his coffee, all at half speed. I got out and waited for him at the back of the car. We were never going to make our meeting on time. I wasn't mad about it.

"I feel like we should take advantage of the situation, but I'm not quite sure how," I said.

"And by situation, you mean what?"

"Jerome obviously doesn't have a secure supply line. He will get one sooner or later."

"So you want to take him down?" he asked.

"Yeah, but the customers will go back to him when he starts selling again. He's selling cheap to intentionally undercut us."

"And his product is cheap crap."

"That too," I said.

"So what do you want to do?"

"I want to undermine him."

"That sounds fun." Nate tripped over his own feet. He barely noticed. When we were finished with this meeting, I was going to feed him and force him to sleep. "That wasn't sarcasm, by the way. It really does sound fun."

"Agreed. I don't have much going on. It's kind of pathetic."

"Well, if you want to help me compile data, I can show you a good time," he said brightly.

"That seems more pathetic than unemployed drug dealer."

Nate held the door for me and I led the way upstairs. We were far too acquainted with this building. The squad room was loud, busy. The first month we were CIs, the detectives were intentional assholes to us, which basically meant they only called us in at the most inconvenient times. Looking at the current population of the squad room, I was suddenly feeling nostalgic for those days.

We headed for the desk Laurel and Reyes shared. Laurel had gone home the night before, which had a positive effect on the range of her wardrobe. She was wearing a thick, cable knit sweater with a blue collared shirt under it. The pop of blue brought out the cool tone of the sweater and the brightness in her eyes. Not that I was cruising her.

I glanced around for Duarte. I didn't think I could handle indulging Detective Junior and his protectiveness yet. I hadn't had enough coffee. I doubted there was enough coffee for me to reach the threshold of tolerance.

"Hey, guys. Reyes said you were coming in. Can I escort you to the conference room?" Duarte asked.

I turned. I'd been looking around the squad room so intently, I'd missed Duarte coming up behind us. "Yeah, that would be good. Thanks."

"Sure. Of course." He bounced a couple of times on the toes of his Adidas. "Want me to get Blackford and Fenton for you? Reyes didn't say who all you were meeting."

"I have no idea who we are meeting with. Nor do I know who Blackford and Fenton are," I said. He nodded a lot. "I just know Kallen said jump so we're here to jump."

"You know how we love to assist law enforcement in any way possible," Nate said.

"Right." Duarte ignored the obvious sarcasm. "Well, let me get you set up and then I'll figure out who needs to know you're here." He led the way to one of the conference rooms. After asking if we wanted coffee no less than three times, he left.

Nate sat and pulled out his phone. "I'll show you mine if you show me yours."

"I'm going to need some context."

"Texts from customers who abandoned us, then came crawling back when the cheap guy turned out to be unreliable."

"Not that you're bitter about it or anything," I said.

"Nope. Definitely not irritated at those inconstant assholes."

I couldn't disagree with him. We both knew we needed out, but we wanted it to be a choice, not the result of Jerome St. Maris managing to unseat us. That was just insulting. I opened my messages to show Nate. It only took a minute of scrolling to find an obvious pattern. Jerome didn't have Adderall. We didn't get to discuss said Adderall paucity because the door opened and a line of detectives filed in. Nate and I stood while they sorted out seating.

Reyes took the seat across from me. Laurel took the seat next to Nate. That was good. Very inconspicuous. No one would suspect we were fucking if she sat next to someone else at the conference table.

Two guys sat next to Reyes. The one on his right was slender and tall. He wore dark, stiff jeans and had his shirtsleeves cuffed to his elbows. The other was also tall but stocky. His beard was gray and full. Impressive, if you were into that sort of thing.

Reyes spoke first. "Xiao, Braddock, this is Detective Travis Blackford." The younger, slim one. "And Detective Lyle Fenton." The heavier, bearded one. "They are from the Sexual Assault and Child Abuse unit. Blackford, Fenton, this is Cash Braddock and Nathan Xiao."

"Good to meet you." Fenton leaned over the table to shake both our hands.

"Yeah, thanks for coming down today," Blackford said.

"Sure," I said. Nate nodded. Our excitement was palpable.

Fenton unlocked his iPad. "I'm not sure what Kallen and Reyes have told you, but we have had five reported rapes at or around Sacramento State in the last two weeks."

Fenton stopped talking when he caught me looking at Laurel. I was pretty sure she'd said four rapes when we spoke on Sunday. I wondered if she had finally told them about Lane. Or maybe her labs finally came back and the hospital had contacted Blackford and Fenton. Forty-eight hours could be a long time. Someone else could have been assaulted over the weekend.

Blackford picked up the thread when Fenton didn't continue speaking. "All five victims were young women who attend the college. The circumstances around the assaults are similar. All occurred at parties at Greek houses." He flipped open a notebook. "All have similar time frames."

"The most notable similarity, of course, is the use of ketamine," Fenton said.

"Aside from the ketamine, why is this unusual? Greek organizations are literally known for being rapey." Nate was clearly not into participating today. I knew he was stressed over writing his dissertation, which was probably why he was short-tempered, but I was also thoroughly enjoying watching him be dismissive.

"Sac State's campus averages two or three reported rapes per year. That's obviously a small percentage of the actual sexual assaults on campus," Blackford said. A muscle below his eye started to twitch. The faster he spoke, the faster it twitched. "Five reported means there are potentially double that amount. Regardless, the increase is unusual."

"Maybe it's just a combination of school being back in session and the recent political climate. More people might be reporting than in previous years," I said. I thought Nate made a good point. Frat boys being rapey was pretty on brand for them.

"Honestly, we thought the same thing. It wasn't until we found out the victims were dosed with ketamine that we connected the cases," Blackford said.

"That's why we brought Kallen and Reyes, and subsequently you two, in on the case. We've seen ketamine used previously, but it's not common," Fenton said.

Reyes spoke up. "I've barely seen any ketamine use in the last few years. And that use was strictly as a party drug, not to facilitate sexual assault. We thought you guys might be able to offer some insight."

Nate looked at me and shrugged. "I haven't seen much ketamine use recently. Molly is more popular for recreational use. And I rarely get requests for date rape drugs."

"Same here. But most people know better than to ask either of us for date rape drugs," I said.

Nate poorly hid a smile. Two summers ago, some dude had asked him for roofies and Nate just bitch-slapped the guy. No explanation, no warning. Just an open-handed slap.

"Sorry we couldn't be more help." Nate stood. I hastened to stand with him.

Fenton and Blackford looked up at Nate, their confusion evident. "But we haven't asked you any questions," Blackford said.

"We didn't deal ketamine or any similar drugs. I don't think we have much insight to offer." Nate shrugged. I did my best to look appropriately saddened that we couldn't help.

"We know. You two focused on prescriptions." Fenton glanced at his iPad screen. "Primarily opioids and stimulants. We still think you'll be able to help us. That's why we asked to interview you."

"Oh." We sat down. It had been a good try. We carefully didn't make eye contact with each other. I knew he had been fucking with them, but the detectives seemed unaware.

They spent a good twenty minutes quizzing us on local dealers who might sell ketamine. They seemed to be under the impression that we didn't understand their line of questioning and if they phrased the question in a specific way, we would suddenly get it. Tragically, they were incorrect. After that, we spent ten minutes reviewing the witness statements from the victims in an attempt to identify the perpetrators. The running theory was if the perps bought drugs from someone else, they might have also bought them from us. The witness statements had all been recorded between midnight and four a.m. and were from twenty-year-olds who had all just been raped while on ketamine. They weren't heavy on specifics.

Laurel finally intervened. "Let's take a break, guys."

Blackford's eye finally stopped twitching. "Good idea."

Nate shot out of his seat and headed for the door. I followed him. Partially because I wanted out of the room, but mostly because I was afraid he wasn't coming back. He headed for the stairs. I started to follow him, but stopped when Laurel grabbed my arm.

I did my best to not fall into Laurel's baby blues because we were at the police station where she would definitely be fired if anyone figured out that we were sleeping together. It didn't work. She still looked hot.

"Got a second?" she asked.

"Maybe we could speak privately?"

"Sure."

CHAPTER SEVEN

"Let's go in here." Laurel led me to one of the dark observation rooms that looked in on an interrogation room through one-way glass.

As soon as the door closed, I pressed her back against it and kissed her. She gripped my shoulders. She started to restrain me, to push me away. And then she gave in. Her hands shifted to wrap around my wrists. I pressed my palms into the door harder. If I touched her, I wasn't sure I'd stop.

Having Lane around wasn't a problem. Being afraid to touch my girlfriend because her sister was pretending to sleep in the next room apparently was a problem.

Laurel whimpered. I pushed the length of my body against hers. Her breath caught. She tilted my head back and kissed down my neck. Her mouth was open, sucking, biting. It felt really fucking good.

Somewhere in the back of my mind, I was thinking about walking back into the conference room with bite marks on my neck and a flushed Detective Kallen. That would probably be bad. But that thought wasn't enough to slow me down. She had my pants unzipped before I realized it. I couldn't stop her. I didn't want to. She slid her fingertips under the elastic of my waistband.

Her phone started ringing. Her hand stilled.

"Fuck."

"Shit." Laurel dug into her pocket and pulled out her phone. "Hello."

I was close enough to hear Janice Kallen's voice come over the line. Laurel curled her hand into a fist, seemingly not realizing that it was still wrapped around the top of my underwear. I only caught half of what her mom was saying, but I didn't have the desire to hear the whole thing. Janice was still angry that Lane wasn't taking her calls or responding to her texts. Her desire wasn't irrational. Her youngest child had been assaulted and she hadn't been there for her. That had to sting. But I was fascinated by the logic that made Lane not answering her phone Laurel's responsibility.

Janice's tirade played itself out in only a few minutes. Laurel made a lot of non-committal noises.

"Are you even listening to me?" Janice asked.

"I don't know what you expect me to do." Laurel's voice was tight with anger.

"Bring Lane home."

"I can't do that."

"We are not the enemy," Janice said.

"No one said you were, Mom." There was a flash of pity in her tone that quickly shifted into authority. "Lane needs to be able to control her own life, her own body, her own decisions. Right now more than ever. I'm just following her lead."

"So she doesn't want to see us."

"I don't know. At the moment, she wants to watch documentaries and eat salt and vinegar chips with M&Ms."

Janice started yelling about Lane's health. I didn't think she was talking about physical. I lifted Laurel's fist away from my waistband and took a step back. She looked at me with an apology as I buttoned my jeans.

"Mom." The yelling continued. "Mom." Laurel pulled the phone away from her ear and shook her head. "Why did I answer this call?" she asked me.

"Because you're the child who answers calls?" I offered a half smile. Laurel gave far more weight to duty than I ever had. It was a quality I didn't understand, but maybe it was admirable.

Laurel sighed and put the phone back to her ear. "Mom, I'm trusting Lane to know what she needs. If she needs help from us or her therapist or her friends, she will communicate it. But I'm not going to assume she's broken just because the first thing she asked for wasn't her mother." There was blissful silence as Janice processed that. When she finally spoke, it was low enough that I couldn't make out what she said. "No, I'm not trying to be hurtful. I'm just trying to get through the day. Listen, I'll tell Lane you're worried about her, okay?" Janice said something else. Laurel's jaw tightened. "I'm at work. I need to go. We'll talk later." She hung up without waiting for a response.

"So are you grounded or not? Because I was really hoping we could get milkshakes later."

She smiled. "I'll sneak out the window. Pick me up at the corner."

I leaned back against the table that had been shoved into the cramped room. "You're a rebel, Detective."

"I know."

"I take it your mom doesn't know Lane is at her therapist's right now?"

"Clearly not. I get why she's upset, but this really isn't about her feelings."

I crossed my arms over my chest. "Hopefully, she'll see that soon. In the meantime, maybe try to get her to meet with a counselor as well."

Laurel nodded, but it lacked conviction. "Yeah. I'll try."

"So before I jumped you, I assume there was something you wanted to talk about?"

"The jumping was far more enjoyable." She grinned.

"We should probably be wary of private meetings in the police department headquarters."

"Shit." Laurel's eyes darted around the room like she'd just remembered where we were. "Yeah. Umm, I pulled you in here to let you know Lane's labs haven't come back yet. The fifth victim was from yesterday."

"Why did her labs come back so fast when Lane's didn't?"

She shrugged. "I'm not sure. I'm guessing Fenton didn't ask them to rush labs on victims that matched the profile until after our conversation Sunday."

"What exactly is their plan here? Even if they identify one of the rapists, he's not going to give up the dealer. And if he does, the dealer won't give up the other potential rapists."

"Actually, they probably will. We'll offer them a plea, which is no loss because the chances they will serve time are minimal anyway."

"What do you mean?" I asked.

"Statistically, the chances that any rapist will serve jail time are negligible."

It was one of those facts I'd heard dozens of times and never entirely registered. "That doesn't bother you?"

"Of course it does."

"Sorry. It just seems like the police should be doing more."

"We are doing our part. Catching the perpetrators won't unrape anyone. At best, it makes it harder for the rapist to offend again. At worst, it slows him down for a couple of months. But that's the part I play."

"Even if the perp is back on the street after only a few months?"

"At least he's off the street for those few months."

"How are you so cavalier about this?"

She let out a choked laugh. "You think I'm being cavalier?"

"Yes. You just said it's pointless to catch rapists." If that wasn't cavalier, I truly didn't know what was.

"I didn't say pointless. I just said it was cyclical. Inevitable."

"Your sister was just raped."

"And if we catch the guy, the uniforms will let me or Lance into the guy's interrogation for ten minutes while the camera is off," she said matter-of-factly.

It took me a minute to figure out what she was saying. It took me a lot longer to comprehend it. "Seriously, Detective? You're going to go vigilante and beat the shit out of some dude after he's in police custody?"

"Yes."

"You didn't even think about it." I was amazed. "You just knew you would get a call from someone and they would arrange for you to have time to beat someone."

"It's not something that requires thought. It was a decision made the moment someone decided to rape Lane." She seemed frustrated at my lack of understanding.

"But all the other rapists just won't serve time? Because it isn't worth it?"

"No. They will also probably get roughed up. Because none of them will serve time. We all know it."

"This is why people don't trust cops. You know that, right?" I didn't know what was worse: beating a perpetrator who hadn't been convicted or the easy acceptance that justice wouldn't be served.

"Please. It isn't just the police. That's why the WEAVE advocates emphasize the need for counseling. Justice doesn't exist for the victims of violent crimes. All the police can do is try to prevent the next one. The counselors can try to keep the survivors from falling apart. Did you know that perpetrators get rape kits too? The victim has a choice. But if we catch the perp, he doesn't get to consent to a kit. And the Sexual Assault nurse is not kind and gentle when she performs those exams. Society is fucked up. We are just holding cotton to the wound."

The door opened and Reyes stuck his head in. "There you are. Duarte just went to get Xiao. We are reconvening."

"We'll be right out," Laurel said.

"No, we're done here." I marched past Laurel. "Thanks for the enlightening explanation, Detective."

She clenched her jaw but didn't say anything. I followed Reyes back to the conference room. A second after I sat down, Laurel followed us into the room. Both of them took a seat. She folded her hands and stared at the wall. Her shoulders were so rigid she was practically at attention. Reyes looked back and forth between us but didn't say anything. I wondered if she had told him about Lane. I wondered if he agreed with her.

Within two minutes, everyone was back around the conference table. Even Nate.

Fenton started us off. "We'd like to review the descriptions of the perps with you guys again. When we're finished, we would like the names of any of your former customers who might fit the profile."

Nate and I exchanged a look. That was going to be a really long list.

"Let me read the descriptions again. Listening to you read them isn't giving me a strong picture," I said.

Blackford thumbed through his file and handed me photocopies of police reports. I spread them out on the table so Nate could see them as well. Part of me hoped that I'd been tuning out the detectives and reading would give me clarity, but I quickly realized the reports lacked just as much information as they had the first three times I listened to them. Nate and I read all of them again. The detectives watched us. It was unnerving.

"They all sound like white guys." Nate said it low, but it was impossible for the detectives to not hear him.

"They are all described as Caucasian," Blackford said. He clearly missed the point.

"Yeah, but you know how all straight, cis, white dudes kind of look the same?" I asked.

Nate nodded in solidarity. Reyes hesitated, then he nodded too. Laurel was still staring at the wall. Fenton and Blackford seemed confused.

"Not really," Fenton said. Just like a straight, cis, white dude would.

"Well, these descriptions all sound like the same guy."

"That's not true." Blackford started reading from his notebook. "One is described as having blue eyes, another as green. One had darker slicked back hair. One had longer sandy brown hair. And another had dirty blond." He was kind of proving my point.

"So lighter eyes and different hair styles. That's not exactly a variety of dudes. I'm just saying they all sound the same to me." I knew I was being an ass, but I was tired of being there, tired of cops.

"But a straight girl isn't going to have the same issues differentiating between men as you do," Laurel said.

Nate shrugged. "She's not wrong."

"Then maybe they are all the same guy and that's why it sounds the same," I said.

They all stared at me. Blackford was the first to break. He started flipping through his files and making notations in his notebook. Fenton followed suit with his iPad. Reyes leaned across the table and collected the reports Nate and I had been reading. He started writing notes on them.

"If you're right, we are dealing with a serial rapist, not an increase in ketamine usage," Fenton said.

"It would account for the similarities in circumstances." Blackford didn't look up from his frantic note taking.

"Shouldn't you have already gotten that information from the rape kits?" I asked. If one guy was responsible, his DNA would match across victims. The detectives looked at me. Their expressions ranged from confusion to pity.

Nate nodded. "Yeah. Unless he didn't leave any DNA. But this guy doesn't seem that sophisticated."

The detectives shifted their looks to Nate. Then they all looked at each other. They seemed confused by the statement.

"The rape kits haven't been processed," Fenton said.

"Oh. Well, how long until they finish processing?"

"They haven't been started. The lab doesn't process the kit until we go to trial."

"What do you mean?" Nate asked.

"Just what I said. The rape kit isn't a tool to catch the perp. It's a tool to convict the perp," Fenton said.

"But if you've already caught them, conviction shouldn't be an issue. Wouldn't it be more useful for catching the perp?" I flashed back to the conversation I'd had with Laurel twenty minutes before. She was still wrong, but she was right about how fucked up the system was. "Never mind. Just tell us what you need so we can go."

"We need a list from you so we can start working our way through possible perpetrators," Blackford said.

"Whatever," I said.

"So what are we looking at?" Fenton asked. The question was directed at Blackford, but we were all present so I took it.

"A white guy in his early twenties. Between five nine and five eleven, approximately two hundred pounds. Light brown or dark blond hair with lighter eyes. Poor hygiene," I said.

"Why poor hygiene?" Fenton asked.

"All the victims mentioned a heavy, musky cologne. Like three of them mentioned bad acne." I shrugged.

Blackford looked up at that detail. "One of them said he had oily skin."

"That could all just be unkempt college boy," Reyes said.

"Okay. Fine. Unkempt college boy."

"So based on that description, can you generate a list of names for us?" Fenton asked.

Nate looked at me and shook his head. "That's like sixty percent of our customers. We couldn't possibly name all of them," he said.

"This isn't the time for you guys to play your uncooperative games," Laurel said.

"We're not being uncooperative. That list would be hundreds of names long. It would be a waste of time for us to create it and a waste of time for you guys to run through it looking for leads."

"What if you include anyone who has asked for a drug that could be used to facilitate a sexual assault?" Reyes asked. He was trying to do us a solid, but it wasn't working.

"So any opioid?" I said.

Reyes grimaced. "Oh. Never mind."

"We might be able to find a local source of ketamine." At Nate's words, I had to force myself not to look at him. Where had that offer come from? "But chances are decent that it was purchased online."

Blackford and Fenton looked at each other. Blackford shrugged. Fenton nodded. "That would be great. If we get any more information on the perp, can we pass it on to you?" Fenton asked.

"That's fine. Just tell Kallen or Reyes and they will contact us," I said.

"Perfect," Blackford said. He and Fenton stood. Reyes and Laurel followed suit. And then Nate and I were free. For the day at least.

Chapter Eight

"You want to tell me what that offer was about?" I asked as soon as we reached the parking lot.

Nate shrugged. "Maybe I'm feeling benevolent."

"Right."

"I don't like rapists."

"True. But you also think the police are incompetent assholes," I said.

He grinned. "Yeah, okay. I figure whoever is dealing ketamine is probably getting drugs online like we are. If we don't keep an eye on supply lines, we won't have anything unique. Or it's Jerome. He would be the fuckwad dealing date rape drugs. Either way, it benefits us to find out, and it benefits us to have Sac PD shut them down."

"That's nice and all, but how do you plan on finding the source?"

"I'll ask."

"Who are you going to ask?"

"Jerome."

"Nate, I'm beat. I just had a fight with Laurel. I'm pretty sure her sister moved in with me. I'm still not speaking with Clive. I'm broke. Can we not do this whole coy, Nate's a genius thing?"

He gaped at me. "I have questions."

"Answer mine first."

"We have Adderall. Jerome needs Adderall. I think we should offer him some in exchange for information about ketamine."

"I really fucking like that idea," I said.

"Okay, wow. I thought it was good, but not brilliant."

"Remember what I said earlier about undermining Jerome?" I asked. He nodded. "Well, what better way than letting him have our clients, but forcing him to use us as a supply line?"

"Oh, man."

"Oh, man is right." I unlocked the car and climbed in.

"So what did you and Kallen have a fight about? You finally remember that she's a cop?"

"Could you not kick me while I'm down?"

"Fine."

"You want to get some lunch?" I turned up Freeport toward downtown.

"Yes. I want drunken noodles."

"That was really specific."

"Remember how I haven't been outdoors in years?"

"Years. Yeah, sure."

"I've been craving drunken noodles. But the only place that delivers Thai to my apartment has the worst drunken noodles. What's the point of becoming fat and lazy while I sob into my dissertation if there aren't any good drunken noodles?"

"That's a lot."

"That wasn't rhetorical."

"Umm. I guess there's no point?"

"You bet your ass there's no point."

I pulled up texting on the screen in my dash and found Lane's name. "You want Thai question mark." Siri sent the text.

Nate turned and stared incredulously. "I'm sorry. Did you just include punctuation in your text?"

"You got a problem with that?"

"I have a multitude of problems with it."

"Siri and I have a genuine connection. So many people misunderstand her, but I know how to speak to her," I said.

"I think I might hate you."

"No. You don't." A text from Lane popped up. I tapped it.

"Yes, please. Vegetarian red curry. And spring rolls."

I nodded even though Lane definitely couldn't see me. "Will you call it in?" I asked. Nate didn't react. "Nate?"

"What?"

"Will you call in the order?"

"Oh. Were you talking to me? I thought you were speaking to your special friend Siri."

"I didn't say question mark so obviously not."

"Obviously," he said in the most mocking tone he could muster. But then he called the Thai place.

❖

"Lane, you here?"

"Kitchen," she called.

While we were waiting for our food, I'd warned Lane via text that I was bringing a boy home. I didn't know how the whole survivor thing worked, and I didn't want to trigger her with a surprise boy.

I led Nate to the kitchen. Lane was pulling plates out of the cabinet. She was wearing leggings and a baggy sweater. I didn't know much about straight girls, but I was pretty sure that was an outfit.

"Lane, this is my buddy Nate. Nate, Lane, Laurel's younger sister."

Nate smiled and leaned forward to shake her hand. He hunched his shoulders to make himself slightly shorter. I wondered if that was conscious or not. It seemed like one of those details I'd never noticed, but in retrospect, he did it frequently with people who were noticeably younger or smaller than him. And most people were smaller than him.

"So I've only been here like three days, but Andy officially has me hooked on La Croix. She says it's gay water. Did you know water could be gay?" Lane asked.

"Yes," Nate and I both said.

"Okay. I wasn't expecting that answer."

"Everything can be gay. Like check this out." I picked up a coffee mug from the counter. "Gay mug."

Lane pursed her lips and watched me. It was like she couldn't decide if I was kidding or not.

"That fridge is gay." Nate tipped his chin toward the fridge. "And the table."

"The table is super gay," I said.

"There are levels of gay?" Lane asked.

Nate set the bag of takeout on the gay table and started unpacking it. "There are always levels. Right now, we are in Cash's house. She's super queer, thus all the objects she owns are inherently queer."

"The La Croix is only gay because it's in Cash's fridge?" Lane sat at the kitchen table and propped her chin on her hand. She was legit ready to discuss this with him.

"No. La Croix is just gay. Like statement tees. Or effective communication," he said.

"So like gay dudes communicate more effectively than you do?"

"No." Nate opened a container and set it aside. "In this case gay is specifically lesbian." He opened the spring rolls and put them in the center of the gay table.

"Why didn't you say lesbian instead of gay or queer?" It didn't seem like Lane was trying to trip him up. She was delving into queer research.

"Because we were talking about La Croix. It was obviously gay as in lesbian." Nate found the red curry and set it in front of Lane.

"I don't know. I think it might be gay as in not cis man gay. So queer and lesbian, but not gay," I said.

Nate pointed at me like I'd offered a really important distinction. "But we still call it gay colloquially."

"Yeah, of course."

Lane nodded slowly. "Right. Got it."

"So do you want a La Croix?" I opened the fridge. There was an excessive amount of La Croix.

"Oh. Yes, please." Lane started to get up, but I waved her back down.

Once we'd distributed food and plates and gay beverages, we all dug in.

"So what are you doing camping out at Cash's? Hiding from the mob?"

Lane chuckled wryly. She pressed her lips together and took a deep breath before speaking. "A couple of nights ago, I was raped. Being on campus is uncomfortable right now."

Nate stopped eating. "Fuck."

"Yeah."

"I'm sorry that happened."

"Yeah."

"Wait." Nate looked at me. I shook my head, but he didn't catch it. "Is she one of the five? Because Kallen—"

"No. It's not the same case," I said.

"What case?" Lane asked.

"Nothing. We can't talk about it."

"Is Laurel investigating my case? I thought she couldn't do that," Lane said.

I set down my fork. This was going to be a long conversation. "She's not. There's another case that's really similar to yours, but I don't think they are related."

"Good. I don't want her on the case."

Nate cocked his head. "Why not?"

"They're probably not going to catch him. I don't want her to carry that guilt." Lane snagged a spring roll and held out the container for Nate. He took one.

I started back in on my food. I didn't know how to say that Laurel had confirmed that fact just a few hours before.

"You don't know that," Nate said.

"No. But it's pretty unlikely. It's been three days." Lane shrugged. "Plus, you know, looking for a specific rapist on a college campus is like looking for a specific piece of hay in a haystack."

Nate choked, then started coughing.

"You okay?" I asked.

"Yeah." He took a drink. "That description was just a little too apt."

"I didn't even want to report it, honestly. My sorority sister bullied me into it. I know she was trying to help, but I wish she would have just let it go."

"But then he just gets away with it," Nate said.

Lane started one of her breathing exercises.

"Nate."

He turned toward me. "Hmm?"

"Maybe this is something you should try to understand on your own instead of quizzing Lane," I said.

"Oh. Right. Yeah, sorry, Lane." He shook his head. "I didn't think that through."

"Actually, it's okay. I can talk about it."

"No. Cash is right."

"Really. It would be helpful. I process things better when I'm asked to explain them. Plus, you're safe," she said.

"How so?"

"You're not part of my immediate circle, but judging by your relationship with Cash, you're trustworthy."

Nate and I looked at each other. I tried to find a flaw in her logic and came up short.

"Okay." Nate readied himself. "So it seems like this asshole won't face any repercussions if you don't report it. Even if the chances of catching him are slim, at least there's a chance."

"What's the best-case scenario there?" Lane asked.

Nate had a list prepared. "He gets arrested. Is actually convicted. Goes to jail."

"Great. Cool. And how does that help me?"

That seemed to stump Nate. "I don't know. But he has to serve his time."

"And regardless if he serves a month or ten years, it doesn't do a thing for me."

"What if the best-case scenario is that he goes to jail and all that, but also learns that it isn't okay to assault women?" I asked.

"Good. Yeah. Still doesn't help me move on. And he is the one who benefits from the lesson. I already knew the lesson."

"Oh, shit," Nate said.

Lane half smiled. "Yeah."

"So what is the best-case scenario for you?" Nate asked.

Her smiled expanded. "Now you're asking the right question. The best-case scenario for me would be to deal with the trauma in a healthy manner."

"That makes sense." I really wanted to ask Lane the same questions I'd asked Laurel, but I was afraid she would confirm what her sister had said.

"Is our justice system pointless then? Should we replace police with trauma centers?" Nate asked.

"Whoa. You went micro to macro instantly," Lane said.

"Sorry. I haven't talked to off-campus humans in weeks. I'm apparently in a very academic head space."

"That doesn't seem healthy. You should probably get out more."

"He's finishing his dissertation. It's been a time," I said.

"Okay. That's less odd."

My phone vibrated. I pulled it out. Jerome St. Maris. I really didn't want to talk to him. Sure, I'd asked him to call me, but I still didn't want to talk to him. "Sorry, I have to take this." They both waved me off. I swiped as I walked down the hallway to my bedroom. "Hello."

"You called," Jerome said.

"Yeah. I've got an offer for you." I closed the door.

"What kind of offer?"

"I understand you're low on Adderall."

"Oh yeah? And where did you get this understanding from?" His tone was fussy.

"All the customers you stole have been calling and asking me and Nate for Adderall."

He didn't say anything for a minute. And then, "Fuck."

"I'm guessing your supply dried up. It happens, man. Maintaining a prescription supply line can be hard," I said.

"Don't be a dick, Braddock."

"I'll sell you a couple hundred pills."

He laughed. "You're going to sell me pills so I can keep the customer base I stole from you?"

"I'm going to gouge you on price."

"No shit."

"Or you could give me some info and I'll only mildly gouge you."

"Fuck." He was silent, presumably pondering that offer. "What do you want to know?"

"Special K. Who is selling it these days?"

"Special K? Shit. No one does ketamine anymore."

"Apparently, someone does."

"All right. I'll find out. But I need at least a thousand pills."

I laughed. He couldn't move a thousand pills. And even if he could, I wasn't setting him up for that kind of success. "I'll sell you two hundred."

"No deal."

"Okay. I'll sell you two fifty, and if the lead pans out, I'll sell you another two fifty."

"I fucking hate you." His tone was full of respect. It was a first.

"I'll take that as a yes."

"Yeah, yeah. Give me a day."

"I look forward to your call."

He hung up.

When I got back to the kitchen, Lane and Nate were in a full-on argument. They both were smiling though, so it was probably fine.

"I'm not suggesting we do away with it entirely. I'm just saying it's deeply flawed and we shouldn't treat it with respect out of obligation," Lane said.

"I don't think it's obligatory respect. I think it's fear. The edifice is built on complex weaponry. Those weapons keep the plebeians in line, for the most part." Nate was waving his hands around.

"Complex weaponry?" Lane laughed. "It's good you're not overly dramatic."

"It is complex weaponry." He was quite riled. "The racism in this country is precise and multifaceted and built with the intention of keeping people of color down."

"Agreed. I'm just not sure racism is that complex. As a weapon, I think it might be more of a fist than a well-oiled gun."

Nate shook his head. "It's both. Depends on what it's used for, who is wielding it, how long they've been using it."

I sat again. "I'm sorry. How did you guys get from punishing assault perpetrators to race in America?"

Lane and Nate exchanged a long look. They grinned and shrugged. "I think it went from no justice for survivors to the justice system still needs to exist even if it's ineffective," Lane said.

"But it needs a dramatic overhaul due to that ineffectiveness. And an overhaul would obviously include appropriate measures to prevent recidivism."

"Especially among violent offenders."

"Of course." Nate half-smirked like he knew she was highlighting the distinction for my benefit.

"But would also need to account for the institutionalized racism in the system, which is difficult to address without addressing overarching American racism," Lane said.

"And you came in as we were figuring out the best way to alter the justice system."

"I was only gone for two minutes," I said.

"How is that relevant?" Lane asked.

"I guess it isn't?" I shrugged.

There was a knock at the front door followed by the sound of it opening. After a moment, Laurel stuck her head in the kitchen.

"Hey, sis." Lane held up her can. "I'm drinking gay water."

Laurel frowned. "Okay."

"What are you doing here? I thought you had to work," I said.

"Can I talk to you?" Laurel asked me.

Nate and Lane suddenly found their food very interesting.

"Sure." I stood and led her to my bedroom. My house was becoming far too crowded.

Chapter Nine

I closed the door. The click of the latch seemed to reverberate through me. I didn't want to have this conversation. I didn't want to hear her justify the things she'd said.

"I owe you an apology," Laurel said.

"Okay."

"I wasn't being entirely honest." Laurel half-sat on the edge of my dresser and studied the wall just to the right of my head.

"How so?" I leaned against the wall and crossed my arms.

"When I said any rapist would get roughed up. That's not true. Same with the whole thing about how they would call me or Lance if Lane's rapist got arrested."

Really? She was going to say she made it all up? "That's kind of a fucked up thing to say, especially if it isn't true."

"Yeah, well, you pissed me off." She crossed her arms. I couldn't tell if she was posturing or protecting herself. "I'm not proud that it was my first response."

"Your first response was to lie?"

"My first response was to lash out. You suggested I was being dismissive about the punishment for rapists. It irritated me."

"Sounded pretty sincere to me."

"I'm not proud of that either." She was still feigning eye contact, feigning calm.

"What?"

"My ability to lie so convincingly."

"Lying convincingly is a huge portion of your job. It's apparently one of your strong suits. Shouldn't you be proud of it?" I asked.

The muscles in her jaw tightened. "You know what I mean."

"Actually, I don't."

"I mean I'm not proud that—I don't know—that I default to lying when I feel cornered."

"I'm confused."

"About what?" She sounded irritated. Granted, most of our difficult conversations were resolved with a beer and conscious avoidance, but this wasn't going to disappear so easily.

"So now you're saying cops don't rough up suspects? That was just for show?" I asked.

"No. Plenty do. But it isn't common practice the way I made it sound."

"So you're not like that?" It was a leading question, but I asked it anyway.

"No. That's not the kind of cop I am." At least there was conviction in her tone.

"So if the guy who raped Lane was arrested, you wouldn't kick the shit out of him?"

She shrugged. "Given the opportunity, I would. But that's not the cop in me. That's the big sister."

I shook my head. "I don't know what to make of this."

"What?"

"You say you're not that kind of cop, but you keep saying shit that makes you one of those cops. Which version of you am I supposed to believe?"

"What the hell does that mean?"

I looked at the solid lines carved into the door. I felt trapped, confined by the room. I wanted to run. "Most of the time I feel like I know exactly who you are, but there are moments when you become someone else. The last time I felt that way about you, I found out my girlfriend was an undercover cop so it's a little disconcerting."

Laurel blinked at me. Anger and hurt swirled in her eyes. "How can you make that comparison?"

"I'm just saying what I see. You aren't acting like the version of you that I know. Getting angry and lashing out. Lying for no reason. Posturing like a brutal cop. Either you're acting extremely out of character right now or you've been putting on an elaborate facade for months."

She met my eyes for a moment, then flicked her gaze away. But it was enough. Her eyes started to fill. "Fuck." She pressed her palms against her eyes. "Fuck."

That was not the response I was expecting. "What? Talk to me." I crossed the room without thinking about it. My anger was momentarily tempered by my surprise. I stopped a foot away. I was afraid to touch her, to invade her space.

"I don't know what the fuck is wrong with me."

"What's going on?"

She dropped her hands and blinked at me through watery eyes. "I don't know."

"I can't help if you won't talk to me."

"I don't know," she practically shouted. Her frustration finally cut through, and I realized her anger was with herself, not me. I didn't appreciate being the recipient of her ire, but at least this appeared honest.

"Okay. Well, try to explain. It doesn't need to make sense."

"I feel like I've been running for miles and I can't breathe. But I can't stop either. I can't focus on anything." She blinked long and slow. Tears spilled out and spread across her eyelashes. "It's like I'm constantly thinking about six things and I can't land on one long enough to get anything done."

That was a lot. "Why do you think that is?"

She shrugged, shook her head. "I don't know. Because I'm stressed and I'm anxious."

I could certainly guess what was stressing her out and making her anxious, but attempting to predict her feelings probably wasn't helpful. Or fair. "What are you stressed about? What's making you anxious?"

"I feel so goddamn guilty about Lane. She got hurt and I wasn't there."

"I think that's a pretty normal feeling." I finally realized that her emotional state wasn't about me and making it so was selfish. I wanted to touch her. I wanted to do something, anything to take her pain away, but I knew I couldn't, and I didn't know if she would want it even if I could. "You didn't do anything wrong. You just need to remind yourself that you can't follow her around and protect her all the time. She wouldn't want that."

Laurel nodded enthusiastically. Tears dropped off her chin. Some continued to drip down her neck. "And then I feel so guilty about you.

You've been there for Lane in ways that I wasn't—ways I didn't even think of. It's like you know what to do and say, and all I can think to do is yell or punch someone. Which makes me feel like an idiot because that's a Lance response."

"Okay, but you don't need to be everything for her. Your feelings are valid too."

That just made her cry harder. "Fuck. And then there's that."

"Sorry." I did my best to keep calm, but I was clearly not saying the right things. "What did I say?"

"That's it. You keep saying exactly what I need to hear, what she needs to hear." She sniffled. "You're doing all this emotional labor and that's not fucking fair to you. You don't need to deal with this bullshit."

"Can I hug you?"

That made her cry more, but she nodded. I pulled her close. Her hands felt warm on my shoulders. The heat from them radiated down my back, up my neck. The front of my shirt slowly became damp. I traced the lines of bone and muscle in her back, smoothed my fingertips over the bumps in her spine. Her breathing started to even out. She leaned back.

"I'm getting your shirt all wet."

I shrugged. "I'm not worried about it. You shouldn't either."

"My nose is running on your shirt. That's worth worrying about."

"It's really not." I chuckled.

"It's still not productive to sit here crying all day."

"I'm pretty sure no one cries to be productive. That's not really a function of crying."

She squeezed her eyes shut and more tears spilled out. "I'm just so tired. I keep trying to move forward and I can't. I can't help Lane. I can't solve this case. I'm stuck."

"Do you need to do all that?"

Laurel's brow wrinkled. "Yes."

"Okay." Seemed inaccurate, but what did I know.

"Why are you putting up with me?"

"Because it's not putting up with you. Same with the whole performing emotional labor thing. I'm not performing emotional labor that you're supposed to handle. There is no supposed to. We're working together to deal with a shitty situation."

"But you shouldn't have to."

"None of us should have to deal with this. It's bullshit. It's the patriarchy come to life. But this is where we are and we're not going to parse out who is dealing with what trauma. We're just going to shoulder what we can."

"You're carrying more than we are."

"At the moment, maybe. Who knows about tomorrow. Maybe it'll be you. Maybe it won't. It's okay. This is where I want to be. This is one of the benefits of loving someone."

She seemed confused. Like there was a trick in what I was saying and she just needed to find it. "How is this a benefit?"

"Do you know how hard it is to convince someone to let their nose run on your shirt? There's a whole fetish culture around it."

Laurel finally looked at my face and realized I was grinning. "You're a dick."

"Being able to do this, talk to someone honestly is a fucking gift. Nothing you've said in the last twenty minutes made a bit of sense. But I got it because I get you. Do you know how cool that is?"

She took a deep breath like she was inhaling me, my smell, my essence. "It's pretty fucking cool."

"I'm sorry I tried to make it about me."

She shrugged. "What you said was shitty, but fair."

"Sometimes I just don't know which version of you I'm going to get."

She nodded. "For the longest time, I've done and said certain things because it was easier to blend with my colleagues than it was to be honest. That was cowardice." She took a step back, but kept her hands on my arms.

"That probably will require some work to unpack."

"Yeah. It will." She slid her hands down so she could hold mine. "But I want to be the person I think I am. I want to be the person you think I am. Well, the person you think I am most of the time."

I half-smiled. "I just want you to be genuine."

"Same."

"Now can we back up a bit?" I asked.

She sighed. "I guess."

"Feeling like you've been running is probably not good. How long has that been going on?"

"Since we were called to the hospital, I guess."

"You've been feeling winded for four days?" I asked.

"I mean, yeah." She shrugged. "It's not a big deal. My anxiety is pretty well under control except when I'm feeling high levels of stress. Or, you know, if there's some sort of predicating event."

"Like being called to the hospital in the middle of the night?"

"Yeah, that'll do it."

"I didn't know you had anxiety."

"Oh." She frowned. "I guess you wouldn't. It's not bad. Not like Logan's. Or even Lane's. Theirs is much worse."

"I'm pretty sure you can't quantify something like that."

"I guess." She sniffed.

"How do you normally deal with it?"

"I'm not sure. I haven't felt this way since I was a teenager. So most of my coping mechanisms involve, you know, studying for finals or whatever."

"Have you spoken to anyone about it?"

"You mean other than you, right now?" she asked. I gave her a look. "Right. No. I've been doing a solid job of ignoring it."

"Laurel, honey, darling."

She scowled at my litany. "What?"

"You've been doing a shit job of ignoring it."

She rolled her eyes at me in an epic fashion. "Okay. I could probably do better."

"What do you need? And can I help?"

"I don't know. I guess I should probably talk to a counselor or therapist again."

"I agree. Do you have one?"

She shook her head. "It's been fifteen years. I'd need to find a new one."

"Okay. We can do that."

Tears started to gather again. "We can?"

"Yes." I pulled her in again. It was such an absurd question. Not like Laurel at all. Or, apparently, it was like her. Just not a side I'd seen before. Part of me was blown away by the openness of her breakdown. She'd allowed me to see something I imagined few were privy to. But I also ached at how raw her pain was. I couldn't absorb it, but hopefully I could ease it. "We will figure this shit out."

"I'm sorry. I really don't know what's wrong with me."

"Nothing." I kissed her head. "This is a normal response."

"Doesn't feel normal." She sat on the edge of the bed. I sat next to her, just close enough so our shoulders could touch. I took her hand in mine.

"It's your response so it's healthy and normal for you," I said.

"You sound like a fucking hippie."

I laughed. "You're not wrong."

"How are you so good at this?"

"Good at what?"

"Dealing with crazy. Talking to Lane. All of it."

"Well, I don't think you're crazy. I think you've got a lot going on," I said. She rolled her eyes. "The Lane thing I just have practice with."

"What do you mean?"

"You remember Shelby? She runs the farm with Clive?"

"Shelby would be difficult to forget."

"Right. Well, she's a survivor. I asked her plenty of dumb questions. I said a bunch of dumb stuff. She called me on it. I listened."

"So you talked to one person once about being assaulted and now you're like an expert?" Laurel sounded rightfully skeptical.

"No, of course not. Everyone knows people who are survivors. But most people don't talk to them about it. Shelby was helpful. She didn't need to take the time to explain to me why what I said wasn't okay, but she did. Repeatedly. I try to value that sacrifice."

"But you're really good with Lane."

"I'm not. Honestly. I'm pretty good at listening and empathizing, but I'm not particularly skilled in dealing with assault survivors. Other people are just really bad. Not you, necessarily. It's just, sexual assault isn't a polite subject so most people don't learn how to talk about it."

Laurel stared intently at her hands for a minute, then two. "Yeah. Okay. That makes sense."

"I'm real smart."

She chuckled. "What do we do now?"

"There's Thai food."

"Just eat Thai?"

"You should wash your face. I should change my T-shirt. Then we should eat Thai. Later, we'll find you a therapist. Do you approve this plan?"

"It sounds like an excellent plan."

Nickels chose that moment to start scratching at my bedroom door. She thought this closed door business was bullshit.

"Nickels thinks you should give her snuggles too," I said.

Laurel laughed at me. "She does?"

"Yes. I can sense it. She's very therapeutic." I opened the door wide enough for Nickels to run in. She went straight for Laurel. "Told you."

Laurel sat on the floor and Nickels flopped so her belly was exposed. "Hi," Laurel said. Nickels purred.

"See? Purring makes everything better." I stripped off my T-shirt and swapped it for a dry one.

"You're right. This is very therapeutic."

"It doesn't negate the need to see a therapist, though."

"Hard-ass."

Chapter Ten

Going on adventures with Laurel held a lot more appeal when they weren't connected to following a drug lead. Unfortunately, we had a lead to follow. At least I hadn't been saddled with Reyes. I'd just have to take my adventures where I could get them.

Laurel was driving. I realized now that her obsession with driving was actually an obsession with her truck. Sure, the cameras and microphones routed to the FBI were a bonus, but she just liked driving her truck. The worst part was she was hot while driving it. She was wearing a flannel shirt and a navy quilted jacket. Her window was down a couple of inches. Cold air blew through the cab. One would think it was more logical to roll up the windows and take off the jacket, but Laurel had her quirks.

The stretch of Highway 70 we were on was mostly farmland. Orchards spread on both sides of the highway. Most of the trees were either barren or changing color. Every couple of miles there was another farm stand. Every farm had one. Some were next to the central house on the property. Most were situated far enough away to give the occupants a semblance of privacy. A handful were already closed for the season, but the majority would remain open until winter set in.

We passed another parking lot set between a farm stand and a house. Laurel did a double take, then braked. Luckily, no one was driving behind us.

"You see that?" she asked.

"See what?"

After a second, she sped up and looked back at the road. "Never mind."

"What the hell was that?" I asked.

"Would you mind dropping a pin?" She pointed at her phone in the cup holder.

"Okay?" I took her phone and launched the map. I dropped a pin at our location. "Want me to label it?"

"Yeah. Truck."

"Huh?"

"Label it 'truck.'"

"You going to fill me in?"

"Did you see that truck back there?"

I looked back, but the lot was long behind us. "No."

"It was eighties, I think. Green and white. Looked pretty cool."

"You in the market for a new truck?" I knew she wasn't.

She looked at me like I was dumb. "No, but Andy is."

"Andy wants a truck?"

She laughed and shook her head. "She told Robin she wants a truck like mine. Robin and I talked about it. A seventies truck will either be expensive because it's a classic, or will require money to make sure everything is running smoothly."

"I take it Robin's got a budget?"

"Yeah. She's telling Andy the budget is a thousand, but she's got double that set aside. She's just trying to make Andy work for it."

"So eighties is the compromise?"

"Yeah. Still a beast. All the cool factor, but you know, not a classic. I mean, technically, seventies isn't classic depending on who you ask, but whatever."

"Why am I just hearing about this?"

"No clue. I could have sworn Robin mentioned it to you. She and I have been on the lookout for like a month and a half."

"I think I'd remember that."

Laurel shrugged. "I don't know. I guess you're getting old."

I laughed. "Yep. That's the first sign of age. Forgetting entire conversations."

"Well, try to retain this one. The truck will probably turn out to be nothing, but we should stop and check it out on the way back. Robin and I have checked like three between us, but none of them were right."

The scenery started to shift back and forth between suburban development and farmland until we crossed the river and were suddenly in Marysville. We circled the man-made lake in the center of the small city as I directed Laurel to Highway 20. The city quickly fell away and we were back in valley farmland. Laurel turned off the highway and onto increasingly dilapidated roads. The asphalt ended and gravel took over.

Laurel rolled up her window. "What are the chances Jerome gave you a bad lead to set you up?"

"Honestly? Fifty-fifty."

"You didn't think to mention that before we came all this way?"

I shrugged. "Maybe sixty-forty."

"Which side is in favor of the set up?"

"Forty. Probably." A dirty road appeared ahead. I squinted at the hand-lettered sign. "There." I pointed. "Feather River Large Animal Clinic."

Laurel slowed and turned. The road widened and smoothed out once we got past the initial tree line. Up ahead was a ranch-style house. The drive split. Laurel took the left fork toward the barn. The wide doors were open. A large wooden sign proclaimed the name of the veterinary practice. This one was newer and more artful. Like it had been commissioned rather than the afterthought of the sign back at the road.

We parked in the small lot next to the barn. Laurel texted Agent Michelson our location and waited for a response. We were out of Sacramento city and county limits. Her Sac PD colleagues wouldn't be much help if this went south. The text telling us to proceed came after a minute. In that time, a guy emerged from the barn. He looked young—maybe early thirties. His brown boots were both sturdy and hipster. His jeans and flannel looked just about as trendy as Laurel's. He waved as we got out of the truck.

"Can I help you?" he called.

I stepped in front of Laurel. She let me. "Yeah. We are looking for Roy Wickham. Can you direct us to his office?"

The guy frowned slightly, then pushed back his floppy blond hair and forced a smile. "Dr. Wickham retired a couple of years ago. I bought the practice. I'm Cory Parrish." The smile became genuine. "Dr. Cory Parrish. How can I help?"

Shit. There was no way this wholesome country veterinarian had continued his predecessor's drug dealing. "Oh, there's a specific prescription medication we are trying to track down," I said. He started frowning again. Hopefully, he never played poker. "We were directed here by a colleague. Jerome St. Maris. He said Dr. Wickham was known for carrying it."

"Right. What medication was it?"

I assumed Laurel and I were about two minutes from being sent packing, but we'd come this far. "Ketamine."

Parrish stared at me for a full thirty seconds. I stared back at him. "How much did you need?" he asked.

"Five vials."

"Did you bring payment for that?"

"We did."

He nodded once, with conviction. "Let me check my supply. I'm not sure I have that much on hand."

I offered a half-smile. Maybe he was a better poker player than I'd thought. "Thank you."

He went back into the barn and ducked into an office.

Laurel leaned close. "Michelson wants us to confirm that he's dealing. That's our only job. They want to make a clean arrest and gather as much solid evidence as possible."

"You guys think they kept records?" I asked.

She shrugged. "It's possible. The more we can get on him, the better our leverage."

"Seems logical."

"Did you actually bring enough money for five vials of ketamine?"

I grinned. "I have no fucking clue. I tried to figure out how much it costs before we came and was wildly unsuccessful. The internet is a weird place."

"Cash." She gave me a sharp look.

"What?"

"That could totally undermine our credibility."

"It won't. I'm good at bluffing. You're good at lying. We'll be fine."

"What if he comes back and tells you it's five hundred a vial?"

"He won't. Even with an insane markup, it won't be that high."

"But you don't know the street value."

"Neither do you, Detective."

She glared. "How much did you bring?"

"Only a grand."

"You brought a grand?" she whisper-shouted.

I grabbed her hand and squeezed. "Should I have brought a roll of sweaty twenties?" I laughed at the visual. "I'm a professional."

"You stress me out."

"No, I don't."

She huffed. "Where the hell did this guy go?"

I tried to see inside the barn, but it was pretty dark compared to the bright, crisp sunlight. "No clue. Want me to go check?" I started walking toward the barn.

Laurel pulled me back. "No. We don't go marching into random barns. We have no clue what's in there."

"Worst-case scenario it's an axe murdering sex cult. Or Republicans."

"You're taking this far too lightly."

"You're taking this far too seriously. This guy is a white-collar criminal. He likes to make a couple extra bucks selling horse tranquilizers to rapey frat boys. He's a jerk, but he's not the kind of jerk who fights back."

"I don't know about that. I've seen way too many entitled men backed into a corner." She looked past me and scowled. "What the fuck?"

I turned in time to see two Yuba County Sheriff's vehicles pull up behind us. One angled behind Laurel's truck, the other parked between us and the open barn. Four sheriffs climbed out of the cars and rapidly surrounded us. We followed their instructions to put our hands on our heads. Laurel watched them move until she figured out who was the superior officer. She made eye contact with him.

"I'm a detective with the Sacramento Police Department. My badge is in my jacket pocket."

One of the deputies patted me down. He was less than kind in doing so.

"We got a weapon." The only female sheriff removed Laurel's service weapon from her shoulder holster. That was why she kept her stupid jacket on.

Laurel sighed. "I have another gun on my ankle. And my badge is in my jacket pocket. May I please show it to you?"

The female deputy squatted and removed a small piece from Laurel's ankle holster. I had no idea why she was carrying an extra gun. Seemed excessive. Finally, the deputy reached into Laurel's pocket and removed her badge and ID. She handed it to her superior officer. He grunted and read the ID.

"You're pretty far out of your jurisdiction, Detective."

The guy feeling me up pulled my wallet out and handed it over.

"We're here following a lead on behalf of Agent Michelson out of the Sacramento FBI office," Laurel said.

"Cash Braddock?" The sheriff reading my ID chuckled. "You couldn't come up with a better fake name than Cash Braddock?"

I ran through about ten smart responses, but years of contentious interactions with cops combined with years of combative dudes with superiority complexes gave me the wisdom to not say anything.

"Ms. Braddock is my CI. Can I put my hands down now?" Laurel asked. Her words were polite, but her tone was not.

The sheriff grunted and nodded at her. He turned and started reading details off our IDs into his radio. The remaining three deputies stood in a loose circle around us. When Laurel reached for her pocket, one of them stepped forward.

"Please don't, ma'am. This will only take a few moments."

"It will go a lot faster if I can contact my superior."

"I'm sure that's true, but we're going to do it our way."

After thirty minutes of standing and an hour of leaning against the side of a sheriff's vehicle, I no longer had faith that sorting everything out would only take a few moments.

They had taken Laurel's cell phone, which made her real fussy. The sun was on its descent, and the temperature was dropping with it. Laurel's dumb jacket was looking more and more appealing next to my thin hoodie.

"Let's run through this one more time." The lead sheriff seemed to be losing brain cells with the sunshine. Or maybe that was my patience. "Who directed you to Roy Wickham?"

"What part of confidential informant is tripping you up?" I asked.

"You're not going to be in trouble for sharing information," he said.

I looked over at Laurel. They weren't asking her questions anymore. She was just leaning against the other cop car and pouting.

"Okay, I'm done. Are you arresting me for anything? If so, I'd like my lawyer. If you're not, I'm going to need my wallet back and you'll need to give Detective Kallen her keys."

"Whoa there." The sheriff put up his hands in what I imagined was intended to be a placating manner. Instead it was patronizing.

"Kallen," I shouted. She looked up. "I've requested my lawyer or to be let go."

She smiled. "Sounds like a plan." She pushed off the car and started to cross the gravel lot to me. The female sheriff got in her way. Laurel shot her a look and she moved.

"Hey, you need to get back over there." The deputy attempting to question me pointed Laurel back to the other car. She smirked and kept walking. "I said get back over there. I am trying to figure out what the hell is going on here and I do not appreciate some city cop acting like she has a right to my jurisdiction."

"I don't give a shit," Laurel said.

"That's too fucking bad."

"No. You have no right to hold us here. Now, give me my badge, my weapons, and my keys."

"Listen, sweetheart, I don't know how they do it in Sacramento, but up here we don't shout and get what we want. You came into my county and tried to buy drugs." His face started to turn blotchy and red. "I have no reason to believe that you're here on official business. So you will calm the fuck down while we sort this out. Am I clear?"

"Sorry, I didn't hear anything you said after sweetheart." Laurel held out her hand. "Badge, weapons, keys."

They probably would have come to blows if a shiny black SUV hadn't turned up the drive. We all watched the vehicle approach. The SUV stopped. Dust from the road settled over the black paint. It looked foreign, as if the car had never been exposed to the outdoors before.

The doors opened. Agent Michelson climbed out of the driver's seat. His newest partner got out of the passenger side. The kid had that fresh out of Quantico look. Too much muscle and too much swagger. Both looked like they'd been developed in the last six months.

"Evening, Sheriff." Michelson held up his hand in a lazy wave. "Daniel Michelson, FBI." He held up his wallet, badge out.

"What the fuck?" the sheriff muttered.

"This is my partner, Agent Orr." Michelson nodded at his partner. The kid held up his badge. "Looks like we have a bit of a misunderstanding here."

"Misunderstanding?" The red on the deputy's cheeks started to spread to his neck and ears.

"Kallen, why don't you and Braddock go ahead and tell Orr what happened. I'll speak with Sheriff…" Michelson's voice trailed off as he read the guy's name badge. "Thibodeaux to get this cleared up."

Christ, no wonder I hadn't retained his name.

"Listen, buddy—"

Michelson cut him off. "I'm looking forward to doing so." He stepped between me and the sheriff.

I skirted around them. Laurel took my elbow and led me to the shiny SUV. Agent Orr brought us to the rear of the vehicle. He opened the back door, rooted around, then handed us each a bottled water.

"Thanks, Alec," Laurel said.

He grinned. "Least I could do. Seems like you're having a shit day."

"How did you know to come out?"

He shrugged. The stiff shoulders of his suit made him look like a cartoon. "Michelson got worried when you didn't check in or respond to his calls. He activated the cameras in your truck and, well, here we are."

She nodded. "Thanks."

"I'm Alec Orr, by the way." Orr held out his hand to me. I shook it.

"Cash Braddock."

"So you guys want to fill me in on what happened?"

Laurel launched into the story. By the time she finished, Orr was struggling not to laugh.

"You know, you could look less gleeful," Laurel said.

"I'm sorry." Orr did not look sorry. "I just love when good ol' boys try to handle you."

"Like you're not a good ol' boy."

"I'm not," he said without any real conviction.

"Kallen." We turned to find Michelson holding Laurel's keys and both our wallets.

Laurel sighed in relief. "Thanks." She pocketed her wallet and keys and handed my wallet over.

Behind Michelson, the sheriffs climbed back into their cars. The slamming doors echoed off the barn and out to the tree line.

"Walk with me." Michelson nodded toward the middle of the lot. Laurel followed him. As they walked, he handed her the weapons the deputies had confiscated. She paused to kneel and stow the smaller gun at her ankle.

They chatted for a few minutes. Laurel's body language was a strange mix of anger and levity. Eventually, they shook hands. Michelson returned to the monstrous SUV. Laurel nodded at me and I followed her back to her truck. We climbed in. Michelson waved us ahead of him. He stayed tight on our asses until we hit Marysville, then left us to fend for ourselves.

CHAPTER ELEVEN

"So do I get to know what the hell happened back there?" I asked once we were back on 70.

"Which part?"

"The part where sheriffs showed up and wanted to arrest us. What else?"

"Oh. That. It's actually funny. Or it would be if that sheriff wasn't such an asshole." Laurel unconsciously shifted her gun, like she was making sure it was back where it belonged. "A couple of months after that vet bought the practice, he had someone show up looking for ketamine. He sent them packing. A few weeks later, it happened again. So he called the cops."

"So Wickham was running a side hustle, but didn't tell his customers when he retired?"

"Basically, yeah. They haven't found him to arrest him, but I don't think they're trying that hard."

"And now the new kid calls the sheriff every time someone comes looking to buy?" I asked.

"Yep. They gave him a special direct number and everything. Sounds like they've made a couple of arrests."

"Jesus fucking Christ. And I don't suppose Yuba County Sheriffs thought it was worth mentioning to Sac County or the local FBI office."

"That did not occur to them." She pressed her lips into a thin, angry line.

"And is it now on their radar?"

Laurel shrugged. "I told Michelson we'd like any info he can dig up on local ketamine distribution, but I'm guessing Yuba won't be too forthcoming with their intel."

"I'm sorry. That's frustrating."

"I'll get over it." She shrugged.

"Your perseverance is admirable."

Laurel just shook her head at me. We finished passing another cookie-cutter development and the traffic fell away. She leaned back and settled into the bench seat. The long shadows from the sunset cast dark lines in the shape of her silhouette against the painted metal door. In the setting sun, her fading summer tan was rich and warm.

"Are we getting close?" Laurel asked.

"I think we're still like twenty, thirty miles out. I don't know. You're the one driving."

She looked at me in confusion. "From the pin?"

"Huh?"

"The pin I had you drop. The truck."

"Oh." I sighed. Loudly. "That's fine. We can stop."

"Calm down. It won't take that long."

"I was almost arrested today. For drugs, of all things. My reputation might never recover from those unfounded allegations." I grabbed Laurel's phone and pulled up the maps. "But it's okay. I'll pull through."

"Very disturbing allegations. I do hope you manage to overcome them."

"Thank you. Your kindness means the world."

"Cash." She sounded irritated.

"What?"

"The pin?"

I rolled my eyes even though she couldn't see me. I believed she could feel the essence of my eye roll. "We're three miles away."

"You're not a great navigator."

"I never claimed I was a navigator, let alone a great one."

"You're the passenger. It's implied that you'll navigate."

"Fine, but I thought I was navigating to Sac. You never mentioned any pit stops."

"I had you drop a pin. There was a whole discussion."

"And I was just supposed to deduce the pit stop from that?"

She sighed forcefully. "Yeah."

"Your turn is coming up." I pointed to the left.

Laurel signaled and pulled into the dirt lot of a massive, closed up farm stand. It had clearly been shuttered for the season. On the other side of the lot was a smaller stand. It was open in back and didn't have a roof. Basically, just a glorified counter. A teenager was sitting behind it, looking at his cell phone.

"You see the truck?" Laurel nodded at a truck parked on the far edge of the lot. It was a big white Ford with a pale green panel running the length of it. The paint on the hood and along the bed were peeling, but overall it didn't look bad. The back window had "For Sale $800" written on it. That price tag didn't bode well.

"That does look pretty cool. Andy would dig it."

"Let's find out if it's in decent shape." Laurel climbed out and headed toward the open farm stand. I hustled to follow her.

"How you two doing?" the kid at the counter called out.

"All right. We're actually interested in that truck over there." Laurel pointed. "Any chance the owner is around?"

"Oh, yeah. That was one of Mr. Copen's. His son is selling them. I can grab him." He pocketed the phone and half-jogged to the house.

For a moment, I was concerned we were about to interrupt the poor guy's dinner, but the kid went past the house to the backyard. A couple of minutes later, he came back with another guy. This one wasn't much older than the farm stand kid, but where the kid's T-shirt was baggy and his slim jeans bunched at his knees and sneakers, the older one's shirt and pants looked painted on.

"Hi there. I'm Brady." He stuffed his hands in his tight pockets. "You ladies are interested in the F-150?" He nodded at the green truck.

"Hey, I'm Laurel. This is Cash. And, yeah, we're looking for a friend's kid."

"Cool. Follow me." Brady waved and walked backward toward the truck. "It's an eighty-five. Starts up pretty easy. Has over four hundred thousand miles, but just about everything in the engine has been replaced at some point in the last thirty years."

We reached the truck. Brady hauled the door open. Look like it required a bit of effort, but not a prohibitive amount. Laurel climbed in.

"Automatic," she said. She touched various points of the dash and peered at the instrument panel.

I quickly realized I had no clue what I was supposed to do. So I went to the back and opened the tailgate. It popped open easy. That was the extent of my car knowledge. I slammed it shut and went back toward the cab. Laurel and Brady had the hood open. They were poking around and making faces.

"What are we checking out, exactly?" I asked.

Laurel grinned at me. "I'm checking the condition of the engine. You can look over the body to see how much rust there is."

"The body is in decent shape, but there's a fair amount of rust under the bed," Brady said.

I nodded and went to look at the underside of the bed. I crouched by the back tire and looked up. It was dark. Not surprising. I slid my phone out and turned on the flashlight. There was an impressive collection of spiderwebs in the wheel well. Beyond that, the bed had three rust spots that were at least a foot in diameter. That was probably bad. I stood, realized there was a spiderweb on my knuckles, and flung my hand around like a lunatic.

"You okay there?" Laurel asked.

I turned and she was smirking at me. "A spiderweb attacked me."

"Are you okay now?"

"No. I'll probably die."

"How's the rust?" She indicated the bed with her chin.

"There are a couple of big spots." I held up my hands to indicate size. "Three about this big."

She frowned. "Hmm." She took out her own phone and shined the light up. "Yeah." She stood, shaking her head. "I think we're going to have to pass."

"Damn." Brady crossed his arms. "Can I ask what you're looking for? I've actually got two others out back."

"It's going to be a first car for a sixteen-year-old so we want safety first. Solid body, engine that won't leave her stranded. If it needs some work, that's okay. She needs to learn basics."

Brady nodded. "And same year approximately?"

"Yeah. Early eighties is better. She wants the aesthetics of mine." Laurel pointed at her truck. "But we're not concerned about cosmetics."

"Okay, I might have what you're looking for. It's more expensive than the eighty-five, but it sounds like you're okay with that."

Laurel looked at me and shrugged. "What do you think?"

"It's your call. I don't know anything."

"Yeah, we'd love to take a look."

"Great. I've got it in the workshop out back." Brady started walking down a path to the back of the house. "One of them is a ninety-four, F-250. Probably not that one. The other is an eighty-two. The engine was replaced eight years ago. Interior is a bit trashed, especially the upholstery."

As soon as the truck came into view, Laurel turned to look at me wide-eyed. We'd found the truck. For the sake of the excitement in her eyes, I hoped this one was in good condition. It had paneling like the other, but the truck was red.

Laurel went right to the hood and looked at the engine. I peered in the dusty windows. The dash was a dull red. "A bit trashed" was a kind description for the bench seat. The fabric was coming off in strips. Upholstery poked up from the passenger side. I circled the truck. Paint was peeling at the wheel wells, hood, and roof. I couldn't find any rust, though. I even looked underneath. The base of the bed looked like it was lined with slats of wood. Most of it was rotted out. It would look really cool with fresh, varnished wood. I wondered how easy that was to do.

When the truck started up, it made me jump. It was loud. Also, I wasn't expecting it to start. Laurel jumped out of the cab and went to look at the engine while it ran. She looked delighted. She needed better entertainment. After a couple of minutes, she turned the truck off. She climbed out and came toward me.

"Find anything?" Laurel asked.

I shook my head. "No rust. But I'm not sure what else to look for. Interior is torn up."

"I saw that." She leaned in close even though Brady was clearly giving us space to talk. "The engine is fucking gorgeous. His dad replaced it, but then he barely drove it. Sounds like the dad died a few years back and Brady's just now ready to sell. She runs great."

"Okay. That's good. I think." I realized I really had no idea if that was good. "It sounds good, right?"

"Yeah. It's good. There are a couple of small issues in the engine. But those will be cheap for a mechanic. Or I can help Andy."

"How much is he selling for?"

"Twenty-one, but I think he wants her taken care of. I can talk him down."

"What about the seat and shit?"

Laurel shrugged. "We'd probably order her a seat cover anyway. And the radio is AM/FM so she'll want to update that. Interior is easy."

"Did you see in the bed?"

"The wood?" she asked. I nodded. "Yeah, that's just cosmetic. It's not like she'll be hauling shit. Not a big deal."

"Want me to call Robin?"

"Yeah. You comfortable with me negotiating price?"

"Totally. What am I going to say? It looks red?"

She laughed and shook her head. "You're useless."

I could live with that. Laurel went back to Brady. I called Robin.

Just when I was afraid she wouldn't pick up, she did. "Hey, friend."

"Hey. Can Andy hear us?" I asked.

"Probably. Give me a minute," she said. The sound of the back door closing came through the phone. A minute later, another door. "Okay, we should be good."

"Laurel said you guys are looking for a truck for Andy?"

"Yeah. I looked at another yesterday, but it was a bust." There was a pause. "Oh, did you find one?"

"Maybe? Laurel seems to think this is the one. All caps. The One."

"No way. Tell me about it."

"Umm, it's red. With a thick white panel that runs the length of the truck." I looked at the silver trim by the driver's door. "It's an F-100. Looks cool."

"How's the engine? Did Laurel look at it? Are the seat belts in good condition?"

"Laurel checked the engine. The owner said it was replaced eight years ago, I think. She seemed pretty stoked about it. Let me check seat belts." I hauled the door open and pulled out the belt. It looked intact, unadulterated. I gave it a tug. How did one check seat belts? "I guess the seat belt is good."

"Manual or automatic?"

"Manual? There's a big gear shift in the floor."

"Manual, four speed," Laurel shouted at me.

"Laurel says four speed manual. I'm starting to understand why you didn't mention this to me," I said.

Robin laughed. "It wasn't a criticism. Just not your area of expertise."

"I'm going to take photos and text them to you, okay?"

"Perfect."

"Just a minute." I went back to the home screen so I could take photos of all four sides, one of the engine, the bench seat, and the dash. "Okay. Photos are sending. It'll take a minute."

"Cash?" Laurel called.

"Just a sec, Robin. Laurel's talking to me." I moved the phone away from my face. "Yeah?"

"I'm going to take her for a test drive."

"Cool."

Laurel climbed into the cab and started the truck again. It was real loud. Louder than Laurel's truck. Once she'd driven off and the noise was at a manageable level, I put the phone back to my ear.

"Sorry. Laurel's taking it for a test drive."

"I thought I heard a truck start up. So I have a final question."

"Yeah?"

"How much is it?"

"Oh, that. I guess that's kind of important." I took a couple of steps away to get out of Brady's earshot. "Laurel is negotiating. He's asking twenty-one, but wants it to go to a good home? I'm not sure what that means, but Laurel seemed fixated on it."

"Oh, yeah. That sounds perfect. Ooh, photos." There was a faint noise as she switched to speaker. Then she gasped. "This is exactly what we were looking for. It's a stepside and everything."

"Huh?"

"See how the back fender has the big wheel well?"

"Sure." Not really.

"And there's that step behind the door?"

"Got it." I definitely did not.

"Never mind." She tapped the speaker off. The audio shifted. "Just tell Laurel it's great."

"Any concerns?"

"Nothing I wasn't expecting. We knew upholstery might be an issue."

"She said you guys could order a seat cover."

"Yep. Oh, I'm so excited. I was getting a little worried. Her birthday is coming fast."

"Andy will freak," I said.

"She better. Call me with updates. Or text. I'll make sure my screen isn't visible."

"You got it." We hung up.

The truck came around the side of the workshop. Laurel stopped and climbed out. She crossed the yard to talk to me.

"Verdict from Mom?" she asked.

"She's in love and she said to go for it. How much?"

"Nineteen hundred. He's excited too." She hooked her thumb over her shoulder in Brady's direction.

"Cool." I thought about the contents of my wallet. "I've got twelve hundred, maybe. Any chance you have cash?"

"How? Why?" Laurel blinked long and slow. "I thought you had a thousand."

"I brought a thousand for drugs, but I carry cash. I'm a drug dealer, remember?"

She shook her head and pulled out her wallet. She fanned out the cash. "I've got forty seven."

I did the same. "Two sixty. Look at that. We've got thirteen hundred and still have seven dollars left for ice cream."

She sighed pointedly. "We still need six hundred."

"Ask your new friend Brady where the nearest bank is. I'll take your truck. You stay here and talk engines. And flash your badge so he knows not to fuck with you."

"You're paranoid."

"I'm honest." I took the cash out of my wallet and handed it to her. "Put this in your wallet. Then offer it as a deposit for while I'm gone. Your big ass badge is hard to miss when you open that thing."

She seemed to think I was nuts, but she put the cash in her wallet. "All right." She led me back to the workbench Brady was leaning against. "We're going to take it," she said.

"Awesome. I hope Andy will love it." He looked at Laurel to make sure he got the right name. She nodded. "She sounds like a neat kid."

"We still need some cash. Where's the nearest bank?"

Brady frowned. "Wheatland and Lincoln both have banks. Both of them are about twenty minutes away."

"That'll do." I turned to Laurel. "Keys? You can stay here and start the paperwork."

"Works for me." She handed over the keys.

"Back soon." They both nodded at me.

I circled to the front of the house and climbed in Laurel's truck. The sky was getting real dark. I turned north, the way we'd just come from. After a couple of minutes, my GPS directed me off the highway onto a wide farm road. The sky was black ahead of me, but in the mirrors it was orange shifting to purple. Every few miles, there was a tree tall enough to be silhouetted against the sunset. Most were pines, but there were a few random palms there to insist we were in California. I abused the speed limit in the hopes that there was a quota for run-ins with law enforcement and I'd hit mine for the day.

Just about everything in Lincoln was, in fact, closed. But the ATMs were well lit at the first bank I went to. Apparently, the limit on my account was four hundred. It had been so long since I pulled cash out of a bank account, I didn't quite know what to do with myself. ATMs had changed. They had cameras and more options than seemed necessary. I went to the next bank I had an account at and pulled out the remaining cash I needed.

The drive back to Laurel and the truck was uneventful. I parked and went around to the back of the house. The truck, Laurel, and Brady were gone. That wasn't good.

I heard them before I saw them. That engine sure did project. Andy wouldn't be doing any sneaking out. They pulled around the side of the workshop. Laurel was driving. She came to a stop ten feet in front of me. When she cut the lights, I could see her face. She looked delighted. They hopped out.

"We finished the paperwork and I wanted to take her for another spin," Laurel said.

"Cool. You seem pretty pleased."

"Oh, yeah. She's a beast."

"I'm so glad she's going to someone who will appreciate her," Brady said.

"Andy will definitely love it. Hard," I said.

We counted out money and signed the paperwork. It wasn't long before we were southbound on 70 again. This time, I was following a red tailgate with big white letters spelling out "Ford." I wondered if Robin was going to put a bow on it.

Chapter Twelve

Nate and I pulled up to the bar Jerome had chosen. It was unremarkable, which was a great quality in a bar when you were dealing drugs. Inside, the majority of the illumination came from neon beer signs and lights projected on the booze behind the bar. We stood at the bar long enough to buy two beers.

Jerome was in a booth against the far wall. The seats were high, the vinyl padding stretched a good foot above Jerome's head. Good privacy. Nate followed me through the crowd. I slid into the booth opposite Jerome. His hair was slicked per the usual. He'd grown an impressive handlebar mustache. Light glinted off the wax keeping the ends curled. He was wearing a leather fanny pack across his chest. I almost got up and left. I couldn't tell if I'd hit my threshold for hipster or drug dealer, but either way it was too much. I glanced at Nate. He studiously did not make eye contact with me.

"How's it hanging, my dudes?" Jerome grinned big and leaned forward.

"Doing all right," I said.

"Chill, chill. So did Wickham fill all your needs?"

"Actually, no. Some new guy bought the practice. He wasn't selling. And he was kind of a dick about it."

"What?" There was a brief moment before he figured out that meant we were only selling him two fifty. "Shit. Listen, that was a good lead. There's no one else selling K. Believe me. I looked."

"I do believe you, but we're still only giving you two fifty."

"Come on, Cash. How about a little professional courtesy?"

"The lead you gave me was a couple years old. Where's the professional courtesy there?"

"I swear. No one is selling it." He rotated the half-full pint glass sweating in front of him.

I glanced at Nate. He shrugged. We didn't have any reason to not believe Jerome. Except for his general shittiness.

"Okay. We have a business proposition for you," I said.

He smirked. "I hope it involves more product."

"You're kind of a dickwad. You know that, right?"

"What's your point?"

"Just making sure you're aware." I took a swig of my beer. I wanted it as a prop more than a beverage.

"I think we should go with the original business proposition," Nate said to me.

"Punching him in the nutsack for stealing our customers is not a business proposition," I said to Nate.

Nate shrugged. "That's your opinion."

"That's not very nice," Jerome said.

"Neither are you," Nate said.

"What's the business proposition?"

I did my best to look serious and bored. "We will provide you with a reliable supply of quality product in exchange for eighty percent of your revenue."

He laughed. Loud. Really more of a guffaw. "Eighty percent."

"The alternative is to just swipe back the customers who keep calling us. You'll get zero percent of that. Twenty is generous," Nate said.

"If you can keep them."

"We can. Our brand is worth a lot more than yours." I shrugged. It was the truth. And a well chosen truth had far more potential to damage than a lie.

"How do you figure?"

"The calls we're getting suggest that your supply line is inconsistent at best. Even when you do have pills, the dosage varies."

"It's downright reckless to buy from him." Nate addressed me rather than Jerome. "At least, that's what I heard."

"Reckless." I nodded. "Unpredictable."

"Okay, okay I get it. And how would people figure out that my product came from you?"

"We'd tell them. But more than that, you have to earn the trust of your customers. After a few deliveries that are actually what you say they are, people will begin to trust you. Our product will make that possible."

"I don't need this condescending shit."

"Okay." I nudged Nate to get him to climb out of the booth. He started to slide out.

"Wait," Jerome said.

Nate paused with one leg out of the booth.

"I can't agree to eighty. I have to pay my guys."

I slid back over. Nate swung his leg around. "We will need something to make up for the difference," I said.

"Like what?"

"Information. Better than the ketamine info. You'll need to prove your reliability to us just as much as the customers."

His brow furrowed as he tried to work out the implications. "That's reasonable. I guess."

"All right." I took another sip of my beer. "Seventy-five percent and information."

"Seventy-five? Jesus fucking Christ."

"After a month, if the information is high quality, we will consider dropping it to seventy," I said.

"You want a little unsolicited business advice?" Nate asked. Jerome gave him a look that suggested he did not want unsolicited business advice. "You should jack up the price. When customers ask why, you say you have a new supply line through Braddock. Win-win. Higher profit and a built in way to spread the word."

Jerome scowled. The fact that it was good advice had to be frustrating.

"Tell you what, here's the two fifty from our original agreement." I slid a sandwich size Ziploc across the table. "See how people react to the product."

He unzipped his fanny pack and pulled out a folded stack of bills. I took the money and handed it to Nate. He discreetly counted it. Jerome put the Ziploc of Adderall in his fanny pack.

"I'll consider your offer." He chugged the remainder of his beer. "I need another." He held up the empty glass.

"It was great meeting with you," I said.

"Sure was." Nate grinned.

"Yeah, whatever."

I'd been home for five minutes. Those five minutes were blissfully silent. It took me that long to realize why. No one else was home.

"Lane?" I called.

Nothing. I glanced in the study. Her stuff was still spread out. I looked in my room. Nickels was passed out on my pillow. Great. Who didn't love a face full of cat fur at bedtime? In the kitchen I found a note stuck to the coffee machine. Lane had clearly figured me out.

At group therapy. Back at 4. –L

It was only three. I adored Lane. I loved Andy. I loved Laurel in an entirely different way. But I'd missed silence. I stood in front of my bookshelf for two minutes before I selected Gloria Anzaldúa.

I stretched out on the couch and opened *Borderlands/La Frontera*. I was two pages in when Nickels jumped onto my stomach. She purred and rubbed her face against the spine of the book. I turned the page again, which she found quite offensive. She flopped into the crevice between me and the back of the couch. Within minutes, she was asleep. And then I spent an hour reading with a warm cat curled against my side.

When Lane let herself back in, she got halfway through the living room before she saw me.

"Hey, you're back. Did you have fun?" I asked.

"Yep. Group therapy is loads of fun." She altered her path from the study to the armchair by the couch.

"Right. Did you gain tons of personal insight?"

"Lots of it. I've got so much personal insight now, I don't even know what to do with it."

"Sell it on Etsy."

"Excellent idea."

I closed my book and set it down. "So listen," I said in the most serious tone I could manage.

She straightened. "What's up?"

"I know we've been doing movies and takeout and generally chilling, but what if we went out to dinner and immediately came back here without talking to anyone?"

She waited for me to get to the serious part then realized I'd already proposed it. Her posture softened. "Are you just using me to maintain your introvertedness but make it seem like you're social?"

"Absolutely."

"Can we go to that cheese place?" she asked.

"Cheese place?"

"You know, the one that only serves cheese?"

"Sadly, that was enough description for me," I said.

"Was that a yes?"

"It was. But it's Friday and that means it will be busy so you have to promise you won't let people make small talk with me."

"I swear on my life."

"Seriously. Only deep, meaningful conversation. If someone mentions the weather, you have to ask them about American masculinity and if the culture of the late nineteenth century is entirely to blame or if there were other contributing factors and it was inevitable."

"That seems like reasonable conversation to make while waiting for a table."

"I think you know by now that I don't make normal small talk."

"True." She nodded wryly. "Follow-up question. If we go in the next hour, are we officially senior citizens?" she asked.

"We would be, yes. That said, we could probably watch a lot more television and play a lot more video games if we do dinner early. Which means we can eat second dinner at the normal time."

"By normal time you mean eleven?"

"It's like you're speaking to my soul."

She grinned. "I like being a senior citizen with you."

"Same, bro."

"Let me go change." She pointed at the study. "I'll be ready in ten."

I looked at her leggings and sweatshirt, but decided not to ask. "Sounds good."

"Are you judging me?"

"No?"

"I can't go to dinner in this." She waved a hand over her torso.

"Of course not." We stared at each other. I broke first. "Can I go to dinner in this?" We looked at my jeans and flannel.

"Yeah. What's wrong with what you're wearing?"

"I don't know. I'm just very unclear on girl clothes." I waved my hand in a vague circle to indicate her outfit.

She rolled her eyes. "Ten minutes."

I carefully slid my hand under the cat and shifted my ribs out from under her. Lane watched me in fascination. "Never wake a sleeping baby." I stood slowly so I wouldn't disturb Nickels.

"You know that's a cat, right?"

"That's what I said. Sleeping baby." I pointed at the cat.

Lane laughed and went into the study.

"So you guys bought Andy a truck?" Lane asked ten minutes later as we walked to the cheese place.

"Yeah. Did Laurel tell you about it?"

She nodded. "She's irrationally excited about it."

"I think she's equally excited about the truck and the fact that Andy wanted a truck. It indicates a certain amount of Laurel-based hero worship."

"Ah, yes. Laurel is a big fan of Laurel-based worship."

I shrugged and refrained from making a sex joke about my girlfriend to my girlfriend's sister so I thought I was doing well. "I'm going to have a stereo installed before her birthday, which I think is like the perfect sixteenth birthday present for a kid getting a vehicle."

"No way." She slapped my arm. "What kind of stereo are you going to get?"

"Umm, whatever the stereo department guy suggests?"

"Cash."

"What?"

"That's not how you buy a stereo."

"Okay. How do you buy a stereo then?" I asked.

"You need to research and make a spreadsheet. Look at the needs of the vehicle. Look at the needs of the vehicle owner. You have to pick out the best speaker configuration." She started ticking off points on her fingers and by the end was waving her hands around to indicate speaker placement.

"It's an eighty-two truck. I think you just get whatever the hell will fit."

"Did Laurel put you up to this?"

"I'm confused," I said.

"Oh my God. Okay, car stereos are like my thing."

I felt my brows pull in and my lip curl involuntarily. "Huh?"

"I'm so good at installing stereos."

"You are?"

"You've probably figured out that me and Lance aren't close," she said.

"Yeah." I was missing something.

"The only thing we've ever bonded over was his car in high school. Mostly the stereo, but other shit after that."

"I'm going to need a lot more explanation." We reached our cross street and I tipped my chin in the correct direction. Lane turned.

"When he was in high school, I was tiny. Like eight or nine maybe. He was piecing together a Frankenstein stereo because our parents wouldn't buy him one. It was basically a tantrum that turned into something useful."

"Okay, that's pretty on brand for Lance."

She gave me a look of enthusiastic agreement. "His door panels were jacked up and my hands were small enough to reach in and detach them. Then, he needed someone small enough to put wiring under the seats. After that, he let me help him with everything."

"So you learned how to install a dope car stereo?"

"I'm generally good with anything electronic, but yes, car stereos were the launching point. They are my root."

"I had no idea."

"That's why I'm studying engineering."

"You are?" My mind was officially blown.

She just laughed. "I was studying criminal justice because, you know, I'm a Kallen, but I switched at the beginning of this year. My father is absolutely livid."

"Aww. Poor Randolf. His youngest is getting an engineering degree. That must be embarrassing at the club on Sundays."

"It's horrifying. And a girl studying a boy subject compounds the whole thing." She shifted her tone to mimic her father's voice. "He's very open-minded, but there are certain fields women aren't welcome in. Why would you want to challenge that?"

"Even though Laurel is a detective?" I asked.

"Oh, yeah. That field opened up years ago. This is just too far."

"Gee, I can't wait to meet your parents."

CHAPTER THIRTEEN

Call me ASAP

That was not a good text to wake up to on a Sunday morning from one's cop girlfriend. It could go quite a few ways, and none of them were good. I rolled out of bed. My phone chimed again.

Did Kallen just send you an ominous text? Nate asked.

I texted him. *Yep. I'll let you know what's up.*

He immediately wrote back. *Remember when we used to sleep in? That was great.*

I groaned. Nickels meowed.

"I know, right?" I said to the cat. She meowed again in understanding. Probably not in hunger.

I tapped Laurel's name.

She answered on the first ring. "Hey. That was quick."

"What's up?"

"There was another last night."

"Fuck."

Her sigh carried over the phone. "Right there with you."

"What do you need from me and Nate? He said you texted him too."

"The vic runs a popular Instagram account."

"She's Instagram famous?" I asked.

"Is that a thing?" she asked.

"That's a thing."

"Right. Okay. She's Instagram famous. She posted a ton of photos last night. We are scouring them to identify people. Can you and Nate help us with IDs?"

"Dammit. Yeah. That's fine."

"We're in the big conference room. I'll see you soon."

I hung up. Nickels meowed again. "I know. I'll feed you in a minute." I tapped Nate's number.

"We're going to have to go to the motherfucking police station aren't we?" was how he answered the phone.

"Yes."

He let out a long list of creative expletives. It would have been impressive, but I hadn't had coffee yet.

"You feel better?" I asked.

"Not really. Dammit. If you make coffee, I'll drive."

"Deal. See you soon."

I tossed my phone on the bed. Nickels watched me get dressed mournfully. It was like she knew the cowl-neck cardigan meant business. When I sat to put on boots, she sidled up next to me and tried to look extra adorable. It was quite unfair. She followed me to the kitchen. I fed her and she started purr-eating. It was one of her signature moves.

I ground coffee and started putting the machine together. The door to the study was still closed. Hopefully, that meant Lane had managed to sleep the entire night. It was the first morning in a week that her door was closed when I got up. While the coffee brewed I wrote her a note explaining where I'd gone. It had been a long time since I'd lived with someone. Laurel slept over often enough that I was comfortable sharing space, but I wasn't sure what role Lane fell in. Was she my temporary roommate? Was I babysitting? Had I somehow ended up with my very own little sister?

Nate's knock saved me from ruminating further. I answered before he started pounding on the door. His stress level was directly related to his maturity. The more stressed he was, the less mature he became.

"I can't believe this shit," he said. Clearly, the distance between his place and mine hadn't dulled his ire.

"Same."

"And I forgot my key." He rounded the corner and saw the closed door. "Oh, shit," he lowered his voice. "Is Lane still here?"

"Yeah. I don't see any reason to send her back to her dorm."

"Agreed. I just wouldn't bust in here shouting before nine if I knew someone was asleep." He went to the cabinet where I kept the travel mugs. He picked out two and filled them with black coffee.

"Thanks." I took the mug he held out. "Let's get this shit over with."

He waited until we were going down Nineteenth before launching in. "I'd be irritated over any case right now, but the fact that it's a serial rapist pisses me off extra."

"I don't know what to tell you. It pisses me off too."

"I'm also suddenly aware that I have a hierarchy of people who fucking suck. Sac PD pretty much dominates at sucking, but rapists definitely unseat them."

"Interesting." I nodded slowly.

"Why are you musing while I'm yelling?" he asked.

"Sorry. It's just that one is a power structure and one is the result of a power structure."

He looked away from the road for longer than I was comfortable with to glare at me. "I hate you."

"No, you don't."

"Dammit. No, but I hate rapists. And cops. And I'm only helping the cops because I hate rapists more and the cops keep fucking up."

"Agreed. Not that it helps, but it sounds like they actually might have a decent approach on this one. The victim is Instagram famous. She posted a ton last night. They're hoping to get a lead off the party photos."

"We are going in to look at Instas documenting a college party?"

"Yep."

"We clearly did something terrible in a previous life."

"Clearly."

"So do they think this is actually going to help? Even if they identify people who attended the party, how do they plan on narrowing down who the perp is?"

"I didn't ask. I want them to catch the perp, obviously, but part of me is fine with letting them fail because I'm tired of helping Sac PD."

"You say that like it's a new feeling."

"Fair point. I never wanted to help them."

Nate pulled into the lot. We slogged upstairs. The squad room was empty, but a fair amount of noise was coming from the open door of one of the big conference rooms. I followed Nate in and we found four detectives sprawled along one side of the conference table. Duarte was the only detective not at the table. He was sitting perpendicular to the wall, next to a large white screen. It looked like the contents of his computer were being projected on the wall while everyone else took notes.

Reyes noticed us first. "Braddock, Xiao, thanks for coming."

Everyone else looked up. Excitement flashed across Duarte's face before he remembered he wasn't supposed to think we were cool. Laurel, Blackford, and Fenton nodded, but that was about it. Nate and I pulled out seats.

"So what exactly are we doing?" I asked.

"We're looking over the vic's posts from last night. Anyone who matches the description of the perp, we are trying to identify," Laurel said.

Nate shot me a look. I shrugged. "You're trying to identify every single guy in the background of photos taken at a college party?" Nate asked.

The detectives looked at each other uncomfortably.

"I still think we should do a brief run through of all the photos and see if that gives us any direction," Duarte said.

Fenton waved his hand. "That's fine. Go back to the beginning."

Duarte clicked back through seven photos. Christ. They'd only gone through seven pictures?

We spent the next hour and a half looking at each photo for thirty to ninety seconds. Every few photos, someone would ask a question. The detectives took copious notes. I couldn't imagine what they were taking notes on, but it seemed to make them happy. The hashtags and attached comments became less coherent as the evening went on, but they were pretty impressive for someone who was intoxicated. When we hit the final photo, Duarte spun in his office chair to face everyone.

Blackford took the lead. "All right. What stood out to everyone?"

"Do we have time stamps on the photos? It would be nice to narrow down our time frame and see who was with her around the time of the assault," Laurel said.

Reyes nodded. "I know the vic already reviewed the photos, but that might jog her memory as well. Looking at ten photos might be easier than however many that was."

"Do we know which of the parties she was assaulted at?" Nate asked.

I nodded. "Yeah, if it's the last one, we'll have a lot fewer people to identify." She'd only posted a handful of photos at the final party. I was guessing the ketamine kicked in and made Instagram less of a priority.

"What do you mean?" Fenton asked.

I was confused by the question. "Well, at the last one, she didn't post as much. So there aren't as many people."

Nate looked at me and shrugged. He didn't get Fenton's question either.

"No, what do you mean by 'which party'?" Fenton tried again.

"I'm assuming the last party is where the assault took place, but I suppose it's possible she continued partying before going to the hospital. I just think we should confirm one way or the other," Nate said.

"There were multiple parties?" Laurel asked.

Nate and I looked at each other, then at the detectives, then back at each other.

"I only saw two locations. Are you sure there was a third?" Duarte started flipping through photos.

"Why didn't you mention this previously, Detective?" Fenton asked Duarte.

Duarte's brow furrowed and he shrugged. "I didn't know. I hadn't seen all the photos."

"That one, there." Nate pointed. "The one with the guy wearing the blue polo. That's where the third party starts."

Duarte clicked between two photos. "Yep. I see it." He turned to make eye contact with Nate. "I'm sure we can look over the victim statement to find out if she went to a different party after being assaulted. Blackford, do you have that?"

Blackford was just as shell-shocked as his colleagues at Duarte's competence and sudden initiative, but he started flipping through paperwork. He held up a report. "Got it. Give me a minute." He read through it quickly. After thirty seconds, he started shaking his head. "Nope. She was assaulted and her friend found her. The friend took her directly to the hospital."

"Okay, so we have the location." Duarte began selecting the photos in question.

"Not necessarily," I said.

"Why not?"

"Well, she posted less throughout the night. Likely because she was intoxicated. It's entirely feasible that she went to a fourth party, but the ketamine in her system prevented her from posting."

"Shit." Blackford tossed his pen on the table. "Okay, how can we figure that out?"

"Does the report say how many parties she went to?" Reyes asked.

Blackford shrugged and dove back into the file. His eye was starting to twitch again. Fenton was the one who found it.

"Got it." He raised his hand a few inches off the table. "It's not in our report, but the Sexual Assault nurse included it in hers. Vic went to four different parties. She went directly from the party where she was assaulted to the hospital. Assault occurred between one thirty a.m. and two fifteen a.m. She arrived at the hospital just before two thirty."

"So these photos are useless?" Laurel asked.

"Basically, yeah." Reyes closed his notebook and rubbed his face.

"Wait." Duarte scrunched his nose and looked back and forth between us and the screen. "She was assaulted at a frat party, right?"

"Yeah," Fenton said.

Duarte spun and pulled up the search bar. "What frat house was she assaulted at?"

Blackford flipped through his reports. Fenton scrolled through his. Blackmore shook his head.

"Nothing?" Fenton asked him.

"Nothing," Blackford said.

Duarte looked over his shoulder. "Okay, do we know any of the frat houses she went to?"

There was a chorus of negatives.

Duarte huffed. "Xiao, Braddock, name any frat at Sac State."

"Pi Tau Gamma," Nate said.

"Zeta Beta Chi," I said.

"Cool. Thanks." Duarte typed *#PiTauGamma* into the search bar.

"Oh, nice, man," Nate said.

"What is happening?" Blackford asked.

"People sometimes tag the frats they are partying at. They'll do the parties too sometimes if it's themed or whatever." Duarte pointed to a photo on the screen. "See? Hashtag Flannels and Handles."

"So we just need to figure out which frat or party or whatever and we can look at the photos from other attendees?" Reyes asked.

"And we can do the same for any of the other previous vics," Laurel said.

"Duarte, you're a goddamn genius," Blackford said.

"I'm glad you're finally recognizing that." Duarte grinned at Blackford.

"So happy we came down here for this," I whispered to Nate.

He smirked. "Great use of our time."

"I'll get in contact with the vic. See if we can get the location." Fenton closed up his iPad.

"If you guys don't mind, we're going to take off," I said.

Fenton and Blackford gave us bare nods. Reyes grinned and shrugged.

"Thanks for helping, guys," Duarte said. It sounded like he was being sincere, which was on brand for him, but kinda weird in the grand scheme of things.

"Sure thing." I smiled at him. I tried for sincere, but I was pretty sure it landed somewhere between patronizing and creepy.

"I'll walk you out." Laurel stood and followed us to the door. She didn't say anything until we were outside the station.

"What's up?" I asked.

Laurel dug in her pocket and pulled out a key ring with two silver keys. She handed them to me.

"Fancy. Are those little Andy's new keys?" Nate asked.

Laurel nodded. "Robin said she was finally able to check out the truck today. I was going to drop those off this morning, but I got called in."

"Cool. I wasn't sure if Robin was going to make it," I said.

"What do you mean?"

"Lane and I are apparently installing a stereo in the truck today," I said.

Laurel started laughing. "Oh, shit. Good luck."

Well, that was ominous. "Anything you want to tell me about your baby sister? Should I not be trusting her with this?"

"No, no. The stereo will turn out exquisite." She continued chuckling. "She told you that it would be a fun project for you to do together, right?"

"Yes."

"Yeah, you're going to spend about eight hours watching her work. She won't let you touch anything or do anything. But you can't leave her unattended because she'll get real mad at you."

"That doesn't sound like Lane," Nate said.

"Maybe she'll be nice." Laurel shrugged and grinned.

Chapter Fourteen

After following Lane around Best Buy for ninety minutes, I was starting to wonder if Laurel maybe wasn't exaggerating. We had been staring at subs for longer than I cared to admit, and I had come to the conclusion that I was dead and hell was real and this was mine. I'd learned in the first hour of our excursion that Lane would not, could not, be rushed. Also, questions would not be tolerated. Lane was, of course, permitted to ask me questions, but there was a wrong and a right answer. I'd yet to figure out how to determine which answer was which, but I was confident I would eventually do so.

The smell of new plastic had faded and returned. I was juggling two spools of wire, a stereo harness, a box of speakers, and a car stereo. Lane was debating between the amplifiers built into two different subs. The kid answering her questions did not seem surprised that subwoofers had amplifiers, unlike some people who were carrying equipment and surprised at how much they were learning.

"What do you think? Is the added power boost worth the upgrade?"

Across the store, a group of teenagers had set up shop with a demo video game system. They were collecting small children who had stopped to watch the game play.

"Cash?"

"Huh?" I looked back to Lane. "What?"

"What do you think?"

"Oh, were you asking me about the power upgrade?"

She rolled her eyes. "Yeah. Obviously."

"Right. What does that mean?" I shifted the stereo box to my other hand.

"The more amplification, the higher the price tag."

"I don't know what amplification is, but that sounds cool," I said. The kid in the blue polo helping Lane started to smile, then tried to hide it.

"We can easily spend over a grand on the sub if you don't care about the price."

"So probably not that."

Lane took a deep, long-suffering breath. "Which is why we're not looking in that range. That seems excessive for a sixteen-year-old."

"Totally. I want her to have a badass stereo, but also not over-the-top because she's a kid. She'll be pleased with anything above average. That said, the chances someone will steal it because she forgot to lock the door are decent."

"Why didn't you say all of this an hour ago?"

I shrugged. "You were asking complicated questions?"

"Are you asking me?"

"Yes?"

Lane laughed and huffed all at once. She turned back to the kid and pointed at one of the subwoofers built into the wall. "That one. Will you bring the box up front for us?"

"You got it." He leaned close to read the item number, then disappeared into a back room.

"Come on." Lane led me back to the car stereos.

"I thought we already picked out a stereo," I said.

"We did." She took the box from me and put it back on the shelf. After a quick scan, she picked up a different stereo box. "I picked a decent sub, but nothing too excessive, which means we are getting her a better stereo because she'll play with that more anyway." As she spoke, we went down the next aisle and swapped the box of speakers for two boxes of speakers.

"Will the stereo light up in pretty colors?"

That earned me a look. "It's not 2005, Cash."

"Okay?" I drew the word out in confusion.

"The stereo is a touchscreen."

"That's awesome." I reached over and turned the box in her hands. It was, in fact, a touchscreen.

"What exactly was your plan for getting a stereo for Andy before I offered to help?" Lane asked.

I shrugged. "I hadn't given it much thought. Maybe ask Nate. He's good at this stuff."

"But Beverly and her whole setup is pretty complex. How did you manage that?"

"Well, yeah, but she started out as just a TV. From there it was research, trial and error. It took years. I need this done now."

We got to the register and piled everything on the counter. Lane did a quick count to make sure we'd grabbed all thirty-seven necessary packages. After the cashier finished scanning, Lane frowned at the total.

"Oh, we're missing the sub." Lane pointed at a bigger box on the back counter. "You guys are holding it for us."

The cashier nodded and scanned the subwoofer.

"We good?" I asked. Lane nodded and I handed over my credit card.

We loaded our haul in the back of my car. Lane didn't say anything until I was almost downtown.

"I missed all my classes last week." Her tone didn't give anything about her state of mind away.

"I assumed. Did you email your professors?"

"Yeah. I didn't give any information though."

"Are you planning on it?"

She started to shake her head, but stopped and shrugged instead. "Maybe?"

"You're not required to. You know that, right?"

"Yeah. I don't feel obligated. But I also don't want it to be some secret. Not in my academics, but my whole life. It's a thing that happened. It colors my perception. But it isn't who I am." She tucked a strand of hair behind her ear. "I don't know if that makes sense."

"It does. You seem pretty contemplative. Self-aware, I guess. So that seems like a very Lane response."

"I'll take that." She half smiled.

"Since we are analyzing, do you want to go back to school?"

She took some deep breaths in what I'd started to recognize as one of her breathing exercises. "Yes. I think the routine will be good for me."

"That's logical."

"And my therapist thinks the routine will be good for me."

"If you both think so, then it's clearly a winning plan."

She laughed. "Thanks. I figure between four classes, one lab, two therapy sessions, and group therapy, my week will be plenty full. Less time to think."

"I'm a little relieved. Netflix is running out of nature documentaries. I was afraid I'd need to order BBC or something."

"It's fine." She waved her hand. "I can rewatch once I get through them all."

"So are you nervous about going back on campus?"

"Not really. I mean, the main campus is way different from the residential buildings. I don't think it will bother me."

"I take it you don't want to move back into your dorm."

She shook her head. "No. I don't think I can right now. I guess I'll have to eventually." She stole a look at me. "But I'll go back to Laurel's. You don't need to keep putting me up."

"Nice try. You're not ditching out on me that easy."

She huffed. "Cash."

I looked away from the road long enough to make eye contact. "I really don't mind."

"Thanks." She turned back to the windshield. "But it's okay."

"Don't your parents keep showing up at Laurel's unannounced to try to find you?"

"Yeah, but I can't keep imposing on you just because I'm afraid of talking to my family."

"You totally can. It'll be better for your mental health, which is better for Laurel's mental health, which is better for my mental health so really I'm being selfish."

Lane laughed. "Fine. But you have to promise to tell me when you get tired of me. I'd rather leave when you still like me than have you resent me."

"Deal."

"Thanks. I know I'm going to need to see my parents at some point, but I'm just not ready for them yet."

"That's valid. See them on your terms."

"Shit."

"What?" I asked.

"What if my parents show up at Laurel's when we're installing the stereo?"

"Hmm."

"That's your response?"

"Calm down. I'm thinking." I turned onto Laurel's street. Lane studied the cars parked along it. "If they show up, tell them you have something disgusting like oil grime on your hands and you need to wash. Then run away out the back door like last time."

"That sounds complicated."

"Or does it?"

"It does."

"I don't know, man. I'll just keep an eye on the street. If we see them, hide. Avoidance is sometimes the healthy option." I parked behind Andy's truck.

"I feel like you're probably really good at justifying almost anything."

"Your sister once compared me to your parents and their ability to argue any side of a debate. I'm pretty sure it wasn't a compliment."

"No. It wouldn't be."

We climbed out. Lane directed me to carry the bags upstairs. I dropped them on the porch so I could unlock Laurel's door. Lane started sorting through them before I could pick them up again. I grabbed the ones she wasn't digging into and put them inside. Lane followed. She started to unpack the bag she was holding onto the coffee table. I followed suit, but she appeared to be sorting according to a system I couldn't decipher.

"How can I help?" I asked.

She looked at me and pursed her lips. "There's no way to say this without sounding like a dick, but you can help by staying out of my way."

"Dude, Lane, I'm excellent at staying out of the way."

She laughed. "But maybe stay within earshot so you can retrieve shit and hand me tools?"

I gave a half-assed salute. "Tool bitch, at your service."

"Great. Laurel keeps her toolbox under the kitchen sink. There's also a drill. Will you grab both?"

"On it."

I grabbed the toolbox, the drill, a beer for me, and a gay water for Lane. Carrying everything down to the street proved to be a challenge. I thoroughly shook both drinks in the process so that was chill.

Lane already had the passenger door opened wide. She was lying on the floorboard to look under the dash. Her sneakers hung out the open door. They were retro with an early eighties vibe. They were real on point for the task of the day.

"Cash?"

"Yeah?" I set down the toolbox, put our drinks in the truck bed, and set the drill on the bench seat.

"Will you run back up and get a flashlight? Laurel has a couple of mini Maglites in the junk drawer. I think."

"You got it." I jogged back up the stairs, remembered why I didn't jog when I got out of breath, found the flashlight, and returned to the truck at a normal pace.

"Thanks," Lane said when I put the flashlight in her hand. She spun it on and directed the beam under the steering column.

After a solid two minutes of watching her, I was thoroughly bored. I climbed into the truck bed, stretched out my feet, and opened my beer. It didn't explode everywhere so I thought I was doing pretty well. It was only when I bent my leg and reclined against the corner of the bed that I realized the layer of dried mud coating the wood slats had transferred to my jeans. I brushed at one leg. A cloud of dust floated up and left me with the faint outline of my hand on the fabric. The dirt was still solid. And my palm was dark and chalky.

"Awesome," I said.

"Huh?" Lane's voice was muffled.

"Nothing. I've got a La Croix for you when you want to take a break."

"I just started."

"So don't take a break right now."

"Thanks for that," she called. She didn't sound very thankful.

"How much would it screw up your vibe if I washed the truck?" I asked.

"As long as you don't spray me with a hose, I don't care."

"This isn't suburbia, kid. There's no hose. I have to use a bucket."

"Then it really doesn't affect me."

I dug out my phone to text Laurel.

You have a bucket? And car wash supplies?

I lounged as I waited for a response. My clothes were already covered. No point in avoiding the dirt anymore. At least I'd traded my sweater for a hoodie.

The condensation from my beer melted circles in the filth and turned to delicate rings of mud. I spun the can, slowly widening each ring before starting a new one. I had marked each individual slat by the time Laurel texted back with directions to her storage space out back.

"Lane?" I called.

"Yeah?" Her voice was less muffled and seemed like it was coming from the curb.

I glanced over the edge of the bed and found her crouched by the open door, prying the panel off. "I'm going to run around back to get supplies to wash the truck."

"Cool."

"If you see your parents, roll under the truck. That's a normal response."

"You're so helpful. Thanks."

I climbed out of the truck bed. As I walked, I tried to beat the dust out of my pants, but it was useless. Laurel's storage locker was clearly marked like she said it would be. Buckets and rags were stacked under the narrow counter. I filled the buckets with icy water at the back spigot.

I alternated scrubbing and rinsing, rotating around the truck so I wouldn't drip on Lane as she worked. It took a good six buckets before I bothered adding soap. My nails steadily turned dark. It was pretty funky.

"Oh my God."

I straightened at the sound of Robin's voice. She was standing in the bike lane, grinning.

"What do you think?"

"It's gorgeous." She slowly rounded the truck bed. "This is perfect. God, how did Laurel find it?"

"I helped."

"Did you?" She smirked.

"Okay, no. Not really."

"Hi, Robin." Lane rolled out of the cab. She was surprisingly graceful.

"Hey, Lane. What are you doing?"

"Installing the stereo," Lane said.

"Kind of looks like you're just dismantling the truck," I said.

Lane gave me a look. "Should I just balance the speakers on the dash?"

"How complex is this stereo going to be?" Robin asked.

"It's more simple than it looks right now. Cash said she wanted above average, but not world ending in the event that it's stolen. It's a good stereo for a teenager. Like better than her friends will have, but not excessive," Lane said.

"Okay. Super." Robin look at me and shrugged. I shrugged back. "How long until you guys are finished?"

"I'm done." I drained the end of my beer. "I was washing it enough to get the first twelve layers of dirt off, but I'm bored now and you're here to play with me."

"I'll be working for a few more hours," Lane said.

Robin turned to me. "Then I need a beer."

"Follow me," I said to Robin. I turned to Lane. "We will be back in a sec."

"Grab me another La Croix?" Lane asked.

"You got it." I headed for the stairs.

Robin trailed after me. "Where's Laurel?"

"She's working. I don't know when she'll wrap up."

"It's Sunday."

"Apparently, police officers work weekends."

"Who knew." Robin followed me to the kitchen.

"Grab a beer. I'm going to change my clothes."

"That's probably wise."

I ducked back around the corner to Laurel's bedroom. I switched my jeans and stole a fresh hoodie from Laurel's drawer. When I got back to the kitchen, Robin was sipping on a beer and waiting for me. I grabbed a beer of my own and another water for Lane.

"So what about Andy? Where is she?" I asked.

"At Sloan's for dinner. They're studying." She paused a beat, then asked, "Can I ask you a question?"

"Sure." I already knew what was coming.

"Sloan uses they pronouns?"

I didn't bother pointing out that she hadn't really asked a question. "Yes."

"Is that common?"

"More common with younger queers. There are other gender neutral pronouns, but 'they' is the most popular at the moment."

"But it's plural."

"It is, but we use it as a singular and have for a centuries."

"We have?"

I nodded. "Like if one of Andy's friends left a backpack at your house, but you didn't know which friend, you'd say 'someone left their backpack here.'"

"Oh." Robin contemplated that for a minute. "Oh," she said with more conviction.

"Does that make sense?"

"Yes. I think I get it now."

"You ready to go back out and heckle Lane?" I asked.

"Absolutely."

The moment we got downstairs, Lane sent me back up for various stereo components. We watched her for five minutes, growing steadily bored. When my phone rang it was an exciting reprieve. The readout showed Laurel.

"Hey. You finally done?" I asked.

"Yeah. Where are you guys?"

"Your place. Lane is still deep in her installation extravaganza. Robin just got here."

Laurel made an excited noise. "What did she think?"

"Of the truck?"

"Yeah. What else?"

"She thinks it's pretty and also that you walk on water."

"That's true. I do walk on water."

"Are you coming home? Watching Lane install a stereo is really boring."

"Yes, I am. And I warned you," she said. I huffed. "You want me to bring pizza?"

I moved the phone away from my mouth. "You guys down for pizza?"

Lane leaned out from under the hood. "Always."

Robin nodded and saluted me with her beer.

"That's an affirmative."

"Cool. Be there in twenty."

Chapter Fifteen

Laurel settled into her favorite corner of the couch, her sock-clad feet perched on the lower edge of the coffee table. Robin was similarly tucked into the opposite corner. Pizza, beer, and plates were perfectly spread out across the coffee table.

"Someone needs to get Lane," Laurel said.

Robin nodded. "It's too bad we don't have shoes on."

"You guys suck." I pushed myself out of the square, mod armchair that shouldn't have been comfortable, but was infinitely so.

"Aw, thanks. You didn't have to do that," Robin said.

Laurel laughed. "Yeah, that's sweet."

I rolled my eyes and headed down to the street. Lane had the hood closed and was back on the floorboards. She was rapidly losing daylight.

"Lane," I called.

She rolled to her back and half sat up. "I'm almost done."

"Finish it later. We've got pizza."

"Fine. Will you look around and make sure I didn't leave out any tools?" She dropped the screwdriver she was holding onto the small pile of wire cutters and socket wrenches on the bench seat.

I walked around the truck, looked in the bed, glanced underneath, but I didn't see any forgotten supplies. "I don't see anything."

"Cool. You think everything will be okay locked in the cab?"

"Yeah. You'll be back down in thirty minutes."

She followed me back upstairs. Laurel and Robin were serving pizza. Robin handed me a plate. Laurel did the same for Lane. I reclaimed my chair. Lane went to sit between Laurel and Robin.

"Oh, no. You're disgusting." Laurel smacked Lane's ass. "You're on the floor."

"What?" Lane looked back and forth between Robin and me like we had the answers.

"You're covered in dirt and spiderwebs and weird patches of grease." Laurel pointed at the floor.

"I am not." Lane looked down. Her jeans did look patchy with filth. She sighed and set her plate on the table. "I'm going to go wash my hands." Instead of going into the kitchen, she went down the hallway toward the bathroom and Laurel's bedroom. The sound of the water running carried. Two minutes later, Lane returned. She had removed her borrowed flannel and was pulling on a newer, cleaner flannel over her tank top.

"So you're almost done installing?" Laurel asked.

Lane nodded and swallowed her bite of pizza. "I'm securing the sub. The wiring is all in place so I just need to hook it up and make sure everything is working."

"Cool. Does that mean you'll be finished tonight?"

"Probably. I hope so." Lane nodded toward me. "I told Cash earlier that I want to go back to class tomorrow."

"That's great, sis."

Lane half shrugged. "We'll see."

"You have Monday classes?" Robin asked.

"Yeah. Monday, Wednesday, Friday."

"That's not bad."

"Are you moving back on campus?" Laurel asked.

"Nope. I called dibs on little sister." I winked at Lane.

"Did you just wink at her?" Laurel asked.

"Yeah. What of it?"

"Winking is creepy. And you can't call dibs on someone."

"I agree with Laurel on this one," Robin said.

"No one asked you." I pointed at Robin.

"Do you want a ride to campus tomorrow?" Laurel asked Lane.

"Oh. Yeah. That would be good. I guess I can't just walk to class like I usually do."

"You could, but it would take a while."

Lane laughed. "I'd rather not."

I debated offering to give her a ride as well, but then I realized Laurel might want time with Lane. Dibs or not, my goal was not to get between them.

After we finished pizza, Lane went back to the truck. Robin followed to take measurements for seat covers and whatever other goofy accessories she was going to get Andy. I helped Laurel gather dishes and empty cans to bring into the kitchen.

"Did you guys make any more progress on the case today?"

Laurel started scrubbing plates. "Not really."

"We don't need to talk about it," I said.

"It's fine. I like talking through stuff like this with you. You're removed from it. That's a good thing, by the way."

I nodded. "I like that you talk to me about your day. So I guess we are all in agreement."

She grinned and shook her head. "Fenton wanted to run through everything again, see if we were missing some connection. Nothing stood out. A couple of flimsy connections, but—" She shrugged.

"Did you guys set up a meeting with the victim?" I started drying the plates as she rinsed soap off of them.

"Yeah. A few of them, actually. Two of the other women explicitly stated that they were at frat parties. So we are going to start with them."

"I thought all the assaults happened at frat parties."

"So did I. Apparently, the others only said party and mentioned a few other details that led Blackford and Fenton to believe they were frat parties." She dried her hands and leaned back against the edge of the sink. "This case is already falling apart, even as it's getting bigger."

"Well, hopefully they'll get specifics to look at. The good thing about social media is that it doesn't disappear. Even if someone deletes it, it exists somewhere."

She gave a little nod at my pep talk. "That's true."

"I assume you can bring in your tech department for help?"

"Yeah. Duarte is good, but that's because he's young. It's not a specialization."

"He did kind of kick all your asses today."

Laurel laughed. "He did."

"Maybe they have a program that will help you sort through the photos."

"They do. But we need a specific pool for them to input."

"Like a specific pool of photos?" I asked. She nodded. "Oh, but you don't know which parties to focus on."

"Exactly. Duarte pointed out that we can probably use geotracking to get solid locations, then work backward and figure out which party and hashtag to focus on for each incident."

"That's kind of badass."

"Assuming people posted photos of the parties. And assuming those photos have hashtags. And assuming the rapist is in any of the photos, let alone enough to tip us off that he's worth noticing."

"So we're going with a glass half-empty approach?" I asked.

She grinned. "Fuck off."

I stepped into her space and kissed her. Partially because she was hot even when she was bitching and partially because it had been far too long since I'd done so. Between my shoes and her lack thereof, our height difference was more noticeable. She stretched to wrap her arms around my neck. I took a step backward and let her push me against the counter. Our lips parted on impact. She kissed me again, her tongue pressing past my lips.

I worked my fingertips under the edge of her sweater. Her undershirt was tucked in, and I worked it up until I could touch skin. Her breathing tripped. She tugged at my hair. The sharp sensation cascaded down my body.

"I take it you two aren't joining us downstairs?" Robin asked.

Laurel pulled away. She looked flushed, but I told myself it was from making out, not having been caught.

"I wasn't planning on it at the moment, no," I said.

Robin laughed. "Well, Lane is still working, but I need to pick up Andy."

"Dammit."

Laurel smacked my stomach with the back of her hand. "That's fine. We would love to head down to make sure Lane isn't alone."

"Yeah. That's obviously what I meant to say," I said.

"Obviously," Robin said.

We followed Robin out and waved her off. Lane didn't seem to notice when we climbed into the now clean truck bed and stretched out our legs. Laurel put her warm hand on my thigh.

"You're crashing at my place tonight, right?" I asked.

"I can't. I need to be in by seven to review the case with Fenton. I volunteered to interview victims with him all day."

"Aren't you supposed to take Lane to school?"

"Shit."

"It's fine. I can take her."

"You don't need to. I'm sure I can take a break and do it."

"I was going to offer earlier. I just didn't want to interrupt your time together, if that's what you were aiming for."

"It kind of was, but I didn't think about my schedule at all."

"Or," I said grandly. I waited until she gave me her full attention. "I stay here tonight. Lane can take my car back to my place and drive herself in the morning."

"That seems complicated."

"It's not. Staying at my place alone will help her develop autonomy in a safe place."

"Are you just advocating for this so you can get laid?"

"No," I said. Laurel gave me a look. "I'm doing it so Lane can develop autonomy and so I can get laid. It's a win all around."

Laurel looked mildly displeased with that answer, but then she called out to Lane.

"What?" Lane shouted back.

"Come here."

There was a thump followed by a clang. The driver's side opened and Lane stuck her head over the edge of the bed.

"What's up?"

"I forgot that I have to be at work by seven. You want to borrow Cash's car in the morning and drive yourself?"

Lane gave me a questioning look. I nodded. "Yeah, that would be great," she said.

"What if you stayed at Cash's place alone tonight? Would that freak you out or engender a feeling of autonomy?"

"I feel like that was leading the witness," I said.

"No, I gave her two opposing options."

"But what if her answer is neither of those options?"

Laurel huffed. "Fine." She turned back to Lane. "How would you feel about staying at Cash's place alone tonight?"

"I feel like it would engender a feeling of autonomy, but I also feel, inexplicably, like someone planted that idea in my head. Isn't that weird?"

I laughed. Laurel scowled, but then she broke and laughed too.

"I'll text Robin to give her a heads up. If you need anything, she'll mother you," I said.

"Cool. You really don't mind me driving your car?"

"Not at all."

"And if you do get freaked out about sleeping alone, call us," Laurel said.

"Yeah. Seriously."

Lane nodded. "Got it. Call Robin for mothering and call Cash for a slumber party."

"Is that what you guys have been doing? A week of slumber parties?" Laurel asked.

Lane and I looked at each other and nodded. "Yeah, basically. Pillow fights, braiding hair," I said.

"Facials, pedicures."

"Dance party night was my favorite."

"You are an excellent dancer," Lane said.

"Thank you. I was classically trained."

That was too much for Laurel. "Cash, if I gave you one million dollars right now, could you define what a classically trained dancer is?"

"Yes. A dancer trained in the classics."

"Nailed it." Lane leaned over and high-fived me.

"I thought so," I said.

Laurel just shook her head.

"Okay, I'm going to finish this shit up." Lane pointed at the cab. "And then I'm going to Cash's place to dance in my underwear."

"Good plan." I gave her a head nod.

Lane climbed back in the cab. About fifteen minutes later, music started playing. The volume grew steadily. Laurel and I looked through the back window into the cab. Lane was watching us and looked quite pleased with herself. She wrestled the back window open.

"What do you think?" she asked.

"It sounds fucking awesome." I high-fived her through the open window.

"Agreed. Very impressive," Laurel said.

"Andy is going to be stoked. I'm stoked. Thank you for doing this."

Lane smiled slowly, quietly. "It was fun. Therapeutic." She tapped the volume down. "It's like those adult coloring books, but with electricity. And if you do it right, you get validation at the end."

"That was some lovely poetry right there," Laurel said.

"Shut up." Lane took the keys out of the ignition and the stereo cut out.

Laurel and I climbed out of the truck bed. I traded keys with Lane, my car for Andy's truck.

We said good-bye to Lane and went upstairs to Laurel's apartment like normal adults. She closed the door and pressed me against it. She kissed me, gently sucking my bottom lip between hers, then releasing it. I walked her backward. We got as far as her big oak desk. She kicked the rolling wooden chair out of the way and pressed herself between my legs.

I tugged at her sweater, pulling until I could shove it over her head. She didn't bother trying to undress me. By the time I'd managed to untuck her shirt again, my pants were unbuttoned and falling off my ass. She pressed her tongue into my ear. The wet sensation was both unpleasant and tantalizing.

"How invested are you in a bed right now?" Laurel asked as she slid her fingers over my clit.

"Fuck."

She pulled back. "You want me to stop?"

I gripped her wrist above the waistband of my underwear and held her still. "Fuck no."

"Good."

She kissed down my neck, her tongue darting out just enough to keep me engaged with what her mouth was doing. I let go of her wrist, hoping she would put her fingertips back where they'd been. Instead, she tugged my jeans and boxers down. She dropped to her knees. The hard edge of the desk dug a line across my ass, but then Laurel licked the length of me and I did not care about the state of my ass.

I gripped the side of the desk with one hand and the back of Laurel's neck with the other. I wanted to hold her close, to fuck her face, but I knew from experience that she wouldn't allow that until she decided I was ready. So I held still and let her have me. She sucked my clit into her mouth and pulled ever so slightly. Certainly not enough pressure for me to come, but enough that I couldn't think of anything else. She teased the underside with her tongue, the gentle lapping made sure any blood remaining in my body would move at her behest. I choked out a plea for her to let me come. She laughed. The soft vibration mocked me in a multitude of ways.

When she finally let me come, I was hyper aware of the warmth of her mouth, the soft hardness of her tongue, the discomfort of holding every muscle taut. Laurel stood and kissed me slowly. Her lips were softer and swollen. I'd never been loved quite so well.

Chapter Sixteen

My phone vibrated with a message from Kyra. *Here.*

I grabbed my phone and Laurel's spare key ring. As I locked the front door, I could hear Kyra's car idling at the curb. She unlocked the door when I approached.

"Is that the truck?" she asked after I climbed in.

"Yeah. What do you think?"

"It's so Andy. She's going to die."

"It's pretty cool."

"When's her birthday?"

"November third."

"That's like two weeks away. You have to keep this under wraps for two weeks?"

I frowned. "I hadn't thought of that. Damn."

"Breakfast at Tower?"

"Heck yeah."

Kyra nodded and turned toward the edge of midtown. She chatted about nothing in a pleasant way until we got to Tower. We parked in the theater lot and circled around to the front of the restaurant.

"Inside or out?" The hostess grabbed menus and waited, smiling.

I looked at Kyra. "I know it's chilly, but it's still sunny."

"I'm down," she said.

"Outside."

The hostess nodded and led us outside. The greenery enveloping the patio made it even cooler, but we were led to a table sitting in a patch of sunlight that had somehow penetrated the jungle. We sat and took our menus. The hostess assured us a waiter would be with us soon and disappeared around a palm. Kyra dropped her menu without looking at it and propped her chin in her palm.

"So."

"So?"

"Did you meet with Jerome?"

"Yeah." I tried not to scowl and failed.

"How did it go?"

"Really well, actually. He agreed to a much higher percentage than we thought he would. He must be desperate."

"That's great. So what's next? Just give it a couple of months and make sure it all plays out?"

"Basically, yeah. We included a stipulation for information too."

"Nice."

"And now I just have to figure out what the hell I'm going to do with the rest of my life." I was aiming for flippant, but Kyra saw right through it. Which was a pretty annoying quality.

"Freaking out?"

"Totally."

A waiter approached the table. Kyra ordered coffee for us and promised him we would look at the menu. We didn't.

"What do you want to do?"

"I don't know, man. I'm almost thirty. My skills include tolerating college students for up to four minutes at a time, counting real fast, and laundering money with a quick turnaround time."

"You're also empathetic and kind and intelligent."

"I'm a snappy dresser."

Kyra looked at my borrowed Henley. It was tight in the shoulders and loose at my waist. "Clearly."

"That didn't seem entirely sincere."

She pursed her lips and raised her eyebrows.

The waiter came back. I picked up my menu like I'd been looking at it all along.

"You're going to order eggs Benedict with extra hollandaise. Why are you pretending otherwise?" Kyra asked.

I shrugged and put down the menu. "Fair point."

"You guys ready to order?" The waiter took out his order pad hopefully.

"She wants eggs Benedict with extra hollandaise." Kyra nodded at me. "And I'll do the blueberry pancakes." She took my menu, stacked it with hers, and handed them to the waiter.

"All right. Anything else?"

"That's it, thank you." Kyra smiled. As the guy walked away, she turned to me. Her expression was a mixture between horror and embarrassment. "I did it again."

"You did," I said.

"I'm sorry."

"Don't be. Makes me feel like a real lady when you order for me."

She laughed. "Should we add that to your list of skills? Real lady?"

"Fuck yes."

"Any other hidden talents?"

"Wealthy housewives adore me," I said.

"Hmm." She appeared to contemplate that. "You have a very specific skill set that doesn't translate much to other fields."

"Thank you, I know. I've been trying to tell you that."

"Okay, what do you enjoy doing?"

I answered without thinking. "Looking at art, hanging with my cat, being sarcastic, dismantling the white supremacist cis-hetero patriarchy, reading poetry."

"Great. So probably like second grade teacher?"

"Yes. Perfect."

"With a series of themed sweaters," she said.

"Of course I'm going to wear themed sweaters. I'm not a fucking idiot." I took a sip of my coffee.

"Okay. What about journalism? Your degree is in English. You're good at telling people why they suck. Why not be an art critic or something?"

"I don't like to critique art. Or poetry for that matter. I just like to look at it and know in my heart that it's awesome or it blows."

"In your heart?"

"Yes."

"You know what I always wanted to do?" Kyra asked.

"Do tell."

"Run a gallery. Or curate a museum. How cool would that be?"

"I guess. I mean, yeah, for you that would be cool."

"You don't think it would be awesome to put together an art show? Pick the people and pieces to create a cohesive whole?"

"I can see why that would be cool, but I'd much rather just chill in a super cool gallery that someone else curated."

The waiter came back with our breakfast. It was clearly a slow morning. Kyra made a delighted noise and started slathering her pancakes in whipped butter.

"Okay. I've got it. For real this time." She pointed at me with a forkful of pancake. "Stockbroker. Ability to deal with douchebros, check. Counting fast, also check. I think. I'm pretty unclear on what a stockbroker does. Money laundering, definitely probably helpful. Ability to buy a gallery and pay someone else to curate it so you can just hang out, fucking check."

"Yep. You win. That is the clear solution."

"Great. I'm glad we had this talk," she said.

"Now I just need to figure out what a stockbroker does."

"I'm pretty sure you just need to have zero moral compunction."

"Yes, but what do they do?" I asked.

"Wear suits? Which, by the way, is another skill you'd nail."

"Again, not a description of their day-to-day activity."

"I can't help you, friend. The entirety of my knowledge base is eighties movies."

Honestly, so was mine. "Right. Well, I guess that won't work then."

"Damn. At least we tried. I guess you just need to be a drug dealer."

"We did our best."

Lane and I shared a quiet evening. She seemed exhausted from her first day back at school and overwhelmed by the amount of work she needed to catch up on. By nine, she was fully ensconced on the couch with a laptop, iPad, and three textbooks. I retired to the patio. Andy had helped me hang the outdoor heaters a few weeks back, but it was the first night I'd lit them. I was halfway through my beer when the door behind me opened. I turned, expecting Lane and found Laurel instead.

"Hey." I smiled. It was involuntary.

"Hey." She leaned down and kissed me.

"You're done late."

She nodded slowly. "Yeah. Today was…" she paused, searching for the right word, "long."

"You want a beer?"

She collapsed into the Adirondack next to me. "God, yes."

"Okay. I'll be right back."

"Cool."

I went in. Lane didn't look up. When I passed, I could see a flash of white from her AirPods under her messy bun. I snagged another beer and popped the cap off. When I went back outside, Laurel had her head back with her eyes closed. I set the bottle on her armrest.

"Thanks."

"You want to talk about it?"

"I don't even know how. It's a complicated story."

"Okay." I put my head back and looked at the four visible stars. Warm air from the heaters drifted across my face. It was undercut by a cool breeze, but the combination was quite pleasant.

The door on the Ward side of the house opened and Andy stuck her head out.

"You're here," she said.

"That is accurate."

"I texted, but you didn't answer."

"My phone is inside," I said.

"Oh, hey, Laurel. I didn't see you."

"Hey, bud." Laurel opened her eyes and grinned at Andy, but it was a weak smile.

"I was just wondering if you could read my essay for English," Andy said to me.

"Is it due tomorrow?" I asked.

"No, Wednesday."

"Can it keep until tomorrow night?"

"Yeah, totally. I'll email you the link. Thanks."

"No problem, tiger."

Andy disappeared back inside the house. I closed my eyes and went back to my contemplation of air movement. Every few minutes, I heard Laurel lift her beer and take a sip.

"Digital Forensics found an app called Locus on two of the vics' phones," she said.

I sat up straight and opened my eyes. "Okay. What's that?"

"It's a stalking app. It's invisible on the home screen, but it runs in the background." Laurel was looking up at the porch ceiling, studying the shadows.

"Doing what?"

"Some apps record and transmit the text messages and phone calls someone makes. Or they will track social media usage. Or location. They're commonly used by abusers who want to monitor their partner. Some stalkers use them, but it's harder to access the phone to install if you don't live with someone or have their password." Her speech sounded rehearsed, like she'd given it twenty times that day.

"So someone was stalking them? Presumably before assaulting them?"

She nodded. "That's one of the theories. It's also possible that he installed the app after assaulting them when they were unable to intervene. But neither of them remember him taking their phones."

"Why would he do that?"

"We don't know."

"Maybe he's trying to monitor if they report him?"

"It's possible. At the moment, it looks like all this app does is transmit location," she said.

"Can you track where it's transmitting to?"

She shook her head. "Not yet. Brika—he's the detective from Digital Forensics—is working on it."

"Wait. You said two phones?" I asked. She nodded. "Does that mean it wasn't on the others?"

"Don't know yet. The young woman who runs the Instagram account was our second interview. We found the app on her phone when we were trying to use that geotracking thing Duarte was talking about."

"Got it. And then you checked the next woman's phone during her interview for good measure."

"Yep. Tomorrow, we are bringing back the first woman as well as all of the others."

"Were they freaked out when you told them?"

Laurel nodded like five times, very slowly. "It was a rough conversation."

"Fuck." They must have felt violated all over again.

"Yep. So that was today." She was still staring up.

"And you get to do it all again tomorrow," I said.

"Hopefully, Brika can track wherever the fuck the signal is transmitting to. The fucked up thing is that this is probably the best lead we've gotten."

"I'm sorry."

"For what?"

"This. The fact I can't make it better."

She finally looked at me. "You do, though."

I decided to take her at her word. "When's the last time you ate?"

"Does coffee count?"

"It does not. Can I interest you in a grilled cheese?"

"Now that you've said it, you have to make me one." She looked very serious.

"On it." I stood.

"With tomato."

"And mustard and turkey. I got you."

She smiled at me. She still looked tired on a visceral level, but she didn't look hopeless anymore.

I went inside. Lane was crashed out, her books piled on the floor, her iPad balancing dangerously on her knee. I touched her shoulder.

"Lane," I said softly.

She woke with a sharp inhale. "Oh, hey."

"Why don't you go crash? This will all be here tomorrow."

"I can't. I need to read two more chapters."

"Okay. I can make a pot of coffee. Or you can crash, knowing you'll retain more information when you're not exhausted."

She rolled her eyes at me, but then she yawned. "Fine. But only because I'm not going to campus until noon tomorrow."

"You going to need a ride?"

She yawned again and shook her head. "One of my sorority sisters is picking me up. I spoke with a few of them today." She started to stack her electronics with her texts. "They were really good. Kind of closing ranks around me. It was nice."

"Good. That sounds good. I'm glad."

"Same here." She stood and a wealth of blankets fell off her. She collected the pile of study materials and crossed to her room. Her fuzzy socks were silent on the hardwood, but Nickels heard her anyway. She darted out of the hall and sprinted into the study before Lane could close the door.

"I see how it is," I said to no one.

In the kitchen, I assembled the ingredients for Laurel's grilled cheese. I dropped the sandwich into the hot pan, careful not to burn my fingertips. The butter crackled and made the air fragrant. When the bread was golden and the cheese was on the verge of melting out, I slid the sandwich onto a cutting board. I cut it in half diagonally like God intended it.

When I went back outside, Laurel's eyes were closed. I thought she was asleep for a moment, but then she lifted her bottle and drained it.

"You want another?" I asked.

She opened her eyes and took one of the cold bottles I was holding out. Her gaze landed on the sandwich and she sat up straighter. I handed it over.

"This." She bit off one of the corners.

"This?"

She closed her eyes and nodded. "Yeah. This."

"Cool."

CHAPTER SEVENTEEN

They all have it," Laurel said when I answered the phone.

"Huh?"

"The fucking app. Locus. It's on every single one of their phones." The sounds of the squad room filled in at the edges of her voice.

"Fuck. Seriously. What the fuck."

"We're all spinning in circles here. It's a shitshow."

"How can I help?" I asked.

There was an indistinct mumble, then the background noise cut off. "Are you asking as my girlfriend or as my CI?"

"Umm. I don't know. Girlfriend, but I can be your CI if you prefer," I said.

"Shit. I'm sorry. That was a dumb thing to say."

"It's fine. Just tell me what you need."

"I need you and Nate to come down to the station and help us sift through Instagram photos. Again."

"Did you guys narrow them down?" I asked.

"Yeah. Well, Duarte did. He took the locations Brika found and cross-referenced them with the frat parties happening on those dates."

"That doesn't seem like a fun task."

"Apparently, it wasn't. But we're kind of all hands on deck over here right now. Even if that means cross-referencing frat parties," she said.

"Sounds like a blast. Do you need anything else? Or just photo sorting?"

"That'll do for the moment."

"Got it. I'll see you soon."

"Thanks, Cash."

I tapped Nate's name. When he answered, he sounded out of breath. "What's up?"

"Sac PD is requesting our presence."

He groaned. Paused. Groaned again to make sure I got the message. "Dude."

"I know."

"What do they want?"

"The same thing as before, basically," I said.

"I cannot sit there and watch them stick their heads up their asses again. That was painful."

"I think the photos will be more specific. Duarte narrowed down the parties."

"They are so incompetent. How the fuck did they catch us?"

"I got distracted by a hot chick."

"Oh, yeah. Right." He laughed. "Thanks for that."

"Anytime, man. Anytime."

"So they think we are going to happen to identify the rapist in Instagram photos?" he asked.

"Yep. But they are also trying to track him digitally. Forensics found a stalking app installed on all the victims' phones."

"Jesus fucking Christ."

"Yep."

"That's skeevy as shit."

"Agreed."

"Okay. I'm stuck on campus for a few more hours, but I can head to the station when I'm done. I'll even bring you dinner."

"Thanks, man." We hung up.

I wrote an ambiguous note for Lane and left it on the coffee machine. I knew I could text her, but this was apparently our thing. Her phone seemed like the last bastion of her youth. Writing her notes made me feel like a grandpa, but in a good way.

It wasn't until I was tying my shoes that I landed on a thought I'd been circling since the night before. If Lane was, in fact, one of the victims in Laurel's case, her phone would have Locus installed on it as well. There was no evidence of ketamine in her tox screen, which was plenty of evidence for me, but Laurel wasn't convinced. I didn't like her job, but I at least respected her ability to do her job. If she thought Lane was one of the victims, then maybe Lane was one of the victims.

"Fuck," I said.

Nickels was unimpressed.

I grabbed my wallet and keys and headed out. Laurel had surely thought about this already. I just needed to ask what her game plan was.

When I got to the station, I went upstairs and paused at the edge of the squad room. I'd seen it busy in the middle of a weekday and I'd seen it utterly still, but this felt different. There weren't many detectives working, but the noise of them working was overwhelming. The air was weighty with their frustration. Across the room, Laurel stopped typing and looked up. Our eyes met and she took a deep, full breath. The skin around her eyes tightened and turned faintly pink like she was about to cry. I pressed my lips together and tried to smile. She gave me a half nod and went back to her computer.

Duarte came out of one of the conference rooms. I crossed the room to him.

"Duarte, hey."

"Cash." He grinned. "Are you here to help with the photos? Kallen said you were going to."

"Yep. I'm excited." I was not excited.

"Cool. Perfect. I just need to grab a laptop. You can head in though. This is the room." He pushed open the door he'd just come out of. "I'll be there in a sec."

"Super."

I went in and realized we'd been assigned the small, shitty conference room. There were stacks of photos on the conference table. I glanced at the first few in one of the stacks. Someone had enlarged and enhanced the people from the background of all the Instagram photos we had looked through previously. I glanced at the next stack and realized it was a different party. They must have been from Duarte's cross-referencing. This was why I never did anything that involved cross-referencing.

An hour later, Duarte and I had settled into a system. The photos were spread in a grid. We were attempting to identify the hundreds of twenty-year-old frat boys and had tentatively identified two. Plus, Digital Forensics had identified three others because they'd been tagged on Instagram. So things were going real well. There were a few dozen guys who were present at more than one party. We were focusing on them.

"Maybe we need a white guy in here helping us," I said.

"Why's that?"

I stared at a set of three photos. I knew they were different dudes because they were wearing different outfits and were at the same party. But aside from the different shirts, I could not tell them apart. There was not one distinguishing feature between them.

"Because clearly all white guys look the same to us."

"No," he said with the barest shred of confidence. "That one has a high nose and distinctive brow. That one might have a tattoo on his hand. And that one has no chin."

"Well, shit. You solved it. Let's go home."

"I'm just saying I can tell the difference between them."

"Good for you, bro. I can't. How the hell are we supposed to identify them if all we are able to do is determine that this dude is probably not that dude?" I pointed between two photos for emphasis.

Duarte shook his head and collapsed into a chair. "I don't know." He crossed his arms and chewed the inside of his lip.

"What?" I asked.

"What?" he asked.

"You're all twitchy. Say whatever it is you want to say."

"No. What? No, there's nothing." He was very convincing. "It's not professional."

"I'm a drug dealer. Professional was gone a long time ago."

He contemplated that with a borderline-comical furrowed brow. Then he nodded. "Okay. It's just that this is useless. I'm all for putting in the work, but we are wasting our time." He stood and started circling the room. "The rapist totally might be in these photos, but we're not going to find him this way. At best, we will catch him, then find him in the photos, which might give us a better idea of the timeline. "

"So why are we doing this?"

He shook his head. "I don't know. Because Fenton and Blackford are hoping he will appear at five different parties and it will be clear that he's our guy."

"That's dumb. Even if that's the case, we still won't be able to track him down."

"I know. But that's a manageable task. If we have an image, we have something to go on."

"It doesn't matter anyway. None of these guys are in your little database."

That comment made Duarte fussy. "It's not my database. NCIC and Versadex are what all law enforcement uses."

"Whatever. It's not helping us."

"Well, your method of looking through your contacts and saying 'he kinda looks like the dude who hung with Matt' isn't exactly working either."

"Hey, I'm just working with what I got. This was not my idea."

"Fuck. This is not going well." Duarte stopped walking, crossed his arms, and glared at the photo spread.

There was a knock on the door and Fenton stuck his head in. "How's it going in here?"

Duarte and I looked at each other.

"Great," Duarte said.

"Yep. Super," I said.

"You making any headway?" Fenton asked.

Duarte nodded in a very chill way. "A bit. We've identified a couple. Mostly just settling into a system."

Fenton glanced at me and I smiled. "He's good at picking out distinguishing features." That was all I could think of to say.

"Okay." Fenton nodded at that neat tidbit and backed out.

When the door shut, Duarte and I looked at each other and grinned. This was an idiotic endeavor, but at least we were playing on the same team. My phone rang. I checked the readout. It was Nate.

"Hey, buddy."

"I'm finally leaving campus. How's it going over there?"

"It's a shitshow. Duarte just had a tantrum," I said.

Duarte gaped at me. "I did not."

"Duarte throwing a tantrum? That sounds hilarious," Nate said.

"Yeah. It was pretty cute."

"So I'm on my way. You want me to stop at that deli you like in Davis?"

"Heck yeah I do."

"Cool. Text me what you want. And Duarte's order. Maybe it'll calm the kid down."

"On it. See you soon."

Nate was right. Food did calm Duarte down. Or maybe it was just taking our third break in an hour to eat said food. Who was to say really?

We were in the middle of explaining our system to Nate when Laurel stuck her head in.

"Braddock, can I steal you for a second?"

I glanced at Nate and Duarte. They looked indifferent. "Sure."

She led me out of the squad room to the stairwell. I'd learned long before that the stairwell was more private than half the station. And it was a lot more quiet.

"I have kind of a strange request," she said.

"Okay."

"I need you to snag Lane's cell phone." Her tone was even. Unencumbered. "Brika said he can run the diagnostic in about twenty minutes. I'm thinking after she crashes tonight, you can grab it and I'll run it over to the station." That was the moment I figured out what she was suggesting. "Brika will figure out if Locus is on it and we'll have it back before she wakes up."

I couldn't even speak for a moment. "Are you serious right now?"

She gave me an odd look. "Yeah. Why wouldn't I be?"

"You want me to steal your sister's cell phone so you can run a diagnostic to see if a stalker put an app on it without her permission?"

"Yes." She looked very confused by my anger.

"What's the difference between the stalker rapist guy and you in this scenario?"

She stepped back and blinked at me. "What?"

"You're doing the same thing. Taking her phone without permission. Doing things to it. Returning it without saying anything."

"That's not the same thing. What the fuck?" She leaned back against the wall and gripped the railing.

"Why not just ask her for her phone?"

"The same reason I'm not adding her name to the list of victims. I'm not traumatizing her further just to prove something I already know."

"What if she knows something that could help solve the case?"

"I've read her statements. They don't add anything new."

"Holy shit."

"What is your problem?" she asked.

"You're acting like Logan right now," I said. Her knuckles turned white and she started to push up off the wall. I put up my hand. "No. You're doing the exact same thing he did. You're deciding what is best for her under the guise of protecting her, but you're taking away her choice."

"Her choice? Telling her traumatizes her. It's that simple. I'm not doing that to her."

"So leave her out of this case."

"I'm not letting her rapist get away. This guy didn't just rape my sister. I owe it to her to catch him, but I owe it to all of those women." Her volume edged up as she spoke.

"How do you know it's the same guy?" I shouted.

"Because it's my job to know," she shouted back.

"Jesus fucking Christ. I can't do this right now." I took a deep breath, but that didn't calm my anger. "I'm sorry. I need to leave." I started down the stairs.

"You can't go."

"I have to. Good night, Laurel." The sound of my boots echoed back to me as I descended.

"Cash, wait," she called.

I looked back. She hadn't moved from her spot on the wall, but her arms were crossed. She looked small.

"What?"

"Don't tell her, okay? Just don't."

I searched her face as if that would tell me what she was actually asking. "I won't. Not tonight, at least. We'll talk tomorrow. You and me."

She nodded once and it looked like it took all her effort.

Chapter Eighteen

The next morning, Nickels and I were snuggling and apparently sharing a bagel. She was more interested in the cream cheese and seemed entirely indifferent to my suggestion that it wasn't good for her. Lane's door opened. She shuffled around for a couple of minutes before collapsing across from me with a cup of coffee. She pulled a pile of blankets around her. As if the oversized sweatshirt and thick socks weren't wearable blankets in their own right. Nickels jumped out of my lap and went straight for Lane's.

"Hi, sweetheart." Lane scratched under her chin.

"Hi, pumpkin," I said to Lane.

Lane rolled her eyes. "You're like a walking Dad joke."

"Is that a good thing? Never mind." I put up my hand. "I know it is."

We spent a good thirty minutes staring at our phones. Nickels abandoned Lane when I set my plate down. She checked it thoroughly for cream cheese, then returned to Lane.

There was a knock at the front door. Lane and I looked at each other.

"Is that for you?" I asked.

She shook her head. "One of my sisters is picking me up, but not for another hour and a half."

"Maybe it's your other sister." I pushed myself out of my chair. "She's mad at me."

"What happened?"

"Nothing." I waved my hand vaguely on my way to the door.

I swung it open and found Judge Janice Kallen. She was wearing a sheath dress the color of juniper and dark, low heels. Her hair fell in absurdly perfect waves. She carried a patina of sexuality, but it was slightly off—a hint of sweet rot below a flowerbed.

"Mrs. Kallen," I said.

"I'm looking for my daughter." She grasped the clutch tucked under one arm and took a step forward.

I shifted my weight slightly to block her way. "I'm sorry. She's not here."

"Don't lie to me. I'm quite aware that she's staying here." She stepped inside and gave me the option of moving quickly or letting her bodycheck me with all her sweet smelling glamour. I moved.

Lane held her mother's gaze. The look on her face was resolute, bored, kind. "Hi, Mom."

"Baby." Janice stopped two feet from the couch and held out her arms.

"Oh, that daughter," I said.

Lane spared me a brief look that was both amusement and reprimand. She stood and allowed herself to be hugged. I took the opportunity to text Laurel.

SOS. Janice is here.

Janice released Lane and guided her back down to the couch. "I'm so glad you're all right. I've been ill just thinking about you. Dad is distraught." She reached out to pet Lane's hair. "It's horrific. I'm so sorry you're going through this."

Lane pressed her lips together and nodded. "What are you doing here?"

"I've come to take care of you. All of this running away isn't going to help you. Logan found a great program for you. It's inpatient, but I think that will help block out a lot of the negativity in your world."

I had to admire Janice's restraint in not looking in my direction.

"I'm not going to an inpatient program," Lane said.

"It's fine if you feel that way. Logan also found a few promising outpatient programs. One is in Tahoe so it's close by." She continued her hair petting.

"Tahoe is two hours away."

"Yes, so it's close by." Janice didn't appear to realize that Lane was disagreeing with her.

"What do these programs treat exactly?"

"They are rehabilitation programs."

"What do I need to be rehabilitated from?" Lane asked.

This was going rapidly downhill. "Mrs. Kallen, would you like some coffee?" I asked.

She nodded in my direction. "Thank you."

"Cream or sugar?" I asked and hoped she didn't take cream. We were out of everything except the cheese variety.

"Honey or maple syrup, if you have it. Sugar if you don't. I don't want to be a bother."

So said the woman who had shown up without warning and forced herself into my home. I ducked into the kitchen to pour another cup of coffee. I stirred in a spoonful of honey.

"I don't need rehabilitation. I need to do what I'm already doing," Lane said.

"Baby, sitting in your pajamas watching television is hardly doing something." Janice watched me return from the kitchen. She held out a hand for the mug, then immediately set it on the coffee table.

"That's not what I'm doing."

"Look, I understand. You're going through a rough patch right now. This," Janice waved at the blanket fort Lane had built on the couch, "is fine for a little while. But you've been struggling since school started. You're clearly not making great decisions."

Lane stiffened and leaned back. "Like getting raped?"

Janice froze. "No. Of course not. I would never—That's not your fault."

"Then what? What terrible decisions am I making?"

Laurel burst through the front door. She was disheveled in that her hair wasn't perfectly tossed and her shirt was untucked, but those weren't the details normal people would see.

"Oh, hey, Mom, I didn't know you were here," Laurel said.

"Where else would I be? I came to take your sister home." Janice leaned forward to pick up her honeyed coffee. She crossed one stiletto-toned calf over the other and reclined ever so slightly as if she frequently lounged about on blanket-covered couches.

"I'll make this easy for you, then. I'm not going home with you and you need to leave." Lane extracted herself from the couch and stood resolutely over her mother. Somehow the fire and poise of the elder Kallen translated to the leggings and mismatched fuzzy socks of the younger one.

Laurel came around the couch. After exchanging a silent nod, she put her arm around Lane's shoulders. "I'm sorry. You can't stay," she said to Janice.

Janice was entirely unmoved. She smiled faintly. "You're deluded if you think I'm leaving my traumatized daughter at the house of a drug dealer."

"Unbelievable." Lane shook her head. "Cash, I'm jumping in the shower. You need anything before I close the door?"

"Nope. Just make sure Nickels doesn't follow you in again."

"You got it." She threw me some finger guns, which clearly proved we had been spending too much time together.

"Lane, stop being petulant. Gather your things and get in the car," Janice said.

"Christ, she's like a frat boy," Lane muttered.

I prayed her mother hadn't caught that line.

"Mom, you need to go." Laurel held out her hand to help Janice stand.

"I absolutely will not." Janice ignored Laurel's hand.

The bathroom door clicked shut and the shower turned on.

"You will. Lane is happy here. She's making healthy choices. She's taking care of herself." Laurel finally let her hand drop.

Janice scoffed. "She's not happy. She's broken. You may think you understand what healthy looks like, but I assure you this isn't it."

Laurel stared at her mother. After a beat, she took a long, deep breath. "There are many conceptions of normal and healthy and happy. Your opinion of those conceptions doesn't make them any less normal or healthy or happy."

"You are correct, which is why I want Lane checked into a program with medical professionals to help her."

"She's seeing a medical professional, not that it's any of your business. Her therapist is pleased with where she's at." Laurel was somehow staying calm during this appalling discussion. It was giving me a lot of insight into how she became the person she was. Watching was fascinating and horrifying. "You don't get to swoop in a week after the fact and run the show."

"I wouldn't have been here a week after the fact if you hadn't been hiding her from me," Janice said.

"We didn't tell you where she was because she asked us not to," I said.

Janice found a focus for her ire. "Don't pretend my daughter needs your protection. Certainly not protection from me."

I sighed. I should have known better than to speak. "I never suggested anything about protection. I'm just doing what Lane asks me to do."

"That's wonderful." She stood and faced me. "You're the hero for doing as she asks, but I'm the villain for getting her concrete help. Lovely."

"Mom, Cash has done more for Lane in the last week than you—"

"Laurel," I shouted. I didn't need Janice to like me or even respect me, but I did need her to not actively hate me.

"No, no, Cash, it's fine," Janice said in the most patronizing of tones. "My eldest is quite fond of explaining my failures to me. I thought she grew out of that in her twenties, but it seems she's feeling nostalgic."

And suddenly I decided I didn't care if she hated me. "Get out of my house."

"Excuse me?"

"Leave. Now." I held up my hand in the direction of the door.

"Laurel." Janice turned away from me.

"I love you, Mom. Please leave."

Janice just chuckled. "Fine."

I wanted to scream at Janice. I wanted to tell her she'd already lost both her daughters. But I saw Laurel's face and realized there would be no winner here. The best we could do was remain standing. I crossed the room to hold the door for Janice. She walked toward me, her heels clicking forcefully against the hardwood. I closed the door behind her. When I went to turn the lock, I realized my hands were shaking. From anger or fear or adrenaline, I wasn't sure.

"Fuck," Laurel said. She got halfway around the couch before she seemed to remember we were fighting. "I'm sorry."

"For what?" I walked back into the living room.

"All of it. I was out of line yesterday. I spent half the night trying to get the courage to call you and apologize."

"Thank you."

"And I'm so sorry for allowing her here, in your home. She's unbelievable." She nodded at the closed front door.

I shook my head. "That's not your fault."

"I still feel responsible."

"Don't waste the effort. Part of me assumed you were exaggerating, but she is everything you described. I don't know how you don't just tell her off."

"Oh, I tried. For years. But now I see how useless that is."

"Is the coast clear?" Lane asked.

We turned toward the hallway. Lane was hanging around the corner.

"She's gone," Laurel said.

Lane sighed and came all the way out. She was still wearing her pajamas. "That was a nightmare."

"I'm sorry, baby sis."

Lane hugged Laurel. "She was in rare form. I'm glad you came over. Wait." Lane drew back. "How did you know?"

"Cash texted."

Lane looked at me and nodded. "Smart."

"She'll come back," Laurel said.

We all stared at each other and contemplated how unpleasant that would be.

"I can just hide. Someone smart once taught me that avoidance is sometimes the healthy option."

"Whoever that was sounds pretty great," I said.

"She's okay," Lane said.

"I'll ask Robin to keep the back door open. That way you can just hide out next door." I pointed my thumb at our shared wall.

Lane lit up. "Would she do that?"

"It's honestly probably open right now anyway," I said.

"Cool. All right. I'm actually jumping in the shower now." Lane took a step back toward the hallway. "Nickels is crashed on your bed."

"Dope."

A minute later, the water came on again. Laurel dropped onto the couch.

"Jesus. You have enough blankets here?" she asked.

"Lane likes blankets."

"No, I like blankets. Lane has an unhealthy need to be buried in blankets."

I couldn't argue that. I folded half the blankets and set them to the side so I could sit next to Laurel. "So your mom is struggling."

"That's a kind way of saying it."

"It's not. There's no kind way to say it. She's self-involved. All she can see is her own pain and she's completely unaware that her pain is irrelevant. I pity her."

"Yeah, see, that's kind. I love her, but I'm struggling not to hate her."

I shrugged. "It's just because I'm removed from the situation. It lends perspective."

"Well, I'm glad you can see it because I can't. Thanks for helping me look at the larger picture. Not just with Mom, but my brothers too."

"Oh, God." I had a sobering realization. "What's your father like?"

"Like Mom, but in a bespoke suit."

"Super."

"Sorry."

"You've got to stop apologizing," I said.

"I know. It's just my gut reaction to the vitriol of the Kallens."

"I don't think they are vitriolic; I think they are sad." I took her hand and rubbed my thumb along her knuckles.

"How so?"

"Lane has plenty of emotional needs right now. Your mom, your dad, your brothers can fulfill those needs or they can make her see with startling clarity how much she does not need them. Ignoring Lane's autonomy just highlights that her autonomy functions without them."

"Because she's relearning how to function?" Laurel asked.

I nodded. "Yeah. She could use their help, but now she's just going for it without them. I mean, she's at an age where she's learning to move through the world anyway and that process is ramped up because of the assault."

"I can see that. College sophomore and all that."

"Yep. By the time your family sees that she needed them on her terms, it will be too late. Their relationship with her will be irreversibly altered."

"Is that what happened with you and your uncle?" Laurel asked.

I'd wondered if Clive was going to enter this conversation. "To some extent, yes. He didn't trust my perception. Your mom doesn't trust Lane's perception."

Laurel leaned her head back and sighed. "Emotions are hard."

"Hecka."

Chapter Nineteen

Laurel waited until Lane's sorority sister had picked her up before getting ready to leave. She was tying her oxfords when her phone started ringing. She glanced at the readout, rolled her eyes, and flashed the screen at me. It was Reyes.

"Hey, what's up?" she asked. He said something in response. "I haven't been looking at my phone. Give me a sec. I'm putting you on speaker." She hit the speaker button, then started scrolling through her messages. "What the fuck?"

"You're reading it?" Reyes asked.

"Yeah. Give me a sec."

I leaned over so I could see her screen. She angled it so I could read. Her browser was open on a *Sac Bee* article. "Sacramento State Rapist: Is there a serial rapist on Sac State's campus?" The article proceeded to speculate if the school was experiencing an uptick in sexual assault reporting as a result of Me Too or if a serial rapist was operating on campus.

"Fuck. How much information do they have?" Laurel asked.

"We think at least one victim talked to the reporter. They know about ketamine, but not about Locus. It's only a matter of time though. You need to get down here now," Reyes said.

"Yep. I'm on my way." Laurel hung up.

"Will you send the article to me?" I asked.

"Yeah." She tapped her phone a few times and my phone lit up. "This is bad. If they report on Locus, we will lose our biggest lead."

"I know. Get out of here."

"Thanks." She kissed me too briefly, then turned to the door. She got about halfway there before turning around, panic in her eyes. "Do I tell Lane?"

"Shit. Well, she needs to know. People will be talking about it on campus. Anyone she's told or anyone she tells today will ask if she's one of the victims."

"Dammit."

"It doesn't need to be a whole conversation, just a heads up."

"Yeah, okay. Good point. I'll call her on my way."

I nodded. "Good luck today."

As soon as the door closed, I sat and read the whole article. I agreed with Reyes. At least one victim had spoken to the reporter, but it appeared she'd withheld significant amounts of information. The article discussed the frat parties and drugs, but that was it. The number of victims was conjecture based purely on tweets, which was interesting. The tweets might have been more accurate because rape survivors were far more likely to discuss their assault on social media than with police, but also it was Twitter. So that was iffy.

My phone rang. It was Lane.

"What's up, buddy?"

"Any chance I can convince you to pick me up in about two hours?"

"Sure. Everything okay?" I asked.

"Yeah. I just got off the phone with Laurel. After my lecture, I was going to hang at the Tri Ep house until my afternoon class, but I really don't want to answer questions."

"Got it. No problem."

"Thanks, Cash."

I checked the time so I'd know when to leave to pick her up. Then I reread the article. Then I did what I thought I'd never do. I downloaded Twitter and made an account. It took me twenty minutes to admit I couldn't figure out how to navigate it. Being a Millennial wasn't all it was cracked up to be. I knew I could ask Andy for help, but she would mock me. Lane would ask why I wanted to use Twitter. So I asked the only other Gen Z person I knew: Duarte. He gave me a thorough two-minute tutorial complete with screenshots. It was great. Kids, man.

I started reading through the accounts quoted in the article. There were a ton of threads specific to the case. Some predated the article.

Most had been posted after the article went live. It didn't take me long to figure out the difference between the legit discussions and the douche bros defending rape culture, probably because they outright said that was what they were doing.

Duarte texted to ask how my foray into Twitter was going and tentatively ask why I was suddenly interested in social media. So I told him the truth, which sucked him right in. I figured out real quick how to send a thread via text and was quite proud of myself.

By the time I left to pick up Lane, I was equally convinced there was a serial rapist at Sac State and that there was no serial rapist because literally all of the guys on campus were rapists. Logically, I knew that couldn't be the case. But at the very least, they all seemed quick to defend rape. Duarte seemed reluctant to jump on board my all dudes are rapists train, but he was wavering.

Like Lane said, a piece of hay in a haystack.

That evening, Lane was back on campus finishing a lab, Laurel was still radio silence at the station, and I had a deep and nuanced understanding of what a Twitter hole was.

My front door opened. I looked up from my phone. Laurel nodded at me.

"Hey," I said.

"Sorry to show up unannounced." She kicked off her shoes and started emptying her pockets. "I was going to text, but I…" She got distracted by the action of stacking her wallet and phone on the table by the door.

"It's cool. Are you okay?"

She nodded a couple of times. It wasn't convincing. "Fine."

"Want some chips and salsa?" I pointed at the spread on the coffee table.

"Fuck yes." She detoured into the kitchen to grab a beer.

"I can make something more substantial, if you want."

Laurel ate a chip and shook her head. "These really are the best tortilla chips ever."

"I know."

"So what did you do today? Tell me about anything that isn't sexual assault or Sac State related." Laurel leaned back and took a sip of beer.

"Umm."

"What?"

"Well, I learned Twitter."

She cocked her head and grinned. "Why?"

"To research the tweets used in the article," I said. She groaned. "Sorry. Not much of a distraction."

"Wait. You're the reason Duarte was all up on social media today."

I shrugged and nodded. "Yeah, probably. He taught me how Twitter worked and I kinda roped him into my research project."

"He's convinced there are at least ten unreported victims."

"At least he didn't tell you my theory."

"Which is what?"

"That one hundred percent of the cis dudes on campus are rapists and you guys are just connecting the dots between the common ones."

She rolled her eyes. "Oh, yes, thanks. That's very helpful."

"Okay, I know they can't all be, but all of them are fueling rape culture. So, you know, they are all at fault."

"I wish I could argue that."

"You can't. I'm very smart."

"The article prompted three more women to come forward today," she said.

"Jesus fucking Christ. Three?"

"Yep. I'm sure tomorrow there will be more."

"Your turn," I said.

"For what?"

"Tell me something that isn't sexual assault or Sac State related."

She looked at me wide-eyed. "There's a world outside of sexual assault and Sacramento State? What's it like?"

I grinned. "We need to get you to a movie or something."

"That sounds great." She took a few long gulps from her beer and settled into the corner of the couch. "Are we allowed to do that?"

"I'm free." I pulled out my phone to look up movie times. I knew there was only a thirty percent chance I'd get her to go to a movie, but I figured it was worth playing out the fantasy on the off chance it worked.

"Actually, I have a much worse idea of how to spend the evening."

"What's that?"

She grimaced. "You want to go to a frat party?"

"That sounds like a terrible idea."

"I know, but we've tried everything else. We just need one idiot with ketamine to build a case."

"It's a Wednesday night. Are there any frat parties happening?" I asked.

Her grimace deepened. "Sig Ep is having a hump day party."

"Imaginative."

"It gets worse."

"Not possible."

"The hump day theme extends to attire. Apparently, it's business casual. Nineties business casual."

I chugged the rest of my beer. "You're so lucky you're hot."

"I know."

Thirty minutes later, we walked into an absolutely idiotic frat party. Laurel thankfully hadn't made me dress for theme, but everyone else seemed delighted to have done so. I was not surprised to find that a bunch of college kids born in the late nineties to early aughts were completely unaware of nineties fashion. There were slim khaki joggers and skinny ties mixed with colorblock windbreakers and wide sweater vests.

"I'm going to find us something to drink," I said.

"Nothing in an open container."

"Oh, really? Why?" I did my best to look confused.

"Cash."

"Laurel."

"Because someone is going around dosing people with ketamine," she said.

I broke into a grin. "I know." I kissed her cheek and dashed off.

When I came back with bottled water, Laurel look relieved. She cracked it open.

"Look at that. It's even sealed," she said.

"Yeah, girl, nothing but the best for you." I slung my arm around her shoulders. "Isn't Sigma Epsilon the frat your mom said was rapey?"

"She did? When?" Laurel leaned to the side so she could look at me. "Was it before I got there?"

"Got where?"

"To your house."

"What?" I replayed the conversation. "Oh, no. She didn't tell me they were rapey. She told you. It was when she showed up at your apartment. You said she kept asking you what frat house Lane was at."

"Oh. That. Yeah, she asked if Lane was at the Sig Ep house." Laurel turned to stare pointedly at the twelve-foot Sigma Epsilon crest painted on the wall.

"So we're in the rapey frat house?" I asked.

"That's somewhat worrisome."

"Mildly."

We sipped our not drugged water and people watched. No one came up and offered us ketamine, nor did anyone ask me for ketamine. So that was disappointing. I started watching the women. Most of them showed signs of intoxication, but it was impossible to tell if it was a result of alcohol or something else.

"Are you watching the girl on the stairs?" Laurel asked.

"No. Which girl?"

"Cream high-cut pleated pants. Like really pleated. And a floral top."

It only took me a moment to pick out the massive cream color pants on the stairs. Laurel was right. They were very pleated. The woman was clinging to the banister to make it up each stair. She finally reached the top and stumbled into the hallway and out of sight. A guy halfway down the stairs started taking the stairs two at a time.

"Is that guy following her?" I asked as he also disappeared into the hallway.

"Yeah." Laurel took a step toward the stairs. I grabbed her hand and pulled her back. "What are you doing?" She glared. "I need to check on her."

"Alone in the rape house? I don't think so," I said.

"Well, come on then." She yanked me forward.

We wove up the stairs as quickly as possible. They were littered with people and actual litter. When we emerged in the hallway, the drunk girl was at the far end and the guy who had followed her was coaching her to walk. He sighed and picked her up. He turned back to the stairs with the now passed out young woman in his arms.

"Finally. Where the fuck were you guys?" he asked.

Laurel and I stopped walking. That was not the response we expected.

"Excuse me." Another young woman pushed past us. "You found her," she said to the frat boy.

"Yeah, but I texted you like five minutes ago." The guy huffed and readjusted his grip on the woman in his arms.

"Sorry. Jill's getting the car because I can't drive. She's pulling up out front." The woman smoothed the drunk girl's hair. "I'm so glad you found her."

"Yeah, same." He rolled his eyes. "Can you clear the stairs so I can take her down?"

"Yeah, sure." The young woman turned again. "Sorry, you two mind moving?" she asked us.

"Sure," I said. We pressed against the wall so they could get past. It took them a minute to get downstairs.

"We might have misjudged that situation," Laurel said.

"Duh."

"I guess all frat boys aren't rapists?"

"Seems unlikely, but okay."

We laughed at ourselves and went back downstairs. We didn't get a lead on ketamine, but we did get our faith in humanity slightly restored so it wasn't a total wash of an evening. A movie still would have been better though.

Chapter Twenty

Duarte and I had been sequestered in the tiny conference room for three hours. In that time, the noise from the squad room had slowly dwindled. We were sitting at the conference table surrounded by a wealth of devices: laptops, iPads, police issue tablets, but we were both on our phones. The door opened. I looked up in surprise. I thought everyone had gone home.

It was Laurel. "Cash? Duarte? What the hell are you guys doing in here?" She stepped inside the room and pulled the door closed behind her. She was staring at the wall opposite us. "What the fuck is that?"

"Oh, uh, hey, Kallen." Duarte locked his phone and set it down. "We made a murder wall." He blushed faintly.

"A murder wall?" she asked.

He chuckled. "Not to catch a murderer. It's just all the information we have. You know, about the serial rapist." He glanced at me for help.

"Some of it isn't official. We wanted to compare the confirmed information with our suspicions. Try to eliminate some of the cis men on Sac State's campus."

Duarte nodded. "We only suspect like a quarter of them now."

"Well." Laurel edged around the table so she could look at the wall up close. "The rookie detective and the CI."

Duarte and I made eye contact and shrugged. We didn't know what that meant. Laurel started in the center of the wall where we'd put up a map of Sac State and the surrounding neighborhoods. The map was where all the facts were. She traced the lines out. She seemed particularly confused by the list of Twitter and Instagram handles. Watching her made me feel strangely nervous. This wasn't even my job. That morning, Duarte had texted me a photo of the mini version of the murder board tacked up in his cubicle. Somehow, ten hours later, we had ended up here. Yet, Laurel was giving me flashbacks to my algebra teacher critiquing a problem I'd solved on the whiteboard. Algebra had never been my strong suit.

"This is insane," she finally said.

"I can take it down." Duarte pushed his chair back and stood. "We just got carried away. I mean, I did. I dragged Cash into it, but it wasn't her idea. I know she's your CI. And I know this isn't even my case. I just wanted to help out with more than identifying photos."

Laurel spun away from the wall. "No. It's good."

Duarte stopped halfway around the table. "What?"

"I mean it, Jeff." She looked at the wall, then back at him. "You did good work."

"Really?"

"Yeah." Laurel pointed at the map where we had marked time stamps. "Explain this to me." She pulled out a chair and dropped into it.

Duarte hustled forward. "Okay. It's color coded, obviously. Each color is a different victim. So this one, the lavender, is Haylee Prosser." He traced an invisible line between silver pins holding cards in place. All of the cards with Prosser's information had a wide lavender stripe at the top. "The assault occurred at the Zeta Beta Chi house between eleven p.m. and twelve fifteen a.m. We don't have hospital records because she didn't report. But we do know that she attended one other party at Sigma Epsilon." He pointed to a different frat house. "She was there until approximately ten p.m. when she and her friends went to Zeta."

"What's up with that?" Laurel pointed at the far end of the wall where a lavender card was tacked under the Instagram list.

I came around the table. "We have three photos from Zeta Beta Chi during the time frame Prosser was there. And seven photos from the Sig Ep party." I ran a finger down the Twitter list. "No tweets that obviously reference either party. From a cursory look, it doesn't look like the vic has a Twitter account."

"It is also worth noting that the information concerning which frat houses the vics were at is pieced together from interviewing them, their friends, their social media and is by no means exhaustive or even necessarily accurate," Duarte said.

"Okay, burnt orange." Laurel pointed at a card.

"Burnt orange is…" Duarte drew the word out as he looked for the name. "Kali Wayne."

"Assaulted at the Sigma Epsilon house between two thirty and three a.m." I pointed at Sig Ep on the map. "She was our second victim. Sexual Assault nurse noted that Wayne was still clearly suffering the effects of ketamine when she was brought in. That observation is one of the reasons the nurse was aware of the drug in the next victim, which is how she knew to ask the lab for that specifically."

"Thank you, Mercy Hospital," Laurel said.

"We only have one photo from Sig Ep, but Wayne and her friends attended a bar and two other parties."

"The bar hasn't been mentioned by anyone else." Duarte pointed at a bar in East Sac.

"But there are twelve photos from Kappa Kappa Tau and nine from Alpha Pi Omicron in the approximate time frame."

"You guys, this is impressive as hell. When were you going to let the lead detectives in on it?" Laurel asked.

Duarte looked at me and shrugged, but I didn't know. This was his job. I was just indulging him.

"We aren't finished yet," I said.

"What else do you need?" Laurel asked.

"We were filling in some of the social media blanks." Duarte nodded at the fringe lists I was standing in front of. "That's what motivated us, actually. The Twitter chatter surrounding the frat houses paints a pretty clear picture of which houses are rapey."

"When was the last time you left this room?" she asked.

"I think I got here around five," I said. Duarte nodded.

"So you don't know about the app installation," Laurel said.

"The what?" Duarte asked.

"Brika figured out what time Locus was installed on some of the phones. He's still working through the list, but I think he figured out four of them."

"Holy shit. What time? Which vics?" Duarte turned to the conference table and started sorting note cards and felt-tip markers.

"I'm not sure. Let me go grab it." She left the room and was back a minute later. "Here." She handed him a short list.

"Ava Nunes, Jordan Sadler, Kali Wayne, and Mackenzie Glas," Duarte read off.

"Okay, that's plum, pink, burnt orange, and lime green, right?" I asked as I collected note cards and pens.

Duarte nodded, then grunted. "Uh, no. Sadler is blue."

"Right, blue." I dropped the pink pen and grabbed the blue.

Duarte handed me a card. "Nunes, plum, the nineteenth. Twelve ten a.m."

I wrote the pertinent information and drew a stripe across the top of the card. Duarte ran through the rest of the list and I filled out the cards. "Where do we want to tack them? On the map?"

Duarte scrunched his nose. It was his thinking face. "Let's see when it happened in relation to the assaults. That might tell us where they were." He took one of the cards at random and went to the map. After a minute, he found the appropriate card. He tapped it on the map. "Forty-five minutes before."

"Check this one." I handed him another and took the blue one myself. Jordan Sadler had been assaulted at Omega Kappa Nu between one and two a.m. Locus had been installed at twelve twenty-nine a.m. "Thirty minutes before."

"Thirty minutes for this one too," Duarte said.

"An hour for this one." Laurel held up the last card.

"So Locus was installed before each assault," I said.

Laurel nodded. "But within an hour."

Duarte grabbed a couple of pins. "Let's put them next to the assault times." He stuck one to the board.

"I assume they were tagged with the app at whatever party they were assaulted at," I said.

"Yeah." Duarte tacked up another one. "Yes? Probably. I don't know." He started mumbling and tracing his finger over various cards.

Laurel started doing the same with the lime green cards. "I think so. This one only attended one party. She was at Zeta Beta Chi, which she arrived at between nine thirty and ten thirty. Locus was installed at nine thirty-eight p.m."

"There's overlap with this one." Duarte held up the plum card. "She was tagged with the app at twelve ten a.m., but she left Omega Kappa Nu at midnight and went directly to Sigma Epsilon where she was assaulted. She arrived at the hospital at one thirty."

"So she could have gotten Locus at either frat house," I said.

"Fuck. I thought this was going to make it easier." Duarte tossed the two cards he was holding back on the conference table.

"Actually, this is good." Laurel picked up Duarte's cards. "Let's note both possible houses where Locus could have been installed. Maybe there will be clear crossover."

"What do you mean?" I handed her my card.

"Well, if we have two potential locations for all of them, but they all have Kappa Kappa Tau or whatever as a possible location, then logic would suggest Kappa Kappa Tau is where we need to focus."

Duarte lit up. "Oh, dude." His ears turned red. "Sorry. I mean, Detective Kallen. You're right." He grabbed a pen and the stack of cards from Laurel. He checked all the cards and wrote down frat houses on each Locus card. The lime green only got one frat, but everyone else got two.

"Which one is the solo one?" Laurel pointed.

"Zeta Beta Chi."

"Is it a potential location for any of the others?" I asked.

Duarte nodded. "Prosser was also assaulted there. Sadler was at Zeta immediately before being assaulted at Omega Kappa Nu."

"Things aren't looking good for Zeta Beta Chi," I said.

"Okay, so Zeta is our focus. Tomorrow, hopefully, Brika will have the rest of the time stamps for us."

"Sounds like a plan." Duarte grinned. He should have. This was all his doing.

"Can we show this to Fenton and Blackford tomorrow?" Laurel asked.

"Yeah. Sure. I guess." Duarte's smiled dropped a little. "Are you sure that's a good idea? I mean, this isn't even my case. I don't want to edge in on their territory."

"Duarte." Laurel looked at the wall pointedly.

"What?"

"Edging in on their territory was twelve hours and a whole murder board ago."

"Yeah, I know, but I don't want to be disrespectful," he said.

Laurel swallowed a sigh and closed her eyes before the full eye roll became visible. "We can show Reyes first, okay? He will tell you how brilliant you are, and then we can show Fenton and Blackford."

"Okay, yeah. That would be all right."

"Is there anything else you two want to add tonight? Or can we go home?" Laurel asked.

I looked at Duarte and shrugged. We'd barely included any Twitter information, which was what had started this insanity, but that info was also the biggest stretch. Most of what was on the wall could be backed by the information in the case files. Twitter was probably not going to hold up in court. Or to Sergeant Ionescu's scrutiny. We might be able to convince Reyes and Laurel that Twitter was valid. We might even be able to convince Fenton and Blackford, but Ionescu would just glare at Duarte.

"Yeah, let's get out of here." Duarte patted his pockets and removed a few pens. He tossed them on the table.

Laurel led us out of the building. Duarte waved and disappeared into the empty lot.

"You want to go to my place?" I asked.

"That sounds good. I'll follow you there."

I texted Lane to let her know Laurel and I were on our way. She offered to order dinner. I hoped, irrationally, that said dinner would arrive in the fifteen minutes I knew it would take to get home. Sadly, that was not the case. I parked in the driveway and Laurel parked on the street. When she climbed out of her truck, she had her phone tucked between her ear and shoulder.

"No, I was driving. I'm not answering the phone while I'm driving." She rolled her eyes and mouthed "Duarte" to me.

I nodded and opened the front door.

"What do you mean?" Laurel slid past me and I pulled the door shut behind us. "About ten minutes, but up to thirty. I'm not positive though. I can find out tomorrow."

"Hey, guys," Lane called from the couch.

"Hey." I rounded the couch to sit with her, but found the entire surface covered in study materials.

"Sorry. I'll move. Give me a sec." Lane started stacking books.

"Don't. You're fine." I collapsed in the chair instead. "See?"

"Yeah, that makes sense," Laurel said.

"What's up with her?" Lane whispered.

I shrugged. "No clue. She's talking to one of the baby detectives."

"I think it's like two. We'll have to check, but—" She started nodding, which was pretty useless for a phone call, but what did I know. "Yeah, I think so too." She listened to him, looked at me and Lane, then quickly dropped her eyes. "No, I think we should wait until tomorrow. Brika will have the rest of the time stamps then. Okay. Good work today." She laughed at something he said, then hung up.

"If you need to go back in you can," I said.

"No." She shook her head. "It's okay."

"What was Duarte calling about?"

"He wanted to confirm the duration of Ketamine. How long it takes to hit full strength after ingesting, whatever."

"Why?"

"Because he thinks Locus was installed at the same time the women were dosed," she said.

"Well, yeah. Probably."

"That was my reaction too. I think he was looking for a bit more excitement."

I shrugged. "Then give him a gold star."

"All of the gold stars." Laurel grinned.

"Hey, guys, what the hell are you talking about?" Lane asked.

Laurel omitted the fuck out of the truth. "Just this stupid case." She shook her head. "One of the baby detectives is finally figuring out his footing."

Lane shrugged, any mild interest gone at the suggestion Laurel might start talking about her colleagues and their work performance.

Chapter Twenty-one

Are you coming to the station today? No pressure. I just thought since you helped build the board you might want to be there when I show the guys. But like I said, no pressure! Let me know.

It was the neediest text I'd gotten since dating in my early twenties. I groaned.

"What?" Laurel sat on the edge of the bed to put on her shoes.

"Duarte." I held up the phone so she could read the screen.

She leaned back and read the text. She laughed and leaned farther to kiss me. "That's cute."

"How is that cute?"

"He wants to be your buddy." She said it like she was talking about a dog.

"I don't need a buddy. I have a cat and a fifteen-year-old neighbor and a Lane. I'm full up on buddies."

"So are you going to come down?"

"I don't know. It's not really my place."

"I get that." She stood. "Well, if you decide to, let me know. I'll put down the puppy pads in the conference room."

"You're a dick."

"I know, but in my defense, I'm truthful. Duarte thinks you're awful swell."

"Whatever. If I go in, it won't be until noonish. I'm taking Lane to class."

"Brika won't have the rest of the Locus installation info until early afternoon, probably."

"I'll keep that in mind."

My phone buzzed again. I sighed when I saw Duarte's name again.

Did Kallen tell you what we figured out last night?

"How do you want me to answer this?" I held up the phone again.

Laurel shrugged. "I don't know. Don't lie to him."

Yep. Ketamine and Locus were probably same time. You're hecka smart, bro.

Thanks!

"He uses a lot of exclamation points," I said.

"I'd make a joke about it, but I'm sure you would just remind me that I'm ageist."

I tossed my phone on the bedside table. "You are ageist. Duarte is a perfectly capable detective. He just gets excited and also uses a lot of exclamation points."

Laurel rolled her eyes, kissed me, and stood. "Maybe I'll see you later."

"I don't know. I'm meeting my best buddy Jeff first, but maybe after that."

She laughed and closed the bedroom door as she left. A minute later, her truck started up.

I pep talked myself out of bed. It was eight in the morning. Laurel had slept in to indulge me, which made exactly zero sense. If sleeping past seven was sleeping in, there was something fundamentally wrong in your life.

I started the coffee and snuggled the cat. Lane woke up at a normal time and the cat ditched me per the usual. No one's mother made a surprise visit.

After dropping Lane off, I realized my day was empty. I hadn't been up to the farm in months and I didn't plan on breaking that streak. I didn't have any deliveries. Nate and Andy were in school.

Clearly, it was time to become a stockbroker. But I still didn't know what they did so I drove to the police station.

Duarte was nowhere to be found when I arrived on the detectives' floor. Laurel caught my eye and shook her head. I was pretty sure she mouthed "puppy" before going back to typing.

"Hey, Cash, you come down to bask in the big reveal?" Reyes asked.

I turned toward him. "Oh, hey. Yeah, I guess."

"Duarte is with Fenton and Blackford in the conference room." He tipped his chin in the direction of the door. "You're welcome to go on in."

"Dope. Thanks." I crossed the room and let myself in.

Duarte jumped up from his seat and gave me a high five that became a bro hug. "Thanks for coming down. I wasn't sure if you were going to make it."

"Braddock, good work with this." Fenton nodded at the wall. He sounded sincere.

"Yeah, we appreciate the help." Blackford did not sound sincere.

"Sit down." Duarte kicked out a chair for me. "We just added three more Locus installations." He dropped into the chair between me and the other detectives.

"And are they all the same time frame?"

Duarte nodded enthusiastically. "And Fenton caught something we didn't."

"Oh, yeah." I leaned forward a bit to look at Fenton.

"The earlier assaults are the ones with longer gaps between app installation and rape. The later assaults appear to have shorter gaps."

"Shit. So he got more experienced," I said.

"Exactly what we're thinking. There are two outliers, but they don't disprove the theory," Fenton said.

"Both of them were unclear on the time of the assault compared to the other women. One didn't go to the hospital. The other passed out and her friends found her so the timeline is hard to pin down." Duarte used a laser pointer to indicate which cards on the wall he was discussing. The laser pointer was a disturbing development. Either someone at the station had been dumb enough to give him one or he brought it from home. Neither option was good.

"Okay, so we are working on the assumption that they were dosed when Locus was installed," Blackford said. We all nodded and made vague noises of agreement. "We know that dosing a drink with ketamine only takes a second so that could happen anywhere, but Brika estimated that Locus installation would take longer."

"And the guy would need physical access to her phone without her realizing it. That's got to narrow it down. How is he taking their phones, returning them, drugging the women, and following them for up to an hour without anyone noticing?" I asked.

"Oh, yeah. That's the other thing," Duarte said.

"What's the other thing?"

"Brika was in here earlier. He said it was possible the phones were hacked remotely, but it would still require being physically close to the phone. Like within five feet?" Duarte looked at Fenton.

Fenton scrolled through the notes on his iPad. "Yeah, about that. And it would take a little while. Between five and ten minutes."

"So he could be sitting on a couch next to them, hack their phones, then dose them?" I asked. That didn't narrow things down at all.

Fenton grimaced from behind his beard. "Theoretically, yes."

"The weird thing is that none of the women remember seeing the rapist beforehand. They didn't notice anyone following them or sitting near them for an extended period of time or anything," Duarte said.

"But they could simply not have been aware of their surroundings. Most of them were intoxicated and party hopping. It would be easy to follow them without being noticed," Blackford said. It really didn't make me feel great about him at parties.

"Not necessarily. Most women are aware of guys in social situations like that," I said.

"What do you mean?" Duarte asked in all of his innocent glory.

"Men are threats. Especially for femme presenting women. Paying attention to the guys around you could be the difference between life and death, quite literally."

Blackford's eye twitched. "Well, obviously they weren't paying that close of attention."

"Are you fucking serious?" I asked before I could stop myself.

"I'm not trying to demean them." Blackford put his hands up defensively. "I'm just saying that someone who is apparently on constant alert for a predator would notice at least one of these red flags."

"Or this guy is really good at being a creepy predator." I raised my eyebrows and dared him to respond.

"Or what if it's like two guys?" Duarte asked. We all looked at him. "Okay, I don't have any evidence of that, but two participants would make it easier to dose, hack, and follow."

"But none of the victims reported multiple attackers. Why would two guys tag team this elaborate scheme if only one of them was going to do the assaulting?" Fenton asked.

"Yeah, okay. You're right."

How the fuck did anyone do a job where they casually discussed tag teaming elaborate rape schemes? None of the detectives seemed thrown by this discussion. I was saved from asking that question when Ionescu let himself into the room.

"All right. I have five minutes. Where are we at?" He frowned and his jaw tightened as he looked at the murder board. Or maybe that was just his face.

"Current theory is that the perp installed Locus on the phones at the same time he dosed the vics with ketamine. It makes sense with just about every timeline we've constructed," Fenton said.

Ionescu grunted.

"We still can't figure out how this guy managed to hack and drug the vics. He would have needed to be in close proximity for about five, maybe ten minutes." Blackford looked at me, then added, "Most women at a frat party would at least notice a guy hovering for that long."

"Explain this." Ionescu walked up to the map and started reading cards.

Duarte jumped up to walk him through a color like we had with Laurel the night before. Ionescu nodded along. At one point he tapped a blue address, made a noise, then tapped the next blue address.

"How are they getting from point A to point B?" he asked.

Duarte looked at me. I looked at Duarte. Neither of us had an answer to that one. We looked at Fenton and Blackford. They clearly didn't know either. Blackford started flipping through his notebook.

"We don't know," Blackford said.

Ionescu grunted again. "Good work here." He tapped his fist against Duarte's shoulder, then left the room.

"Do any of the interviews discuss it?" Duarte asked as soon as the door closed.

"I've got one that said they caught a ride, but that's it. No indication of the ride," Fenton said.

"I don't even have that." Blackford closed his notebook with a huff.

Duarte was staring at the board. "Most of these are walking distance, but it would be a long walk. Especially for someone intoxicated."

"Would intoxicated women want to walk or would that be too dangerous?" Blackford asked me. At least he was catching on.

"I think most of them were in groups." I looked at Duarte and he nodded. "So walking wouldn't be as dangerous. That said, would you want to walk five or ten blocks if you were trashed?"

Blackford shook his head. "Not if I had another party to get to. If I was trying to sober up on the way home, maybe."

"All right. It sounds like we need to speak with all our vics again." Fenton parsed out the names into three lists. He handed Duarte and Blackford each a note with three names.

Blackford and Fenton left to make calls from their desks. Duarte hung back.

"Listen, I know you've probably got better things to do and you're not my CI, so if you want to go, you're welcome to. No hard feelings." He pursed his lips, but didn't drop eye contact. "But it's Friday and I think we're all afraid that if we don't get this guy real soon, we're going to have to add more colors to that board."

"It's cool. I want to catch this guy." How could I not?

"You do?"

"Yeah. Nate said it best when you guys first called us in. Cops are assholes, but a serial rapist is definitely more of an asshole."

Duarte nodded, then broke into a grin. "Well, okay. I'll take that."

"Go. Call." I grabbed the folder of Instagram photos we had yet to identify. "I'll be here."

Thirty minutes later, I'd identified exactly one more person out of the hundred in the backgrounds of the photos. Fenton had struck out on all his calls and was searching databases with me. Blackford burst into the room looking more excited than I'd ever seen him look.

"We got it." He held up his notebook triumphantly.

"You got the girls on the phone?" Fenton asked.

"Yeah. And they all said the same thing."

The door flew open again and Duarte strutted through. "You guys, I got it."

Blackford spun and stared at him. "So do I. Safe Streets?"

"Dude, you killed my big reveal." Duarte sat down and did a solid impression of a sad puppy.

"What's Safe Streets?" Fenton asked.

"Isn't that the ride share thing?" I asked.

Duarte nodded. "Kind of. It's a service operated on campus."

"And in the surrounding neighborhoods," Blackford said.

"Yeah. It's intended to reduce drunk driving. It's really similar to Lyft and Uber except it's free. You just have to show a Sac State ID." Duarte typed on one of the laptops as he talked. After a minute, he jumped up to turn on the projector and pull a screen over the murder board. "Here's the Sac State website for the program."

The projector flashed and hesitated, then turned on. We were looking at a page on Sac State's student center website. Duarte scrolled past the description of the service until we got to the requirements for drivers. Apparently, they drove in pairs for safety and both operators wore photo IDs. They also underwent fingerprinting and background checks. Everyone in the room held their breath as we read and reread the description.

"If our guy is a driver, then we fucking have him," Blackford whispered.

"Where is their office?" Fenton asked.

"I'm not sure, but here's the contact info." Duarte highlighted the appropriate phone number and email address.

Fenton typed it out in his notes. "I'm going to call. Blackford, will you fill Ionescu in? We need a warrant. Duarte, let Kallen and Reyes know we might need backup."

They nodded. I followed Duarte out to the floor. Blackford kept walking to the other side of the room where Ionescu's office was. Duarte dragged a chair over and planted it next to the desk Laurel and Reyes shared.

"What's up, pup?" Laurel asked.

I leaned against Laurel's desk and tried not to laugh.

"We might have gotten a break." Duarte propped an elbow on the desk and leaned forward. "We talked to five of the women and they all used Safe Streets for transportation."

"Hey, nice work." Reyes leaned forward to fist-bump Duarte.

Duarte shrugged. "I didn't actually do anything. Ionescu figured out where we needed to focus."

Laurel squeezed his shoulder. "No, man. Without you, he wouldn't have been able to see the gap. You did good."

He smiled. "Do you think Fenton and Blackford will let me tag along when they arrest the guy?"

Laurel took a deep, pitying breath like she was about to break a heart. Reyes just barely shook his head at her.

"Yeah, probably," Laurel said.

"Cool." Duarte grinned.

"Duarte," Ionescu shouted.

Duarte jumped out of his chair and went to Ionescu's office.

"There's no need to kill his buzz. He will figure out that the case isn't wrapping up tonight on his own," Reyes said.

Laurel sighed. "Yeah, I realized that."

My phone buzzed. It was Lane telling me her lab had been canceled.

"I think I'm going to take off. There's nothing else for me to do. And it sounds like you guys actually have a handle on this," I said.

Laurel slid her hand an inch to the left so her pinkie just barely touched mine. "Okay. Thanks for coming down."

"Yeah. That board is quite impressive," Reyes said.

I shrugged. As long as they reduced the number of entitled men going around raping people, I was happy to be of service.

CHAPTER TWENTY-TWO

Big Friday night plans?" I asked Lane as we drove home. "Oh, God, I do sound like a dad."

She laughed. "It's good. You're an endearing dad. And, no, parties haven't been appealing recently."

"That's fair."

"It's weird. The Tri Ep social calendar generally dictates my schedule. I'm not really sure what to do without it."

"Are the sisters giving you shit for ditching out?" I asked.

She shook her head. "They've been great. I talked to a couple of the older girls who are survivors. They shared some really helpful stuff. You know, just about taking care of myself and that sort of thing."

"Huh. That's cool, I guess. I mean, it's horrifying that they need to be well versed in assault, but it's nice that you have that system. That's not really how I thought sororities operated."

"Oh, there are plenty who do the shit you've read about. But that's why I like my sorority. We try to operate as an actual sisterhood."

My phone buzzed, and a message from Andy popped up. "Sorry." I tapped Andy's name to listen to the text.

"Alejandro went home sick so I'm not going to his house tonight. Can you pick me up after school?"

"Damn," I said.

"It's fine. What time does she get out?" Lane asked.

"Three twenty." I looked at the time. It was three. "You don't mind?"

"No. This is our thing. Actually, it's your thing. You've officially transitioned from drug dealer to soccer mom." She laughed at her own joke.

"Shut up. But that reminds me. I scheduled your dentist appointment for Tuesday at eleven." I turned on 19th to get back down to Freeport.

She stopped laughing. "How did you know I needed a dentist appointment?"

"Umm, I didn't know?"

"No shit. I'm fucking with you. And I officially just out-sarcasted the most sarcastic person I've ever met."

"Sarcasted is not a verb. Or a word."

"Don't regulate my language. What are you, the fucking patriarchy?"

I started laughing. "You sound like me."

"It's obnoxious, isn't it?"

"Yes. I'm sorry. I think I need to call Ms. Trumbauer from tenth grade and apologize." I tapped Andy's name. "Be there soon." Siri sent the text.

"So your big Friday night is hanging out with a fifteen-year-old whose friends stood her up and a sorority girl who is afraid of parties?" Lane asked judgmentally.

"Well, yeah, but the babysitting money is dope. I'm saving up for a princess phone."

"A what?"

"You don't know what a princess phone is?" I asked. She shook her head. "God, I'm old."

"You're not even thirty."

"And, yet, I'm old." I pulled into the parking lot of the coffee shop down the street from the high school. There was already a line of parents parked and waiting for their kids. "We need to switch seats."

"You want me to drive?" She gave me a weird look. "Oh, no, you want Andy to drive."

"Yep. And you are not a driver over the age of twenty-five."

"I had no idea you were such a stickler for the rules."

"Jeez. You make a living as a drug dealer and suddenly people think you don't follow laws."

"People." She rolled her eyes. "Am I right?"

But then she climbed into the back seat. I got out and went around to the passenger side.

Lane leaned forward between the seats. "I take it Laurel is still working on the big case she refuses to talk about with me?"

"Yep." I turned so I could see her. "It has to do with sexual assault. That's why she's not talking."

"I assumed. Is it the case from *The Bee* story?"

I nodded. "And I'm not going to talk to you about it either because she asked me not to."

"That's fine. But, for the record, I'm okay talking about assault."

"I know. And I trust you to know your limits. She does too, mostly. But it just seems unnecessary to talk about it."

"Assault in general or my assault?" She leaned her head against the driver's seat and watched my reaction.

"Both? I don't know." I searched for an accurate answer to her question. "I guess I figured if you wanted to talk, you'd let us know."

"Okay. It's kinda weird. I feel like I'm not that different than I was before. Like it was an inevitability and the inevitability tempered my reaction. I don't know if that makes sense."

"It does. And I didn't really know you before so I don't know if you're different."

"My life hasn't shifted all that much. I don't know what I was expecting, but status quo wasn't it."

"Well, you did move off campus, cut off most of your family, and stop attending Greek events."

Her eyes got big. "Oh, shit."

"What?"

"You're right. This isn't status quo." She shook her head. "Whoa. I had no idea."

"You're still maintaining status quo with other shit. Attending class, studying, checking in with your sorority sisters, therapy."

"That's wild. How do you do that?"

"Do what?"

"You kind of just blew up my perspective, then reconstructed it."

I shrugged. "I just think about things differently than a lot of people do."

"I guess I do as well. There's the whole fact that I don't really care what happens to the dude who raped me. I'd like an apology." She shrugged. "That's dumb, isn't it?"

"Fuck no. An apology would acknowledge that your autonomy was violated. You said you want to be able to move on in a healthy manner. That's the only real contribution he could make to that end."

The passenger door opened and I almost fell backward out of the car.

"Oh shit." Andy put her hand on my shoulder to make sure I wasn't going to tumble out.

"Hey, tiger." I laughed and turned to sit properly in the seat.

"Hey, Andy." Lane waved.

"Lane, hi." Andy grinned at her. She looked back at me. "You want me to drive, don't you?"

"Oh!" I feigned shock. "What a good idea. Especially, since I'm already sitting over here."

"You're so good at ideas," Lane said.

Andy rolled her eyes and dropped her bag on my lap. She closed the door and walked around the front of the SUV. I turned to put the backpack in the back seat.

"Can we continue this later?" I asked.

Lane nodded. "I'd like that. You're a good friend." She squeezed my forearm.

Andy climbed into the driver's seat. "All right. Home, I assume?"

"Unless you want to go to Hollywood Video and pick up a VHS," I said.

Andy dropped the keys on the floor. "Huh?"

"Won't that cut into your princess phone fund?" Lane asked.

"No. The parents left twenty bucks for pizza and a video rental. They said I could keep the change. This babysitting gig is dope," I said.

Lane laughed. "I thought Blockbuster was the movie rental place."

Andy shook her head, but it didn't help her brow unfurl. "What the hell are you guys talking about?"

I clasped Andy's shoulder. "Nothing. We're just screwing around."

"Whatever." Andy started the car.

"Cash asked me about my Friday night plans. Apparently, in the Stone Age that's what people did. Blockbuster and pizza."

"No, no. Hollywood Video," I said.

"Oh, sorry."

"Blockbuster refused to carry certain morally objectionable titles. So like they didn't carry *Rocky Horror*. The cool kids all went to Hollywood."

"The cool kids." Lane's tone was less than sincere.

"Okay, guys. I'm driving. Don't distract me." Andy reversed out of the space carefully. She pulled into the street. Lane and I maintained perfect decorum. Once we were out of the after-school traffic, Andy asked, "What's a princess fund?"

"A what?"

"You mean a princess phone fund?" Lane asked.

"Oh, yeah. That."

"They were these phones marketed to teenage girls in the sixties," I said.

"I thought cell phones weren't a thing until the eighties," Andy said.

It took everything in my power not to laugh. "They weren't. Actually, cell phones were more like the nineties for most people. Princess phones were rotary phones. You know how old landline phones had the thing you had to turn to dial?" I did the motion of dialing.

"I've seen those." Lane smacked the back of my seat. "My grandma had one when I was a kid."

"Mine too," I said.

"Isn't that way before your time?" Andy asked.

"Yeah. Not landlines, but rotary phones were definitely before me."

"So what you're saying with all of this is that we are ordering pizza and watching movies tonight?" Andy asked.

"I'm not not saying that." I looked back at Lane.

"I'm so in."

"Can we wear footie pj's?" Andy asked.

"I don't have footie pj's," Lane said.

"Neither do I." I clearly had made poor life choices. "Loop back down to Broadway." I pointed at the next cross street.

"Okay." Andy turned on her blinker. "Why?"

"We need to stop at Target."

Lane gasped. "Shut up."

"No, if we're doing this, we're doing it right."

"Doing what?" Andy was getting irritated.

"We all need onesies. And probably candy."

"It's not a proper sleepover unless we have candy. Someone needs to find a sticky Skittle stuck to their pj's at three in the morning," Lane said.

"Can we make a pillow fort?" Andy asked.

"Heck yeah we can make a pillow fort," I said.

Five hours later, Andy was sandwiched between me and Lane on the floor. The dining chairs on either side of us were doing a bang-up job of holding the sheets Andy had somehow attached to the TV. I was just hoping I wouldn't find duct tape stuck to the back of Beverly.

The front door opened and Laurel called out, "Hello?"

I grabbed the remote and tried to pause the movie.

"We're in here," Lane said.

"I figured that out. What the hell are you guys doing?"

I finally managed to find the proper button. "Just a sec. We're coming out."

"I'm already out." Andy grinned and elbowed me.

"Hilarious. I love a good closet joke." I wiggled out and held the edge of the blanket up so Andy and Lane could crawl out. I was definitely too old for wiggling and crawling.

"You guys made a pillow fort?" Laurel looked at my outfit, then her eyes slid to Lane and Andy. "What the hell are you guys wearing?"

"I'm an astronaut!" Andy's onesie was printed to look like a space suit. Mine had dinosaurs all over it. Lane's was a unicorn complete with a metallic horn attached to the hood.

"I can see that."

"Mine glows in the dark," I said.

"That's neat." Laurel's tone was somewhere between mockery and wonder.

"But don't worry, Laurel. We didn't forget you." Andy sprinted down the hallway and slid the last three feet into my bedroom. She came running back with a onesie in Laurel's size. It was covered in cowboys riding broncos with split rail fences and lassos and cowboy hats.

"Oh, wow."

"Now, we were aiming for a sheriff theme, but they just didn't have any that fit what we were going for so we got you these too." Andy whipped a pack of sheriff badge stickers out from behind her back.

Laurel started laughing. "You guys nailed it. I mean, there will be no disputing that I'm the law in town."

"Obviously. Here." Andy held out both items. "Suit up. We're only twenty minutes into *The Hunger Games*."

"And pizza will be here any minute," I said.

Laurel's smile dropped. "I can't. I wish I could. I need to go back to the station."

"Oh, man." Andy frowned dramatically. "It's okay. You can come to the next sleepover."

"Which will be soon, I hope. I'm not waiting to wear this bad boy." Laurel took the cowboys onesie and held it against herself.

Andy leaned forward and held the sticker pack high on Laurel's chest. "Rad."

Lane nodded enthusiastically. "You're going to be the best sheriff."

"I'm not now?"

"No, but that's not your fault. You didn't have the proper equipment," I said. Andy and Lane nodded. We all agreed that it was quite tragic Laurel hadn't been set up for success until now.

"I'll let you guys get back to your evening. I just need to grab a few things." Laurel pointed down the hallway to my room. "And can I steal Cash for a second?"

Andy shrugged. "Sure."

"Come on." Lane led Andy into the kitchen where they started getting out plates and napkins for dinner.

I followed Laurel to my room. She shut the door behind me.

"Have you seen my big shoulder holster?"

"Your big shoulder holster?"

"Yeah."

"There's a big one?"

"Yes. Usually I carry the smaller one because it's easier to conceal, but the bigger one holds extra clips."

"Umm, you left a holster here a couple of weeks ago. It's in the closet. I don't know if it's the big one."

"Thanks." She went to the closet and came back out a minute later with a leather holster the color of espresso crema. "This is it." She set it on the bed.

"Something going down tonight?"

She nodded. "We're just backup, but I prefer to be prepared. Plus, Reyes still isn't cleared for active duty so it's me and Duarte."

"What are you backing up?"

"Fenton and Blackford. They are arresting two Safe Streets drivers tonight."

"That was quick."

"Yeah, we didn't expect the organization to be so cooperative, but they were extremely helpful."

"I'm sure they want to maintain their reputation."

"Yep. And a rapey driver targeting their riders is terrible optics. No one will use them once word gets out." She set her gun on the bed, then shrugged out of her jacket and shoulder holster. "They have a huge pool of drivers, but they also keep amazing records. The time and date narrowed it down to three pairs, but they also have GPS to track driver locations. The whole program runs just like Lyft." She pulled on the bigger holster and started adjusting the fit.

"Can they tell which car the victims rode in?"

She grinned and nodded. "Yep. The first name we ran confirmed the timeline." She put her gun in the big holster and clipped it in. "So at the very least, we can place the two operators' cell phones in the same vehicle as the victim's cell phone at the time Locus was installed. Brika is running all the rest of the names to confirm."

"But you guys have him?"

"Yep." She sat on the edge of the bed. Her posture was an imitation of casual, relaxed in everything except the obvious rigidity of her muscles. "The judge already approved our arrest warrants."

"Why tonight? Wouldn't it be better to wait until you have all the information possible?"

She shook her head. "They are scheduled to drive tonight so we're picking them up when they report for their shift. We can't risk them going out this evening, obviously."

"Shit. Yeah. Got it. Who are they?"

"Grant Osborn and Malcolm Darby. Both in their third year at Sac State. Neither is a fraternity brother, but Duarte says their social media suggests they have friends who are. We don't know which one is our guy, but the warrants give us access to their apartments, vehicles, laptops, phones, the whole deal."

"Dope. The laptops should give you a better idea about why he installed Locus."

"Yeah. That's the one piece none of us can figure out."

"Well, whatever motivated him, I hope you fucking bury him."

"We plan to." She stood and put on her jacket. "It's going to be a long night. I'll call you in the morning."

"Do I need to be worried? I don't know how this whole dating a cop thing works."

"You know enough to realize I'm only going to lie in response to that question."

"Awesome," I said with exactly zero conviction. "Try not to get hurt or anything because I'll be fucking pissed."

"Noted. Don't get hurt or Cash will throw a tantrum."

"You're a dick." I pulled her close and kissed her.

"Romantic as always."

CHAPTER TWENTY-THREE

Hey." I tried to fight my grin when I answered my phone, but quickly realized that was pointless. I'd missed her.

"God, I've missed you." Laurel sounded tired.

"We haven't seen each other for almost twenty-four hours so that probably explains it."

"That's definitely it. I've been missing you for about twenty-three hours."

"I know you're being sarcastic, but I'm going to take it anyway," I said smugly. "So how's it going? Did you figure out which one of them is the rapist?"

"Fuck. Umm, a lot has happened."

"Okay."

"Neither of them is the rapist." Her tone was matter-of-fact but lacked the ire I would have expected.

"Shit. Fuck. How? Do you know who is?"

"Yes. It's a long story."

"Can you come over? Or are you still tied up?" I asked.

"Actually, I'm calling for an official reason. There are a couple of frat houses we need to get into quietly tonight. They are having parties, but they're effectively invitation only."

"Uh, yeah. Sure. Which frats?"

"Kappa Kappa Tau, Sigma Epsilon, and Pi Tau Gamma all need invites. And Delta Delta Theta isn't necessarily exclusive, but they might not let in randos."

"I've got an in at all of them except Kappa Kappa Tau, but Nate might know someone there."

"I was hoping you'd say that. Reyes is calling Nate right now. Can we all meet in like an hour?" she asked.

"Sure. Here? Or do you need us down at the station?"

"God." She groaned. I didn't hate it. "I'd love to go to your place. I've been here since six this morning."

"Cool. Come now."

"Is Lane there? Or Andy?"

"Lane is at a study group." I glanced at the time. "For another couple of hours. Andy is being all social like a teenager on a Saturday night."

"Perfect. I'll be there in twenty."

"I'll start the coffee."

It wasn't that long before Laurel showed up. She even beat the coffee maker.

"Hi, how's it going?" I asked.

Laurel didn't answer. She just kept walking into me. I wrapped my arms around her.

"Fuck, I'm tired," she said into my neck.

"Physically or emotionally?"

"Yes, both."

"Did you actually sleep last night?" I squeezed her shoulders.

"That feels good." She melted into me. "I went home for about two hours."

"That's not enough sleep."

"Tell me about it."

"What do you need right now?"

"Twelve hours of sleep, a shower, a meal that isn't fried or made of cheese, all of the coffee. Failing that, maybe I just need to try cocaine. Everyone says it's great."

"It is great, but it doesn't last long and you apparently have a long night ahead."

"I'll just keep doing more blow. That will make me fit in, right?"

"Totally. Solid plan," I said. She chuckled. "Or how about you drink some water because hydration is good. And then jump in the shower. I'll order non-fried food and you can drink coffee while it's delivered."

"Yeah, okay."

"Go jump in."

She nodded and started down the hallway. "Gosh, I wish I had some fresh clothes. Maybe someone could pick some out for me."

"You're fucking needy."

She tossed her shoes into the bedroom. "I know." She closed the bathroom door behind her.

I debated what food to order before realizing that fried food and cheese were a large portion of my diet. I landed on deli sandwiches and judged myself for having memorized Reyes's and Duarte's orders in addition to Laurel's and Nate's.

Thankfully, there wasn't much effort needed in order to pick out Laurel's clothes. She only had navy boxer briefs and white T-shirts in her drawer so that narrowed the options. Detective Kallen did not mix her base colors.

I was sorting through my flannels to find one for Laurel when she swaggered into my bedroom with a towel slung around her waist.

"Okay, that's just not fair." I tossed the two flannels I was holding onto the bed.

"What?" She looked down. "Calm down. They're boobs, and Xiao, Reyes, and Duarte will be here in ten minutes."

"While I see your point, I'd like you to consider mine."

"Is your point boobs?" She arched an eyebrow at me, dropped the towel, and, in an extremely unfair move, put on her underwear.

"It was, but now that I've seen your ass, I think I have a much more nuanced argument." I crossed the room in a few long strides, kissed her, and used my momentum to take us down to the bed.

Her lips, damp still from the shower and tasting of the clean purity of water, slid against mine. She opened her mouth enough to suck my bottom lip between hers. I palmed her tits, which were just as exquisite as I remembered.

I groaned. "I missed your boobs."

"Who the fuck says shit like that?" She grabbed the waistband of my jeans and pulled me tight against her crotch.

"Me?" I lifted up just enough to take her boxer briefs off.

She took a deep breath. "You have to be fast."

"Not a problem." I kissed down her neck. Her skin had a hint of salt and cedar like it always did. I'd thought it was her soap when we first started up, but I knew now that she just smelled that good all on her own.

She arched up into me to try to move my hands. I was all for teasing, but I really didn't want to get caught by Laurel's colleagues. That was a little too much danger for me.

I slid my hand between her legs. She was slippery. Thick wet strands clung to my fingertips as I pressed on either side of her clit. Her hips started to shift, thrusting against my hand. I only teased her for a moment before pressing inside her. She laced her hands behind my neck and pulled me closer. We kissed as her muscles clenched around me. With my free hand, I grabbed her ass, held her just still enough to fuck her slowly.

She moaned into my mouth. Her breathing sped up and she dug her fingertips into the muscle in my shoulders. I curled my fingers forward, pressed the spot I knew would make her come. She went taut beneath me.

When she started to relax, she pulled me against her. Her rapid breath was warm against my neck. Her muscles slowly loosened, but she just held me tighter.

"We have to get up, don't we?" Laurel asked.

"Yeah, about five minutes ago."

"Time is a bullshit construct."

"Agreed. But, you know, until the rest of the world agrees, maybe we should go with it."

She chuckled. "Fine."

I slowly rolled away from her but took her hand. "I missed you."

"Same." She lifted our joined hands and kissed mine. "Did I see you picking out a shirt for me?"

"We are currently lying on them."

Laurel half sat up and looked at the two shirts I'd picked out. "You've stolen four of my flannels, but you picked out two of yours for me to choose from?"

"I have not stolen four of your flannels."

"The marine blue one, the red and yellow, the one with the bright orange, and the olive."

"Yeah. I don't have any like that." I grinned at the lie.

"So none of those are hanging in your closet right now?"

"Nope. I don't even wear flannel. I don't look very good in plaid."

Laurel started laughing. "You're the worst."

"I know." I kissed her and jumped up. "You've got like two minutes until they get here. Get dressed and I'm going to go out there and try not to think about your boobs."

"That's admirable."

I nodded solemnly. "I know."

Nate and Duarte and I piled onto the couch. Reyes and Laurel took the chairs that bookended either side. Reyes and Laurel looked like they very much needed their coffee. Duarte's eyes were overly bright and his hands were shaking. He'd already clearly had too much coffee.

"So what's the deal? You said neither of these guys were the rapist." Nate leaned forward like that would get the detectives talking.

"They aren't. In fact, there isn't just one rapist," Laurel said.

"What?"

"Seriously?"

All the detectives nodded.

"Each rape was committed by a different perp," Reyes said.

"Holy shit. So Fenton and Blackford were right initially?" Nate looked at me wide-eyed.

I didn't know what to tell him. I was just as surprised. "That's crazy. How could so many dudes be buying ketamine without anyone realizing it?"

"They aren't. It's just two guys," Laurel said.

"That doesn't make sense," I said.

"Do you want to tell the story?" She held out her hand palm up like she was giving me the floor.

"Sorry. We'll try not to interrupt."

Nate nodded. "Promise."

"The two guys we arrested last night are Safe Streets drivers. They were dosing female riders and installing Locus to track their location post drugging. Then they were selling that information to their buddies," Laurel said.

I stared at Laurel. Beside me, I could feel Nate doing the same thing.

"That's fucking gross," Nate finally said.

"It really is," Reyes said.

"So the rapists are all guys who bought the location of a drugged woman to rape?" I asked.

The detectives responded with a chorus of yeses.

"Seriously. That's disgusting," Nate said.

"Who the fuck thinks up something like that?" I asked.

Laurel shrugged. "Grant Osborn and Malcolm Darby?"

I fought an eye roll. "Yeah, but how does anyone conceive of something so sick?"

None of them had an answer for that.

"How does someone even advertise that?" Nate asked.

"We have DMs discussing the transactions," Reyes said.

"Direct messages," Duarte said.

Laurel huffed. "We all know what DMs are, Detective."

"You didn't three hours ago." Duarte held her stare.

Laurel half smiled and waved at Reyes to continue.

"The messages suggest the guys don't think of the interactions in terms of assault. Osborn and Darby are promoting it as a way to help out their buddies," Reyes said.

"The clients don't seem to comprehend the implications either. At no point do any of them ask about consent or willingness. It's just women who are easy." Duarte kind of shrunk into himself as he spoke. "That's by no means an excuse, by the way. They are all scumbags."

"Can you confirm the transactions from the DMs?" Nate asked.

Laurel made a semi-affirmative noise. "For the most part, they aren't explicit."

"But they are very clear despite the lack of specific language. They aren't exactly using sophisticated codes." Duarte grabbed his iPad off the table and unlocked it. "Do you want to read some of them?"

Nate shook his head and glanced at me. "I don't need to read that shit."

"Same." I had no desire to read a conversation where young men bought drugged young women.

"Right." Duarte locked the iPad and set it back down.

"How do you know they were drugging them?" I asked.

"Osborn and Darby were carrying five drugged water bottles when we arrested them," Laurel said.

Reyes chuckled without conviction. "Plus, Osborn had a stockpile of ketamine in his apartment."

"And their YouTube history was a bunch of videos on how to remove a water bottle cap without breaking the seal. Which made it real easy to identify the paraphernalia all over Darby's table because he basically just had the supply list from the video spread out." Laurel spread her hands to show the space occupied by said paraphernalia.

"This is what's wrong with entitled boys. They just assume no one will ever stop them or question them," I said.

Reyes slowly shrugged. "At least their arrogance makes it easy to get charges to stick."

"Yeah, these two aren't getting off easy. It's catching the others that's the challenge now."

"Which is why you need to go to frat parties tonight," Nate said.

"Exactly. I assume from your presence at this meeting that you're comfortable helping us out?" Laurel asked.

"Sure."

"Yep."

"Cool. Reyes will be back at the station managing all the teams. He can walk you through the structure."

Reyes flipped open his notebook. "Laurel and Braddock will obviously be together since we have that relationship established, which means Duarte and Xiao are paired up. Fenton and Blackford are each heading their own team with an undercover officer. The remaining team will be comprised of uniforms since they will be going to private residences."

"Wow. You think that will cover us?" I laughed.

"No, actually. Each of the detective teams will be assigned a pair of officers as backup. They will be plainclothes in case they need to enter any of the locations without arousing suspicion."

"Good." Laurel nodded. "I'm glad Ionescu approved us on that."

Nate choked out a laugh. "Guys, isn't five teams overkill for arresting nine dudes?"

Duarte shook his head. "We're arresting more than that though."

"Oh, yeah. Darby's laptop showed more than nine Locus installations," Laurel said.

Nate and I exploded into a litany of not very creative expletives.

"How many?" I finally asked.

"Digital Forensics is still working to give us an exact number. They are sorting through DMs and pairing them up with the app installations. When I left the station, they had found fourteen cases," Reyes said.

"Jesus fucking Christ."

He read from his notebook. "Six of the women who came forward are included. Presumably, the three other women will also show up in the search. There were also two victims who reported, but that we didn't connect to this case. The remaining women didn't report being assaulted."

"So what do we need to do?" Nate asked.

"Vouch for us so we can get in the door. Acting as an extra set of eyes would be helpful, but you are not obligated to do so. You must not engage with the perps at all," Laurel said.

"That's reasonable."

"Are we wearing wires again or anything?" I asked. Not that I wanted to repeat the last time Laurel had put a wire on me, but I wouldn't necessarily be opposed to it.

"Nope. Those are more for information gathering operations. This is simple smash and grab," she said.

"Without the smash," Reyes said.

"Yeah, there will be absolutely no smashing."

"Duarte has the photos of the plainclothes officers you'll be working with." Reyes waved toward Duarte's iPad.

"Oh, right. Yeah." He unlocked it and brought up photos of police officers in uniform. It was a pretty unfortunate reminder of who I was dealing with.

"The operation begins at twenty-two hundred hours," Reyes said.

"You are such a douche. What the fuck is twenty-two hundred hours?" I said.

"Ten o'clock," Nate whispered.

"I can do the math. I'm just saying it's douchey to talk that way," I whispered back.

The doorbell rang, announcing the arrival of our dinner. "Is that food?" Laurel asked.

"Yep. Not fried or smothered in cheese." I turned to Duarte. "Except for yours, of course. I understand that you are seventy percent cheese."

He pursed his lips and nodded seriously. "I appreciate that you know who I am."

CHAPTER TWENTY-FOUR

Fraternity parties were the pinnacle of American douchbaggery. I couldn't stand college parties as a general rule, but at least the hipster kids tried to provide craft beer. The frats just had kegs of domestic crap. And maybe it was the ketamine talking, but I didn't feel very comfortable drinking from a Solo cup.

Laurel leaned back against me and tilted her head so her lips were against my ear. "Hey, you think we might be in Pi Tau Gamma?"

I chuckled. "Naw, why would you think that?"

I'd wondered how all of the survivors had been so certain about which frats they had been to, but after two minutes inside Pi Tau Gamma, I no longer wondered. There was a massive tapestry that took up one wall in the central room with the Greek letters for the house. Eighty percent of the guys were wearing Pi Tau Gamma clothing. They definitely didn't have a problem with branding.

"You see our guy yet?" she asked.

"I promise you'll be the first to know when I see him."

I scanned the room again. Our perp was Drew Novak, six feet, two twenty, with a dark blond fade. He was a brother who lived in the house, which made it inconvenient for cops who wanted to arrest him on the night of a massive party. Laurel had a warrant, but if she used that in lieu of an invitation, Novak would be warned and gone by the time we got inside.

"Has Lane texted you yet?" I asked.

We had left a stack of photos of the nineteen perps for Lane to look through. Her phone wasn't on the list of Locus installations and

Brika and the Digital Forensics team assured us they had found all the victims.

Laurel shook her head. "I know it's a long shot."

I squeezed her shoulder. "At least you know she's not part of this case."

"Yeah."

She was dejected. I totally understood why. The chances were slim that the guy who had assaulted Lane was among our list of rapists, but it was entirely possible. Most rapists were repeat offenders. At least Laurel could feel like she was doing something.

Thirty minutes in, Laurel texted Reyes back at the station for a status update. He responded that Duarte and Nate had already arrested their guy at Delta Delta Theta. I mentally crossed him off the list of nineteen names and faces Laurel had made me memorize.

"Dammit."

"You realize it's a good thing that they made an arrest, right?" I said.

"Yes, but we need to round these guys up quickly. As soon as one of them texts another or posts something on social media, we're fucked."

"Okay, we can split up to look or I can ask one of the frat boys where Novak is and tell him I have a delivery."

"That's dangerous."

I considered her point briefly before deciding she was incorrect. "It's not. I'm a drug dealer. I'll flash a bag of pills and introduce myself. They will tell me where he is. Simple."

"Yeah, but the more you do shit like that, the more likely someone will realize you're helping the cops."

"Oh, no." I used the most sarcastic tone possible. "But then my cover will be blown and I won't be a useful CI anymore."

Laurel chuckled. "Fine. Go see if you can find him."

"Thank you." I slid out from between her and the wall I'd been leaning against.

I snagged a Pi Tau Gamma in the kitchen. He looked younger than the others and a bit unsure of himself. I hoped he was a pledge. Or whatever. One of the fresh members. I didn't know how frats worked. I probably should have asked Lane for a lecture on structure and terminology.

"Hey, man, I'm looking for Drew. You know where he is?"

"Drew? Which one?"

"Novak. Tall dude, blond."

"Right. Yeah. Yeah. He's still upstairs, I think. Should I tell him you're looking for him?"

"Actually, if he's in his room, that's better anyway." I pulled a bag of Adderall out of my pocket and turned my cupped palm so the kid could see it. "I have a delivery for him."

His eyes got big briefly, then he became cool. Overcompensating levels of cool. "Totally. I got you, bro. Come with me."

He led me back out of the kitchen and through the central room of the house. Laurel made eye contact with me. I tipped my chin toward the stairs and she started walking in that direction.

The stairs were as unimpressive as the house. I'd expected the inside of a frat to look like they did in movies, but it was just an old tract home, built up to create more rooms. The stairs were carpeted in low pile beige, which probably allowed for easier vomit cleaning. It was also a great metaphor for frat houses.

We turned at the landing to go up the second half of the stairs and I glanced back. Laurel was only a couple of steps behind us. I followed junior to a door where he knocked before opening.

"Hey, Drew. I brought up your delivery."

Once the door was fully open, I could see Novak and two other guys sprawled in beanbags playing Xbox. I was obviously shocked to find that beanbag chairs were still in use, which was why it took me a second to realize that one of the other guys was Gabe Sumner. He wasn't one of the guys Laurel was responsible for, but he was on the list of arrests that needed to be made that evening.

"What kind of delivery?" Novak asked.

I pulled out my phone and feigned a call. "Sorry. Give me a minute." I stepped away from the doorway.

"He in there?" Laurel asked quietly as she came even with me.

"Yep. With Gabe Sumner."

"Oh, shit. That's great."

"I think we need some Scotch," I said in the most casual, not a code for backup sort of way.

"Agreed," Laurel said in an actually casual way. She pulled out her phone and texted Reyes.

Junior came out of the room. "Hey, I thought you had a delivery for Drew?" the kid said. I turned so he could see the phone I was holding to my ear. "Oh, sorry." He backed away. "Well, he's in there."

I nodded and the kid went back to the party. I wondered how long I could keep my fake phone call up. I also wondered what the chances were that Novak and Sumner would stay in that room playing Xbox. It would take two to five minutes for the plainclothes cops parked outside to get upstairs. There were a handful of people in the wide hallway, but not enough to draw attention away from me and Laurel.

There were shouts downstairs. I took another step away from the open door and leaned against the wall. Laurel shrugged and went into the room.

"Drew Novak?" she asked.

"Yeah?"

"You're under arrest. Please put your hands on your head and face the wall," Laurel said.

"What the fuck? For what?"

"Sexual assault. Hands on your head, please."

"Be quiet, bro," a different masculine voice said. "Just don't say anything."

"Call my dad, okay?" Novak asked. He sounded scared.

Laurel started giving Novak instructions. Her voice layered over the guy who had told Novak to keep quiet. It sounded like he was calling Novak's father.

Chen and Hawkins, the two plainclothes cops I'd been introduced to earlier, sprinted up the stairs. They were six feet tall, well muscled, and conventionally handsome. The only noticeable difference between them was their race. They were being followed by a group of four or five frat boys who were red-faced, either from anger or beer or both. I tipped my chin at the open doorway. Chen and Hawkins went inside.

"Hawkins, take Mr. Novak downstairs please."

"You got it." A moment later, Hawkins led Novak out of the room.

The frat boys jumped forward and surrounded them

"What the fuck is going on?"

"You okay, my dude?"

"Hey, man, what are you arresting him for?"

"Gabe told me not to talk. He's calling my dad." Novak was trying to sound confident, but it was undercut by the low volume of his voice.

That was the moment Laurel said, "Gabe Sumner, you're also under arrest. Please turn around and put your hands on your head."

That led to a lot of shouting inside and outside the room. The frat guys tried to go in, but Chen stepped into the doorway.

"Step back, guys. You need to let the detective do her job."

"What the fuck am I being arrested for?" Sumner asked.

"Sexual assault," Laurel said.

"This is bullshit."

"Yeah, this is bullshit," one of the frat guys in the hallway shouted.

"Maybe don't rape people and you won't get arrested," Laurel said.

"I didn't rape anyone," Sumner said.

Chen cleared the frat boys out of the doorway so Laurel could lead Sumner out. I glanced in the room. The remaining guy was standing against the wall, trying to look invisible. It wasn't working.

"You can't just accuse people of sexual assault." One of the frat boys stood at the top of the stairs so Laurel couldn't get down them.

"Move."

"Why the fuck should I?"

"Because I'll arrest you too if you don't move." Laurel's restraint was admirable. Her tone was measured. Her stance, relaxed.

The frat boy moved. Laurel and Chen led Sumner downstairs. The frat boys followed. I trailed after them, doing my best to look disinterested and removed from the situation. Outside, Hawkins already had Novak in the back of a police car. Chen and Laurel loaded Sumner in as well. Laurel called Reyes to give him an update. He told us to continue to our next location.

Laurel and I climbed in her truck. Chen idled behind us in his Crown Vic. Hawkins took Novak and Sumner to be booked. It was a Saturday. Even if their drunk brothers remembered to call their parents, those guys wouldn't get bail until Monday.

"How is everyone else doing?" I asked Laurel.

"Six arrests so far. Two of the teams didn't find their perp yet."

"Six is damn good."

She nodded. "And it's not even midnight yet. So we got time."

"And it doesn't hurt that you got lucky and arrested an extra dude."

"I don't hate that." She grinned.

She parked down the street from the Sigma Epsilon house. Chen parked half a block away. The house was bigger than Pi Tau Gamma and had more of a fraternity aesthetic. Five-foot tall Greek letters were painted on the brick facade, just in case we weren't sure which house this was.

"Okay, you know who we are going in for?" Laurel asked.

"Jonathan Ferguson. Caucasian male, five nine, one hundred and eighty pounds. Brown hair. Has a full sleeve tattooed on his left arm."

"Nailed it."

"Fuck yeah, I did." I followed Laurel up the walkway, ready to charm my way in with drugs if necessary.

We didn't have any issues getting in the house or finding Ferguson because he was the guy who opened the door. I felt Laurel stiffen beside me.

"Jonathan Ferguson?" she asked.

"Yeah."

"You're under arrest."

Ferguson's face fell, then he started laughing. "Oh, fuck me up, my man." He turned back to shout, "Shit, Thornton. Fuck me right up."

I wondered if frat boys ever listened to themselves speak. Apparently not, because then they would know how dumb they sounded.

"What?" someone inside shouted back. "What is it?" A moment later, the dude shouting ran into Ferguson, stopped himself from falling by throwing an arm around his shoulders, and stared at me and Laurel. "Who are they?"

"Detective Kallen." She flashed her badge, tucked it in her pocket, and exchanged it for her cuffs. She snapped one bracelet on Ferguson and spun him out from under Thornton's arm and against the doorjamb before he could respond.

"What?" Thornton said.

"Uh, are you not fucking with me?" Ferguson asked.

"I am not fucking with you, I assure you." Laurel maneuvered Ferguson's other arm down and snapped the second cuff on him. "This way, please." She led him back down to the street.

Thornton started laughing. "Okay, okay, I get it. Good one."

"Bro, I think it's real. It's not a prank," Ferguson shouted.

"What?"

Ferguson tried to stop walking and look back at his buddy, but Laurel kept him moving. "Call my lawyer."

"I don't know your lawyer." Thornton started following us down to the street.

"It's my mom, dude. My mom's a lawyer."

Chen pulled up in front of us and opened the back door to his car. Laurel handed Ferguson off to Chen. He started patting him down.

"Hey, wait, Officer." Thornton grabbed Laurel's arm.

"Do not touch me," she said in a voice that was deadly.

"I'm sorry," Thornton stammered. He took a careful, respectful step back. "Can you give me any information?"

Laurel softened. "He's going to be booked into County. If his mother is a lawyer, she'll be able to take it from there."

"Okay, thank you, ma'am."

Laurel and I waited until Thornton went back inside and Chen drove off with Ferguson. We walked back to Laurel's truck.

"It's good you brought me along, huh? I'm super helpful."

"Oh, yeah. I particularly like how you stood there."

"Thanks, I've been working on using both feet."

"Then great work."

"Our next is Garrett Benson?" I asked.

"Yep. I should check with Reyes to confirm." We climbed into her truck. "Give me a sec." She pulled out her phone.

"Nice tag." Reyes answered the phone.

"Thanks." Laurel started the truck, effectively drowning out anything else Reyes said. "Garrett Benson?" She waited for his instructions. "Cool. Just have Hawkins meet us there." They hung up.

"What's the count?" I asked.

"Ferguson put us at eight." She checked her maps app to look up the destination of the next guy.

"Cool. That's like halfway."

She put down her phone and stared at me. "How is eight half of nineteen?"

"Well, eight is almost nine and if you double nine, it's eighteen, which is almost nineteen."

"What kind of jacked up arithmetic is that? I thought you were good at math."

"I am good at math."

"Right." There was a distinct lack of confidence in her tone.

Chapter Twenty-five

We drove to the next house. This one wasn't a fraternity, but judging by the number of cars outside, they were having a party. As we got out of the truck, Laurel checked her phone again. She stopped in the middle of the street to read a message.

"Everything okay?" I asked.

"Hmm? Yeah. Fine." She pocketed her phone and hustled the rest of the way across the street.

"Should we wait out here for Hawkins?"

"No." She waved a hand. "He'll be here soon."

We went up to the walkway. Music poured out the open door. It was mellow, but bass heavy. This was the type of party I normally attended. Inside, the lights were low, but there were multicolored Christmas lights on all the walls. I couldn't tell if they were going for a *Stranger Things* theme or a Christmas vibe or if this was just the cheapest rave I'd ever been to.

We posted up in the living room. After about five minutes it became clear that Benson wasn't present.

"Should we check the rest of the house?" I asked.

Laurel nodded. She took my hand and led me to the kitchen. There was a variety of booze, but no Garrett Benson. From there we checked all the bedrooms in the hallway. More skin and awkward teenage fumbling than I needed to see, but also no Benson. We looped back to the living room.

"There." Laurel's grip on my hand tightened.

"Where?" I had to lean close to hear her. She smelled crisp and fresh, per the usual.

"Across the room. He's wearing overalls and a bright blue beanie."

I searched the area she was staring at and found two dudes wearing overalls. Only one with a bright blue beanie though. "Oh, wow. That's a choice." It was definitely Benson.

"Come on." She tugged me forward.

We wove through the warm, dancing bodies until we got to the other side of the room. Laurel dropped my hand and stepped up to Benson.

"Garrett Benson."

"Yeah?" He glared at her.

"You're under arrest."

He laughed. "No, I'm not."

"Hands on your head. Turn around and face the wall."

"Fuck that." He shoulder checked her and tried to walk away.

Laurel grabbed the back of his overalls and spun him around. He slammed face-first into the wall.

That escalated quickly.

"Fucking cunt." Not the smartest thing to say to a cop.

Laurel shoved him against the wall. She kicked his feet out. Her palm was wide across his back to keep him stationary. When she reached for her cuffs, he pushed hard off the wall to break her grip, then sprinted down the hallway. She took off after him. I took off after her. This was not turning out fun. Not that arresting rapists was fun, but any interaction that went south so quickly was distinctly unfun.

Benson went for the backyard. As I was sprinting out the back door, I saw his overalls disappear over the fence. Laurel ran straight at the fence, leapt up, and hauled herself to the top. It would have been hot if I didn't know I was going to have to do the same thing. I managed to get over the fence and found myself in someone else's backyard. The sound of the gate flying open let me know which way to go.

I ended up on the street parallel to the one where we'd parked. Benson was booking it up the street and Laurel was gaining on him. They turned a corner. I could hear the pounding of their feet against the pavement.

"Fuck." I kept running.

As I turned the corner, Laurel tackled Benson in someone's front yard. They both went down. She landed on top of him. He struggled to shove her off and wriggle out. When that didn't work, he slugged her. All the police training in the world was no match for a drunk, testosterone-filled twenty-year-old dude. Laurel went sprawling.

Benson rolled on top of her. He punched her in the face a few times. She returned the blows. He was winning. Suddenly, Benson raised up and went stiff. Laurel had clearly kneed him in the balls. He angled his shin over her thighs so she couldn't do it again. They grappled as he tried to grab her hands.

I stopped running at the edge of the manicured lawn. I didn't know if I should intervene. I didn't know how to intervene. But then Benson caught both Laurel's wrists in one hand and shoved her hands down above her head. I ran and tackled him. We rolled off Laurel. Benson kept us rolling until he was on top of me. He was fucking heavy. I punched his jaw hard enough to make my hand throb. He appeared mildly inconvenienced. I hit him again. He punched me twice, which was enough to make my head spin. Sharp pain radiated through my cheek and nose.

Laurel was shouting at us, but it was difficult to understand her. I saw her standing behind him. My vision was blurry. She swung her elbow hard into the side of his head. He dropped. Onto me.

"Fuck." Laurel grabbed fistfuls of his clothing and hauled him off me.

"Thanks." I took a few deep breaths to calm down. The blood dripping down the back of my throat inspired me to sit up. I coughed and sent a spray of blood over the immaculate lawn.

"Motherfucker." Laurel stood over him, but instead of reaching for her cuffs or her phone, she kicked him solidly in the ribs. Fully fucking kicked him. Her second kick—in the exact same spot—must have broken something.

"Oh, fuck." I forced myself to my feet so I could face her.

She leaned over Benson and hit him a few more times.

"Laurel," I shouted. Nothing. "Laurel, stop." I grabbed her and tried to pull her off him.

"No. I have to—" She fought against my grip until I let go and she fell on him again.

"Laurel, you got him. Stop." I grabbed her biceps and hauled her back. My grip was high enough on her arms that she couldn't break it easily.

"Let me go. He raped Lane. I'm going to kill him."

I yanked her farther away from him, forcing her to turn and look at me. "It's okay." I eased my grip and rubbed my hand over her shoulders instead. "Try to calm down. You just lost it. It's okay."

She took a long, shaky breath. "I didn't lose it."

"You kind of did. But it's all right." I was lying, but this felt like the appropriate moment to lie.

"No." She took a step away from me. "I meant to."

I put my hand on her arm to ground her and restrain her, if necessary. "Why?"

"I told you. He raped Lane."

"Why would you think he assaulted Lane?"

She turned back to me. "Lane texted. She looked through the photos we left. When we got here, I got a message from her that it was Benson."

"How? The odds are seriously low that it was actually him."

"That's what she told me." Laurel wrestled her phone out of her pocket. Her hand was starting to swell. "Look."

I looked at the screen. There were three unread messages from Lane.

Never mind. I think it's Brenden Santos.

Or Jonathan Ferguson.

I don't know. I'm sorry. They all are kind of blending together.

"Fuck," I said.

"What?"

I glanced at Benson. Thankfully, he was still passed out. I handed Laurel the phone. My hand was throbbing just from gripping it.

"Oh God." The phone slid out of her grasp and bounced on the grass. She swayed on her feet. When her eyes met mine, she burst into tears and fell into me. "Oh, fuck. I'm sorry. I'm so sorry."

I took her hands and squeezed until she looked at me. "It's all right. You just need to cool down."

She took a deep breath and nodded. "I have to call Reyes. Give him our location."

"Yeah. Good idea." I picked up her phone and gave it to her.

She took a final look at Benson, then stepped away from me, from him. She put the phone to her ear. "I need backup now." She looked around until she found a street sign to read to him. "Yeah, I got Benson, but he resisted arrest. We need an ambulance. Benson is unconscious, and Braddock and I took a couple of hits."

When she said it, I realized my nose had stopped bleeding. That was nice. It still pulsed with each heartbeat, but the pain had dulled. I inhaled slowly. My eyes started to water again. I decided to stick with being a mouth-breather.

After hanging up, Laurel checked Benson's pulse. He stirred at her touch so she cuffed him. The trees around the corner lit up red and blue a moment before Hawkins pulled up. He jumped out of the car and sprinted to Laurel's side.

"Reyes has an ambulance en route," Hawkins said.

"Good. Pulse is strong. He'll probably wake up soon. That's why I cuffed him."

"I'll babysit him if you and Braddock need first aid."

"Thanks." Laurel came back to my side as another cop car arrived, followed by an ambulance.

Hawkins waved the EMTs over. The uniform driving the second cruiser checked in with Laurel. I watched them speak without bothering to listen. Laurel's hands were trembling. She kept glancing at Benson.

The uniform went back to his car and pulled out a first aid kit. He handed me a pack of baby wipes. After one swipe, my nose started bleeding again so I just stopped. As the EMTs loaded Benson up, Hawkins and the new uniform had a whispered conversation about accompanying him to the hospital.

"I assume one of them can take us to your truck before we head back to the station?" I asked Laurel.

She looked at me strangely. "What do you mean?"

"Like you're not going to leave your truck here, right?"

"No. But why would we go back to the station?" She seemed genuinely confused.

"Because we clearly need to pack it in for the evening." I was also confused.

"Why?"

"Because we're both on edge and no longer impartial." I included myself in the statement to make it seem less accusatory, but I was pretty sure we both knew I was talking about her ability to remain impartial. Behind her, the ambulance pulled away as did one of the cruisers.

"I'm not calling it early just because one arrest didn't go as planned. There are still guys out there."

"But you're not operating at full capacity." I kept my voice low.

"I'm fine. I'll ice my hand on the way to the next location."

"I'm not talking about your hand. You're looking for a fight."

Laurel looked pissed, but she kept it together. "I know I behaved badly. But I also know myself and I'm fine."

I trusted her to be honest about herself, which meant she had no concept of how far she'd gone over the line. "Okay. I'm not going with you then."

"What?"

"I can't. I'm sorry. If you want to go out, that's your choice, but I can't participate."

"Are you trying to punish me?"

"Not at all. I just think you need to cool down. Until you do, you're not safe."

"Whatever." She was pissed. "So you're fine with the remaining rapists just walking?"

"I didn't say that. There are still four teams out there. They will get them."

"But you're not going to help? Seems like you're fine increasing the odds they will walk."

"I'll just go back to the station and help Reyes. Still contributing, but in a more appropriate manner."

"Kallen, Withers said you needed this." Hawkins came up behind Laurel with an ice pack. He cracked it and manipulated the bag before handing it to her.

"Thanks." Laurel took the pack and draped it over her knuckles. "I need a ride back to my truck. After that, do you mind taking Ms. Braddock back to the station?" She carefully didn't look at me.

Hawkins glanced at me. "Sure."

"Thanks."

We climbed into his cruiser. I could see Laurel's face in the rearview mirror. I scooted over until I could see Hawkins instead. "So you're done being in the field tonight?" Hawkins asked.

"It's good to know your limits," I said sagely as blood dripped off my chin. Laurel didn't respond.

Chapter Twenty-six

We drove in heavy silence to the station. Hawkins seemed nervous, but I couldn't tell if that was because I was a hardened criminal or because he just wanted to get back out there, arresting rapists with his buddies. He stopped in front of the station and I waved as I went inside.

Reyes came out of the conference room where he was monitoring the operation. He grimaced when he saw me. "Christ, Braddock, what the fuck?"

"We had an altercation."

"Are you okay?"

I shrugged. "Yeah. My nose keeps bleeding at random, but it doesn't feel broken."

"Is Kallen all right?"

"She said she was fine."

He didn't seem concerned by my evasive answer. "You hurt anywhere else?"

I held out my hand. "I could use some ice. I'm not used to hitting people."

He whistled. "That doesn't look great."

"You think I'll ever be a hand model again?"

He chuckled. "Go clean up and I'll grab a first aid kit." He pointed at the bathroom. "When you've washed up, meet me in the conference room. I'll take a look at your hand."

I did as he said. I was obviously relieved about not having to answer questions, but also the blood had dried and there was a funky blood crust on my face, which tended to shift one's priorities. I cupped my hands to fill them with water and submerged my chin and nose. The sensation of warm water seeping up my nose was not great. I dropped the handful of water and watched pink splash over the white sink. I folded a rough, sharp paper towel and scrubbed at the line of dried blood running from my nose to my chin. The blood flecked away. The smell of water and copper and cheap paper filled my nose. My T-shirt and flannel both had spots of blood, but I couldn't do much about that. My hands were still shaking. I stared at the drips of water as they trembled off my fingertips.

Laurel had crossed a line. I felt reasonably confident that she would realize it and do something stupid like tell Ionescu. There was a small part of me, however, that wondered if she wouldn't admit it, even to herself. Maybe I didn't know her as well as I thought I did.

I found Reyes in the conference room. He had a digital map projected on the wall with a list of locations.

"How many have we caught?" I asked.

He looked at me and shook his head. "Eleven. Blackford got a triple. It seems a fair number of these guys know each other."

"Not surprising. Osborn and Darby's business plan must have relied heavily on word of mouth." I sat next to him.

"How's your hand?"

"Hurts like a motherfucker."

"Let me see it."

I held out my hand. Reyes walked his fingers over the bones in my hand. When he did the same to my fingers, I jerked. "Ow. Fuck."

"That hurt?" He pressed the knuckle at the base of my ring finger.

"Yes. Stop doing that." I tried to pull my hand away.

"Can you fully extend it?"

I slowly stretched out my hand. "Yeah."

"Okay. Make a fist." He held up a closed fist to show me. Very helpful.

I tried to close my fist, but stopped about halfway there. "Nope. Can't do that."

"It just looks like a sprain to me. I don't think it's fractured." He extended my finger.

"How the fuck did I sprain my finger?"

Reyes opened the first aid kit. "Did you punch someone?"

"Yes, but how do you sprain a finger by punching someone?"

"It would appear you're bad at punching."

I was going to dispute his opinion, but I didn't have any evidence to the contrary. "You're not wrong."

Reyes opened the first aid kit and pulled out some medical tape. It was flesh colored. Flesh colored was bullshit. Mostly because of racism, but also it was boring. Reyes wrapped my middle and ring fingers together. Then he cracked an ice pack, wrapped it, and set it over my hand.

"Keep it elevated." He dragged a massive stack of files over from the end of the table and set my hand on them. "You want an ice pack for your eye?"

"What's wrong with my eye?"

"It's turning color."

"Oh." I lifted the hand without an ice pack and prodded around my eye. Yep, quite tender. "It's fine. Do you have some ibuprofen?"

"Yeah." He dug through the kit until he found a small bottle.

I shook out a couple and Reyes handed me a bottle of water. I tried to open it, but couldn't get a good grip on the lid. I groaned.

"Can you open this?"

He shook his head and took the water back. The seal cracked. He set it on the table.

"So why did you come back here?"

"I did as much as I could out there." I shrugged. "Plus, I'm a wimp."

He chuckled. "For the rest of tonight, you can play CI here and answer any questions that come up. Laurel is with Duarte and Xiao so we only have four teams out there."

"Sounds like a plan."

Reyes's phone rang. He answered it. "Reyes." He clicked and typed on his laptop. The projected screen shifted from the digital map to a spreadsheet. He selected the row for Jake Ramsey. "Okay, secondary location is the Alpha Pi Omicron house if his dorm room is empty. Fenton had a team at the frat house earlier. They didn't make any arrests, but we still don't want to tip the brothers off." Reyes disconnected the call and typed in a few updates on the spreadsheet.

"What happens if you guys don't get all of them tonight?" I asked.

"We will put out an APB and have uniforms posted at their residences. That will likely be enough to catch the stragglers unless they run."

"What are the chances they will run?"

He smiled wryly. "Pretty high. Ionescu has a meeting with the press tomorrow. He hasn't decided if we're going to release the rapists' names, but we probably will."

"Why wouldn't you?"

"Well, we can only charge eleven of them with sexual assault. The remaining guys we are using a bunch of inflated charges around the online transactions just so we can hold them. We still need to find their victims and convince them to press charges."

"How does that affect the releasing of names?"

"It can compromise the privacy of the victim. It gives the perpetrator an opportunity to threaten his victim so she won't press charges. It just complicates things."

"Ergo, attempting to arrest all the perpetrators in one night."

"Nice use of ergo, and, yes."

"Remember when you offered me an ice pack for my eye?"

"Yeah."

"Is it too late to take you up on it?"

"No. I can arrange that." He stood. "Keep an eye on my phone."

"Will do."

He returned a couple of minutes later with a baggie of ice wrapped in a threadbare hand towel.

"Thanks."

"You're welcome. And I promise the towel is clean."

"It didn't occur to me that it might not be, but that's great nonetheless," I said.

"Did my phone ring?"

"Nope." I set the ice pack against my eye. "Oh, I love ice packs."

"Did the EMTs look at you?"

"No. They were focused on the unconscious perp."

The phone rang. Reyes answered it. He clicked the row for Brenden Santos. "No, we only have three locations for him. The apartment, the Omega Kappa Nu house, and the student center where he works." I could hear the voice on the other end of the call. He sounded frustrated, but I couldn't make out what he was saying. "Go ahead and move on to Simon Price. I'll try to come up with more information on Santos." He hung up.

"So we need to find a location for Brenden Santos?" I asked.

"Yep. Any chance your murder board will help?"

I dropped my face ice pack on the table. "Let's find out." I retracted the screen covering the board. Reyes hit a button to stop his laptop from projecting.

"He's Omega Kappa Nu," Reyes said.

I found all the cards that referenced his frat, but they didn't give me any information. I moved over to the social media side of the board. Duarte had added the handles for all nineteen rapists. Most of them had Instagram. Many had Twitter. All of them had at least one. I pulled out my phone and typed Santos's handle into my Twitter search bar. He hadn't posted in a week. I closed that out and pulled up Instagram. Santos had posted four times that evening.

"Call them back. Tell them he was at Royal Oak Tavern on Folsom Boulevard as of twenty minutes ago."

Reyes blinked at me in surprise, then picked up his phone. "Fenton, he's at a bar on Folsom Boulevard. Royal Oak Tavern." He glanced at me and I nodded. "Braddock is looking at his social media. He posted twenty minutes ago."

"I'll keep watching," I whispered and held my phone up.

Reyes nodded at me. "Yeah. Keep me updated." He hung up. "Okay, that's impressive. Can we look up someone else?"

"Sure. Who?"

The phone rang again. "Sorry." He answered it. "You got him? Okay. That's Jake Ramsey?" He clicked on his laptop. "Great. Your next is Colin Hammond. He's Kappa Kappa Tau. Duarte picked one of the brothers up there earlier, but Hammond wasn't there. He's probably working." Reyes typed. "Yeah, it's H and Fifty-sixth. He's one of the cooks so he'll probably be in the kitchen."

I looked up Hammond's handle and checked it. He'd posted on Insta a week previous and tweeted the day before. No useable information though. I sat back down.

Reyes hung up. "Sorry."

"Hey, no worries. Jake Ramsey makes twelve." I held up my good hand and Reyes high-fived it. "Nothing on Colin Hammond's social media."

"Oh, yeah. Will you check Simon Price? He's next in the lineup."

I pulled up the pertinent information. He'd retweeted someone else's photo at Iota Mu. I turned the photo so Reyes could see it. "Is he Iota Mu?"

"No, but that's him." Reyes pointed out a young looking guy with no shirt on and a face full of acne. He clearly worked out to make up for his unattractive face. Or maybe he just worked out a lot and hadn't gotten the memo on properly washing one's face after a session at the gym.

"It is?"

"Yeah. I think so." Reyes turned on the projector again. He half stood, but I stopped him.

"I got it." I skirted the table to pull down the screen.

As soon as the screen was down, Reyes clicked open a file of photos. Simon Price's driver's license photo popped up. He hadn't aged much since his license photo had been taken. Maybe he didn't just look young. Maybe he actually was that young.

"That's him, right?" Reyes asked.

His skin was unblemished in the older photo, but it was definitely the same guy. "Yeah."

"So he's at a party at Iota Mu?"

"He was when the photo was taken."

"How long ago was that?"

I checked when the photo had been posted. "Three hours ago. I mean, the photo could have been taken before that."

"Well, it's at least somewhere else for them to check."

Within the hour, twelve became fourteen. Fourteen became fifteen around one thirty in the morning. I missed that high five because I was stretched across three conference chairs asleep.

"When do we call this?" I asked. My eye was throbbing. My hand was sore. My most recent ice pack had been melty when I started to fall asleep and was now dripping on the floor.

"You can go home. I'm going to try to convince them to come in, but it might take a while to get them to listen."

"How many teams are still out there?"

"Fenton and Blackford are together as are Kallen and Duarte. Xiao went home. The uniforms went off shift, but we brought on fresh guys to back the detectives."

"So two teams?"

"Sorry, yes. To answer your question, two teams."

"And how many rapists?" I asked. Reyes raised his eyebrows. "How many rapists for this case specifically?"

"Four left."

"Okay. I'll stay for one more."

"We're not talking baseball innings. Go home, Braddock."

"Come on, Dad. One more rapist. Just one." I stuck out my bottom lip.

"You are so goddamn weird."

I shrugged. "Hey, if I go home, the patriarchy wins."

"Wouldn't want that."

Chapter Twenty-seven

The next morning, I sat on the back porch drinking coffee and studiously not checking the news. I knew I needed to go to bed, but I was paralyzed by a combination of exhaustion and anticipation. I didn't know exactly what I was waiting for, but I was waiting for something. I needed to know the final three rapists had been rounded up. I was equal parts concerned and scared to find out whether or not Laurel was ready to admit the line she'd crossed was a big fucking deal.

So I waited, watching the light slowly change. There was a hint of fog that dissipated with the sunrise. Unseen birds filled the air with indistinct noise.

I finished my cup of coffee, but couldn't find the motivation to go inside for a refill. The empty mug slowly turned cold in my grip. I set it on the armrest of my chair. The moisture in the wooden planter boxes started to steam in the scant warmth of the sunlight.

The detectives were chasing a rumor at that point. They knew it. That was why they'd sent all the uniforms home. Knocking on doors at six a.m. wouldn't turn up anything but trouble. But Fenton and Blackford wanted to wrap up the case with a tidy little bow. And Laurel and Duarte were just treating rapists like collectors' items. So I watched the yard slowly turn in the sunshine because I couldn't do anything else.

One of the doors behind me opened. "What are you doing up?" Robin asked.

I turned toward her and smiled. "Haven't gone to bed yet."

"Honey, what happened to your face?" She crossed the porch and leaned over to inspect me.

"Huh?" I grumbled. She brushed her thumb below my eye, which started the throbbing back up. "Oh, yeah."

"You forgot about your black eye?"

"Kinda. I'm pretty tired."

"Maybe you should go to bed."

"Yeah. I will. Soon," I said.

"How did you manage to get a black eye?" She angled the other chair so she could see my face when she sat.

"There was an operation last night. Laurel needed to get into some college parties so I went and vouched for her. She and some other detectives were rounding up rapists."

"Rounding up rapists?"

"Yeah, it's the newest, hottest game. Round up the rapists. Like a scavenger hunt, but with much higher stakes." I laughed. I was funny.

"Okay. Time for you to go to bed." Robin took my arm and tried to haul me up.

"Not yet. There are still three."

She sat back down, exasperated now. "Three what?"

"Rapists." I took a deep breath and tried to find a way to speak lucidly. "You know that case Laurel's been working on? They ran that story in *The Bee*?"

"Yeah, the serial rapist on Sac State's campus, right?"

"Yep. Except it turns out it's not a serial rapist. Sac State has one of those free ride share type services to prevent drunk driving, Safe Streets," I said. Robin nodded at me to keep going. "Two of the drivers were stocking their vehicle with ketamine-laced water bottles, installing tracking apps on the drugged women's phones, and selling the coordinates to 'guys who need help' at parties."

She stared at me in horror for at least a full minute. "What?"

"Yeah. It's repugnant."

"How many? I remember the article said there were like five."

"After the article, it was like ten. By last night, it was nineteen."

"You're saying nineteen rapists were arrested last night? That's impressive as hell."

"Only sixteen, but still impressive. They are still out looking for the remaining three."

She nodded. "So you're waiting for Laurel to come home?"

"Yeah, I guess. I'm not really sure what to do with myself."

"Bed seems the obvious option."

"Yeah. I just want to talk to Laurel before."

"Aww, being in love with a cop is doing strange things to you, Cash Braddock."

I realized she was focusing on Laurel's safety, which I was obviously concerned about, but it was everyone else who needed protection. Or maybe I was overreacting. "Yeah, I guess so."

"You should at least put some ice on that eye."

"I did earlier. It got cold."

"Ice does that. I'm still unclear on how you got hurt."

I shrugged. "One of the guys resisted arrest. It got heated. It was a thing." I stretched out my hands. My finger hurt.

"Can I re-bandage your finger? It looks pretty pathetic."

"Do I have to move?"

"No, honey. You stay right there." Robin kissed my forehead and went inside. She came back out a minute later with her first aid kit. It was much more impressive than the one Reyes had. And it had one hundred percent more glitter stickers on the outside.

Robin slowly unwrapped the tape, careful not to jostle my fingers too much. I'd been picking at the edges of the tape all night so it was dirty and awkwardly rolled in on itself. She set the dirty tape aside while shaking her head in a very mom-like way.

"Reyes said he thought it was sprained, not broken," I said.

"I agree, but have me check it tomorrow. If the swelling doesn't go down, I might tell you to go for an X-ray."

"Yes, ma'am."

She rewrapped my fingers. Her tape was hot pink. Much sexier. "Now, try not to pick at it this time."

I flexed my hand slowly as she packed up. "Thanks."

"You want more coffee?"

I moaned and nodded. "You're the best."

"You bet I am." She took my coffee mug inside and returned a minute later with hot, fresh coffee.

"If we weren't neighbors, I'd ask you to marry me."

"My straightness isn't a problem for you?" she asked.

"I try to be open-minded."

"I have an uncomfortable question and I don't know how to ask it."

"Go for it."

"Is the guy who raped Lane among the twenty-something rapists who were arrested last night?"

I shook my head. "No. Apparently, he's just a random guy. They don't have any leads on him."

"You guys know for sure?"

"Yep."

"I'm sorry."

I shrugged. "I don't think she's invested in the legalities of sexual assault. Her approach is unique."

"That is very true."

"I like her," I said.

"So do I."

We drank coffee and watched a faint breeze move through the trees. The leaves were just starting to change. Sacramento had more trees per capita than any other city in the US. It was one of those childhood facts we'd all learned in elementary school. I never really thought about it until fall every year when I had to pay Andy to rake leaves for hours on end.

"We have an interesting little family, don't we?" Robin said.

I nodded. "I like it."

"Is Lane going to stay here?"

"I don't know. We kind of talked about it a week or so ago, but it was mostly just me telling her she didn't need to leave."

"Do you like having her live with you?"

"I do. She's a good kid. And she makes good coffee."

"So why don't you ask her to stay instead of telling her she doesn't have to leave?"

I felt like I should understand what she was saying, but I was too tired to make the connection. "What's the difference?"

"One is an assurance that she's not a problem. The other is a declaration that she's an enjoyable human."

"Right." I thought through the implications of asking my secret girlfriend's little sister to move in with me. I couldn't find a flaw. "Okay. I'll talk to her."

"Good." Robin stood. "I have to get ready for work. You should go to sleep."

"I'll consider it."

She kissed my head again and went inside.

I texted Laurel for an update, but didn't get a response. I dozed in the sunshine until my phone buzzed.

Still out searching.

I wrote back, *You guys all need some sleep. And we need to talk. You should take a break.*

Can't. We'll get them soon.

I knew better than to push. I suspected she was fixating on the remaining arrests so she wouldn't have to think about anything else, but I also wasn't going to judge her defense mechanism.

I collected my coffee cup and phone and went inside. I rinsed the mug and fed the cat. As I walked by Lane's room to go down the hallway, I heard faint crying.

I tapped on her door. "Lane?"

"Yeah." Her voice trembled.

"You okay?"

There was a long pause. "No."

"Can I come in?"

"Okay."

I opened the door. She was sitting on the floor with her back against the couch and her knees pulled tight to her chest. She rocked back and forth.

"Can I sit with you?" I asked.

She nodded. I sat close to her, our legs, hips, shoulders lightly touching. After a moment, she leaned into me. I put my arm around her shoulders. She turned to thread her arm around my waist. We stayed like that for a long time. Her breathing slowly evened out. When she shifted, cool air rushed against my shirt and I realized the shoulder of it was soaked.

"Sorry," she said.

"There's nothing to apologize for. Can I do anything?"

She shook her head. "This is helping."

"Good." I squeezed her shoulder lightly.

"I had a dream."

"Shit."

"Not…that." She took a long breath. "I was at the Tri Ep house with a group of my sisters. We were just hanging out. It was totally innocuous." She shrugged, an aborted movement since she was pressed against my body. "But there was a song playing. I don't know what song it was, but the cadence of it was familiar. It sent me right back there. And then I woke up having a panic attack."

"How are you feeling now?"

"Still shaky. But I can breathe."

"Breathing is good. Can I get you some water?"

"In a second."

After a minute, she unclenched the hand at my waist. She'd apparently twisted it into the material of my shirt. She slowly drew back and sat upright. When she nodded, I stood. I brought back a glass of cold water. She drank it in one go, then handed back the glass.

"More?" I asked.

"No. I'm good."

I set the glass aside and sat back down. "What do you need?"

"I'm tired, but I'm afraid to go back to sleep."

"Do you want to try? I'll sit here until you crash."

She looked like she was going to start crying again, but a different sort of tears. "Yeah, okay." She stretched out her legs and slowly stood. She climbed back on the couch and pulled the blankets tight around her. After she was settled in, she freed one hand. I took it and squeezed.

"I've been thinking. And you don't need to answer right now. But I'd like it if you moved in here. Officially. It can just be for the semester or whatever," I said.

She chuckled warily. "Even after this?"

"Especially after this. We can't have you sleeping on a couch forever. We need to get you a bed."

"Thanks, Cash."

In a matter of minutes, she'd fallen back asleep. I gently took my hand back.

I left the doors of both our rooms open. That way she'd know I was close by. I changed my clothes and climbed in bed. Nickels jumped up and burrowed under the blankets with me. She started purring. I fell asleep about as quickly as Lane had.

Lane let me sleep until early afternoon. When I got up, she was spread out in the living room with approximately one thousand textbooks. Laurel hadn't called or texted.

"Afternoon, sleepyhead," Lane said.

"Now who sounds like a dad?"

"Fair point." She nodded at the kitchen. "I just started a fresh pot of coffee."

I could already smell it. I groaned. "Thanks." I poured each of us a mug and joined her in the living room. I found it amusing how quickly we had adapted to each other. She purposefully left the chair I liked to sit in untouched, but had no compunction about taking over the couch and coffee table.

"Thank you for this morning," she said.

I was going to wave her off, but I realized that would minimize her experience. "You're welcome. I'm glad I was there." I smiled at her and she smiled back. "How are you feeling? You look much better."

"I am. I'm showered and hydrated and caffeinated. All of those tend to improve my mood."

"Good."

"Were you serious earlier? About me moving in, I mean."

"Yes. I like having you here. I don't generally like sharing my space with people, but you're different."

She pursed her lips and nodded. "Okay then."

"You'll move in?"

"Yes."

"Awesome." I grinned. "We'll need to order a bed and some furniture."

"The couch in there is fine."

"You're young and I appreciate that you think sleeping on a couch indefinitely is fine, but you're wrong."

She laughed. "Okay. I'll also need to pack up my dorm room."

"No problem. If you don't want to go back there, Laurel and I can do it."

"I think I'll be okay. Especially if you'll go with me."

"That I can do."

After Lane finished studying, we spent our evening playing board games. I grew increasingly worried about Laurel. She wasn't answering my calls and she responded to my texts dismissively, at least an hour after I sent them. By my count, she'd gotten about ninety minutes of sleep in the past three days. I didn't care if she didn't want to talk about Benson right away. I just didn't want her operating a firearm or a motor vehicle.

It was well after dark when I got a call from her.

"Hey. Where are you?" I asked.

Lane whispered, "Needy." She chuckled to herself and started setting up Battleship. I flipped her off.

"Hey." Laurel's voice was raw and gritty. "I'm on I-5 with a patrol unit."

"What? Why?"

"We got two more today, but Colin Hammond took off. Bakersfield PD picked him up hiding at his dad's house. They are holding him."

"Are you going to get him?" It felt stupid when I asked it, but it seemed even dumber that she would drive three hundred miles on no sleep to pick up a felon that any officer could retrieve.

"Yeah. Fenton and Blackford are buried in paperwork so I volunteered."

"But you haven't slept in three days."

"It's okay. I'm not driving so I'll sleep on the way down. That's the advantage of hitching a ride in a patrol car." Her tone was mellow, measured. It was a lie.

I could think of a ton of reasons why her plan made no sense, but I knew she'd already thought of them and decided to go anyway.

"Fine. Whatever. What time will you be back?"

"Probably around five in the morning. It depends on how long the transfer paperwork takes."

"Okay. I guess I'll see you tomorrow." I knew I sounded dejected and didn't bother to hide it.

"Yeah."

"Bye."

"Hey, wait," she said urgently.

"What?"

"I'm okay. I just need some time and some sleep." It was the first honest thing she'd said since she left me in a police cruiser almost twenty-four hours previous.

"Promise?"

"Yeah. I promise."

Chapter Twenty-eight

Laurel had assured me she would be at my place at two to pick me up for our appointment at the district attorney's office. I'd spent more time than necessary styling my hair. My button up and sweater made me look appropriately non-drug dealery. I'd even pulled a Laurel and polished my shoes. There was nothing else to distract me from waiting. Lane was in class. Nickels was hiding. I was pacing.

We still hadn't talked. I had no clue where she was at emotionally. And without knowing her state of mind, I felt like mine was up for debate. Also there was the whole "*We have an appointment at the DA's office. I'll pick you up at two*" thing. That had been a worrisome text to get without context.

When she finally let herself into my place, I was slouched on the couch, feigning calm. I stood and went to her.

"Hey." I stood in front of her, unsure.

"Hi." She hesitated, then stepped forward and wrapped her arms around my shoulders.

We stood like that for a long minute. She smelled like salt and cedar and hair product. I loved the way she smelled. She pressed her face into my neck. Her lips were touching my skin. Not kissing, just pressing. I started to let go, but she squeezed so I held on. When she finally pulled away, it was slow. A retraction in inches. She pressed my hand, then stepped away. She picked up a folder she had set by the door, then led me back to the couch. She was wearing a navy suit with a crisp white shirt and a tie the color of dried blood. It was rare that I saw her go totally formal. It was hot.

"I spent the morning with Brian Walton. You remember him? He was the deputy district attorney who handled our initial agreement." She unbuttoned her jacket and sat on the couch.

"Yeah, I thought you hated him."

"I do. But I can handle a morning of being called sweetheart by a gross dude to get a decent deal worked out." She held up the folder. "Your lawyer is going meet us at the DA's office, right?"

"Yep. And Nate and his lawyer, just like you asked."

She nodded. "Okay, good. Thanks."

"You okay? You seem nervous." Or maybe I was projecting.

"Sorry. It was a bitch to get an appointment on a Monday. I just want it to go as planned." She smoothed her tie, which was unnecessary because there was a tie bar holding it in place.

"So what's so urgent?"

She tapped the edge of the folder against her open palm. "I negotiated a release of your CI contract."

"You what?" I grinned. "How the fuck did you manage that?" I leaned forward and kissed her. She leaned into the kiss, cradling my lips with hers.

"I argued that your cover had been compromised because I arrested multiple people while at a social engagement with you. Nate's cover was compromised in the same way so he will be released as well." She handed me the folder. "Anyway, like I said, you guys will need to review this."

"Thank you."

She shrugged. "It was the least I could do. I got you into this mess in the first place."

"Actually, as you have so aptly pointed out, I got myself into this mess. I'm the drug dealer, remember?"

She looked down and nodded. "Right. Yeah."

"We need to talk about the Benson thing," I said.

"Yeah, I know." She picked a piece of lint off her knee. "And I'm ready to have that conversation, but it'll need to wait." She was clearly avoiding eye contact.

"I take it we need to head over to the DA's office?" I checked the time.

"Yeah. I'll drive." She stood and closed the top button of her jacket.

I gathered my wallet and keys. If she wanted to wait, we could wait. But we were having a conversation about her behavior, dammit.

"I have to tell you something," I said as we drove.

"What's that?"

"I asked Lane to move in with me. I didn't really think about talking to you first, but now I realize I probably should have mentioned it."

She chuckled and finally looked at me. "I can see why that's problematic, but mostly I think it's an excellent idea."

"Really?"

"Yeah. You guys have a weird bond. I think you'll be good for each other."

"Dope. Because that could have been awkward."

"You realize this probably means seeing a lot more of my parents, right?"

"Oh, swell."

Laurel pulled into the lot for the DA's office. She led me upstairs to the appropriate floor. She was a very useful person to have around while navigating legal institutions.

When we got off the elevator, my lawyer and Nate's were waiting. Both women stood. Nate's lawyer towered over mine, but that could have been because she was wearing insanely tall heels while Joan Kent was in oxfords.

"Cash." Kent shook my hand. "Detective Kallen." She shook Laurel's hand.

The elevator opened again and Nate walked out. He'd showered and put on chinos and a nice shirt. He still needed a haircut, but it was an improvement.

"Hey, man," I said.

Nate nodded at me. "What's going on? Why have we been summoned?"

Laurel opened the folder. Inside were two sets of paperwork. She handed one to each of the lawyers. "I asked Walton to release Braddock and Xiao from their CI contracts." Nate and both lawyers turned to stare at Laurel. "Once you guys look over the paperwork and get everything signed, they will walk out of here free."

Nate caught my eye. He looked like he had questions, but luckily he was smart enough to wait to ask them.

"Do we have time to meet privately with our clients before we all sit down with Walton?" Nate's lawyer asked.

"That's an excellent idea," Kent said.

"There are rooms you can use down this hallway." Laurel held out her hand to guide us. She put me and Kent in one room, then led Nate and his lawyer to the next room. Laurel took a seat in the hallway.

The room we were in had a small round table and four unimaginative chairs. That was about it. I sat and Kent closed the door.

"What changed?" Kent sat across from me and folded her hands on the tabletop. "And talk fast."

"You've read about the serial rapist at Sac State that was actually nineteen different guys who bought access to drugged girls?"

"Yes. How did you get mixed up in that?"

"Nate and I were called in so they could ask us about ketamine distribution since that's the drug they used. Kallen and her partner were assisting on the case. Then, on Saturday night when all the arrests were made, the detectives needed me and Nate to gain access to a few frat parties."

"And with the high volume of arrests, there was a high volume of witnesses."

"Yep. So we are compromised and I guess they decided to let us go."

"What are you not telling me? Police departments aren't known for letting CIs go so easily."

"Do you actually want to know?"

Kent sighed. "Yes, but only because I want to be prepared for any legal ramifications you're not seeing."

"Oof. Okay. Kallen and I have been romantically involved since the start of summer."

She groaned and shook her head. "God, Cash, why?"

I shrugged. "I love her?"

"So she convinced her superiors to release you as a result of your romantic relationship?"

"Yeah. So that definitely won't have any legal ramifications. It's fine."

Kent blinked slowly and visibly restrained herself. "Just for my own peace of mind, I do need to tell you that's untrue. There are a number of potential legal ramifications."

I grinned. "I know. And you've done your duty in informing me."

She flipped through the paperwork Laurel had given her. "The good news is, she appears to love you back."

"I kind of already knew that."

"This deal is beautiful. Pure charity."

"Walton is like her mother's best friend."

"Her mom is Judge Kallen, right?" she asked.

"Yeah. And I got to tell you, she's kind of an asshole."

"Judge Kallen is an asshole?"

"Yeah."

"Got it." Kent shook her head. "Well, I recommend you take this deal. I also suggest that you stay far away from any drug dealing."

"Okay."

"All right." She gathered the paperwork and stood.

When we emerged into the hallway, Nate and his lawyer were sitting with Laurel. They all stood. Laurel guided us down the hallway to a larger conference room. Walton stood when we entered. The man did love his ill-fitting beige suits. We sat around the table, this time with far fewer cops, which made me a lot more comfortable. Walton pontificated a bit, called Laurel approximately four different pet names, then let us sign a bunch of forms. It was unremarkable in every way. Ten minutes later, we were out front, blinking in the sunshine.

"Is that it?" Nate asked.

I shrugged. "I guess so."

"What are we supposed to do now?"

"Not deal drugs, that's for sure."

"Good call." Nate held up his hand for a high five. "You're so smart."

I smacked his hand. "I know."

"Are you going to tell me the actual story behind your black eye?"

"Yeah. But later." I heard the door open behind me. I turned in time to see Laurel walk out. She shook her sunglasses open and slid them on.

"You ready to go?" she asked.

"Yep."

Nate hugged me briefly. "We'll talk later."

"Yeah, man." I squeezed him back.

I followed Laurel to her truck. "This is weird. We don't need to pretend there's a case to discuss for me to ask you to stay over tonight."

She laughed, but it seemed restrained. "Yeah. We're not breaking any rules. Does that take the fun out of it?"

"I was never into you because it broke the rules. I'm not even a rule breaker."

"Right." She arched an eyebrow.

"I'm not. I just disagree with certain rules. I never break rules I believe in."

"Yeah, that's fair."

We drove back to my place with the windows cracked and the heater cranked. Laurel's jacket was unbuttoned. The end of her tie fluttered in the air moving through the truck. She put her elbow up on the door and draped her other arm over the steering wheel. The stance pulled her jacket farther open. I realized she wasn't wearing her shoulder holster. The jacket was probably tailored without the holster. I wondered if her gun was at her ankle or somewhere on her waist I couldn't see.

She seemed relaxed. More so than I'd ever seen her. But there was also a tension around her, a reticence. I wondered how much of her odd mood was relief that our relationship probably couldn't get her fired and how much was fear that we might need to acknowledge that our relationship was real.

"You okay?" I finally asked.

She gave a curt nod. "Yeah. Fine." She took a deep breath. "There's still some stuff we need to talk about."

"Okay."

She pulled up in front of my house. "Let's go inside."

Inside, we moved around each other. I kicked off my boots and took off my sweater. Laurel shrugged out of her jacket and hung it on a kitchen chair. The dress shirt pulled tight across her shoulders. She rolled her sleeves with a series of practiced movements. I sat on the couch. Nickels came out to say hi and immediately ran off. Laurel handed me a beer.

"You okay? You seem subdued. You realize all this is a good thing, right?" I asked.

She forced a smile. "It is."

"Then what's the matter?"

She sat next to me. "I'm leaving."

"What do you mean?" I grinned stupidly.

"I quit this morning. I told Ionescu I couldn't be a cop anymore."

"Okay. That's a big decision."

"It is, but it was inevitable. I quit this summer when I fell in love with you." She picked at the label on her bottle. It was a nervous tic unlike her. "I compromised myself. I've made so many decisions since then that were about you or me or us that a year ago would have been about being a cop."

"Do you blame me for my role in that?" I asked, afraid of the answer, but more afraid of not knowing.

"No. Never."

"Then what's the matter?"

"What I did to Benson, I don't want to be that kind of cop. I don't want to be that kind of person."

"So don't beat people up."

She shook her head. "I crossed a line that I can't uncross. Maybe someone else could, but not me."

"Okay. That's good then." I grinned. Both of us released from Sac PD in one day. It was more than I'd dared hope for.

"It is good, but I'm not just leaving the department. I'm leaving everything. I put in notice on my apartment. I'm leaving Sac," she said. I didn't understand. "I need to know who I am when I'm not a cop."

"How does that translate to leaving Sacramento?"

She shrugged. "This city has always been steeped in law enforcement for me. My parents, my family. I can't move on here."

"And me? I'm in this city."

"I can't be with you."

Well, that was it. I stood and walked across the room, but there was nowhere to go. Nowhere that didn't have her. "That's bullshit."

"Maybe."

"No, it is. You're running away. Finding yourself doesn't require a new city, it just requires you. Location is irrelevant."

She shrugged and held her shoulders up, tight. "Yeah. Maybe. I don't know."

"How can you not know?" I shouted.

"I'm sorry. If I knew, I wouldn't need to do this." She set down her beer and scooted forward to the edge of the couch. "You have such conviction. I don't always understand it or agree with it, but it's real and tangible and defensible. I am so envious of that."

"So read a philosophy book." I was angry. Distantly, I was aware that I wasn't handling this well. But it was really, really distant.

"It's not that simple. My entire moral code is constructed with law at the center. You've shown me how shortsighted that is, but I can't borrow your morality or someone else's. That would just be a stopgap."

"Leaving is selfish as fuck."

"It is, but I need to start fresh." She laced her fingers together. Her joints went white as she pressed her hands together. "You were right when you said Lane's trauma would be traumatic for me. I didn't understand then, but I see now how much it fucked me up. I need to deal with that, which means being strong enough to leave, being strong enough to choose myself."

"Don't dress this up like it's some grand journey. We broke each other's hearts and still managed to build a solid relationship." Or I thought it was until about ten minutes ago. "I love you so fucking much. You love me. It's simple."

"Please, Cash, don't." She refused to drop her eye contact with me even as tears gathered in her eyes and spilled over.

"Don't what? Tell the truth?"

"You can't just play love like an ace. That's cheap."

"I'm not. That's how relationships work." I sat next to her and took her hand. "Right now, you're struggling and I'll support you. But you don't need to run away to find yourself."

"No." She took back her hand and swiped at her eyes. "I love you. I'm sorry." She kissed the corner of my mouth, then stood.

"You're fucking serious?" I looked up at her.

"Yes." She looked at me with pity. "Honestly, I thought you would understand it more than anyone." Tears spattered onto her white shirt. "This is me trying to leave behind an institution that molded me to be something other than myself. I thought you would—" She shrugged and looked away.

"Right. You realized that society is a lie and you came to me for a cookie." I frowned and nodded. "Got it."

"Why are you being an ass?"

"Because you disrupted my entire life. You turned my whole world upside down and now you're just leaving," I shouted.

"I'm sorry."

"That's it? You're sorry?"

"I'm sorry I'm selfish. And I'm sorry I hurt you." She turned away.

I watched her slowly unroll her sleeves and fasten the cuffs. She slid on her jacket and buttoned it. She turned her key ring over a few times, then set my key on the kitchen table. I realized I was crying when it became difficult to see. I blinked away the tears and stood, but I didn't know what to say. It clearly didn't matter what I said.

Laurel turned back when she got to the door. We stood there and stared at each other across an impossibly distant space. And then she left.

About the Author

Award-winning author, Ashley Bartlett was born and raised in California. Her life consists of reading, writing, and editing. Most of the time Ashley engages in these pursuits while sitting in front of a coffee shop with her wife. It's a glamorous life.

She is an obnoxious, sarcastic, punk-ass, but her friends don't hold that against her. She lives in Sacramento, but you can find her at ashbartlett.com.

Books Available from Bold Strokes Books

A Bird of Sorrow by Shea Godfrey. As Darrius and her lover, Princess Jessa, gather their strength for the coming war, a mysterious spell will reveal the truth of an ancient love. (978-1-63555-009-2)

All the Worlds Between Us by Morgan Lee Miller. High school senior Quinn Hughes discovers that a broken friendship is actually a door propped open for an unexpected romance. (978-1-63555-457-1)

An Intimate Deception by CJ Birch. Flynn County Sheriff Elle Ashley has spent her adult life atoning for her wild youth, but when she finds her ex, Jessie, murdered two weeks before the small town's biggest social event, she comes face-to-face with her past and all her well-kept secrets. (978-1-63555-417-5)

Cash and the Sorority Girl by Ashley Bartlett. Cash Braddock doesn't want to deal with morality, drugs, or people. Unfortunately, she's going to have to. (978-1-63555-310-9)

Counting for Thunder by Phillip Irwin Cooper. A struggling actor returns to the Deep South to manage a family crisis, finds love, and ultimately his own voice as his mother is regaining hers for possibly the last time. (978-1-63555-450-2)

Falling by Kris Bryant. Falling in love isn't part of the plan, but will Shaylie Beck put her heart first and stick around, or tell the damaging truth? (978-1-63555-373-4)

Secrets in a Small Town by Nicole Stiling. Deputy Chief Mackenzie Blake has one mission: find the person harassing Savannah Castillo and her daughter before they cause real harm. (978-1-63555-436-6)

Stormy Seas by Ali Vali. The high-octane follow-up to the best-selling action-romance, *Blue Skies*. (978-1-63555-299-7)

The Road to Madison by Elle Spencer. Can two women who fell in love as girls overcome the hurt caused by the father who tore them apart? (978-1-63555-421-2)

Dangerous Curves by Larkin Rose. When love waits at the finish line, dangerous curves are a risk worth taking. (978-1-63555-353-6)

Love to the Rescue by Radclyffe. Can two people who share a past really be strangers? (978-1-62639-973-0)

Love's Portrait by Anna Larner. When museum curator Molly Goode and benefactor Georgina Wright uncover a portrait's secret, public and private truths are exposed, and their deepening love hangs in the balance. (978-1-63555-057-3)

Model Behavior by MJ Williamz. Can one woman's instability shatter a new couple's dreams of happiness? (978-1-63555-379-6)

Pretending in Paradise by M. Ullrich. When travelwisdom.com assigns PR specialist Caroline Beckett and travel blogger Emma Morgan to cover a hot new couples retreat, they're forced to fake a relationship to secure a reservation. (978-1-63555-399-4)

Recipe for Love by Aurora Rey. Hannah Little doesn't have much use for fancy chefs or fancy restaurants, but when New York City chef Drew Davis comes to town, their attraction just might be a recipe for love. (978-1-63555-367-3)

Survivor's Guilt and Other Stories by Greg Herren. Award-winning author Greg Herren's short stories are finally pulled together into a single collection, including the Macavity Award nominated title story and the first-ever Chanse MacLeod short story. (978-1-63555-413-7)

The House by Eden Darry. After a vicious assault, Sadie, Fin, and their family retreat to a house they think is the perfect place to start over, until they realize not all is as it seems. (978-1-63555-395-6)

Uninvited by Jane C. Esther. When Aerin McLeary's body becomes host for an alien intent on invading Earth, she must work with researcher Olivia Ando to uncover the truth and save humankind. (978-1-63555-282-9)

Comrade Cowgirl by Yolanda Wallace. When cattle rancher Laramie Bowman accepts a lucrative job offer far from home, will her heart end up getting lost in translation? (978-1-63555-375-8)

Double Vision by Ellie Hart. When her cell phone rings, Giselle Cutler answers it—and finds herself speaking to a dead woman. (978-1-63555-385-7)

Inheritors of Chaos by Barbara Ann Wright. As factions splinter and reunite, will anyone survive the final showdown between gods and mortals on an alien world? (978-1-63555-294-2)

Love on Lavender Lane by Karis Walsh. Accompanied by the buzz of honeybees and the scent of lavender, Paige and Kassidy must find a way to compromise on their approach to business if they want to save Lavender Lane Farm—and find a way to make room for love along the way. (978-1-63555-286-7)

Spinning Tales by Brey Willows. When the fairy tale begins to unravel and villains are on the loose, will Maggie and Kody be able to spin a new tale? (978-1-63555-314-7)

The Do-Over by Georgia Beers. Bella Hunt has made a good life for herself and put the past behind her. But when the bane of her high school existence shows up for Bella's class on conflict resolution, the last thing they expect is to fall in love. (978-1-63555-393-2)

What Happens When by Samantha Boyette. For Molly Kennan, senior year is already an epic disaster, and falling for mysterious waitress Zia is about to make life a whole lot worse. (978-1-63555-408-3)

Wooing the Farmer by Jenny Frame. When fiercely independent modern socialite Penelope Huntingdon-Stewart and traditional country farmer Sam McQuade meet, trusting their hearts is harder than it looks. (978-1-63555-381-9)

A Chapter on Love by Laney Webber. When Jannika and Lee reunite, their instant connection feels like a gift, but neither is ready for a second chance at love. Will they finally get on the same page when it comes to love? (978-1-63555-366-6)

Drawing Down the Mist by Sheri Lewis Wohl. Everyone thinks Grand Duchess Maria Romanova died in 1918. They were almost right. (978-1-63555-341-3)

Listen by Kris Bryant. Lily Croft is inexplicably drawn to Hope D'Marco but will she have the courage to confront the consequences of her past and present colliding? (978-1-63555-318-5)

Perfect Partners by Maggie Cummings. Elite police dog trainer Sara Wright has no intention of falling in love with a coworker, until Isabel Marquez arrives at Homeland Security's Northeast Regional Training facility and Sara's good intentions start to falter. (978-1-63555-363-5)

Shut Up and Kiss Me by Julie Cannon. What better way to spend two weeks of hell in paradise than in the company of a hot, sexy woman? (978-1-63555-343-7)

Spencer's Cove by Missouri Vaun. When Foster Owen and Abigail Spencer meet they uncover a story of lives adrift, loves lost, and true love found. (978-1-63555-171-6)

Without Pretense by TJ Thomas. After living for decades hiding from the truth, can Ava learn to trust Bianca with her secrets and her heart? (978-1-63555-173-0)

Unexpected Lightning by Cass Sellars. Lightning strikes once more when Sydney and Parker fight a dangerous stranger who threatens the peace they both desperately want. (978-1-163555-276-8)

Emily's Art and Soul by Joy Argento. When Emily meets Andi Marino she thinks she's found a new best friend but Emily doesn't know that Andi is fast falling in love with her. Caught up in exploring her sexuality, will Emily see the only woman she needs is right in front of her? (978-1-63555-355-0)

Escape to Pleasure: Lesbian Travel Erotica edited by Sandy Lowe and Victoria Villasenor. Join these award-winning authors as they explore the sensual side of erotic lesbian travel. (978-1-63555-339-0)

Music City Dreamers by Robyn Nyx. Music can bring lovers together. In Music City, it can tear them apart. (978-1-63555-207-2)

Ordinary is Perfect by D. Jackson Leigh. Atlanta marketing superstar Autumn Swan's life derails when she inherits a country home, a child, and a very interesting neighbor. (978-1-63555-280-5)

Royal Court by Jenny Frame. When royal dresser Holly Weaver's passionate personality begins to melt Royal Marine Captain Quincy's icy heart, will Holly be ready for what she exposes beneath? (978-1-63555-290-4)

Strings Attached by Holly Stratimore. Success. Riches. Music. Passion. It's a life most can only dream of, but stardom comes at a cost. (978-1-63555-347-5)

The Ashford Place by Jean Copeland. When Isabelle Ashford inherits an old house in small-town Connecticut, family secrets, a shocking discovery, and an unexpected romance complicate her plan for a fast profit and a temporary stay. (978-1-63555-316-1)

Treason by Gun Brooke. Zoem Malderyn's existence is a deadly threat to everyone on Gemocon and Commander Neenja KahSandra must find a way to save the woman she loves from having to commit the ultimate sacrifice. (978-1-63555-244-7)